,06

THE MOON'S
OUR HOME

THE MOON'S OUR HOME

FAITH BALDWIN

Thorndike Press • Chivers Press
Thorndike, Maine USA Bath, England

This Large Print edition is published by Thorndike Press, USA and by Chivers Press, England.

Published in 2001 in the U.S. by arrangement with Harold Ober Associates, Inc.

Published in 2001 in the U.K. by arrangement with the author.

U.S. Hardcover   0-7862-3280-3   (Candlelight Series Edition)
U.K. Hardcover   0-7540-4519-6   (Chivers Large Print)
U.K. Softcover   0-7540-4520-X   (Camden Large Print)

The text of this Large Print edition is unabridged.
Other aspects of the book may vary from the original edition.

Set in 16 pt. Plantin by Rick Gundberg.

Printed in the United States on permanent paper.

British Library Cataloguing in Publication Data available

Library of Congress Cataloging-in-Publication Data

Baldwin, Faith, 1893–
    The moon's our home / Faith Baldwin.
        p.   cm.
    ISBN 0-7862-3280-3 (lg. print : hc : alk. paper)
    1. Inheritance and succession — Fiction. 2. Actresses —
Fiction. 3. Explorers — Fiction. 4. New England — Fiction.
5. Large type books. I. Title.
PS3505.U97 M66 2001
813'.52—dc21   2001027106

LIST OF CHAPTERS

CHAPTER ONE

REDHEADED MINX

"I won't! I won't! *I won't!*"

Whatever it was it was apparent that she would not. The husky voice which had swayed thousands from the silver screen and an approximate number from behind the footlights was raised in passionate rejection. And the slightly angular, redheaded girl with the green eyes and the sixty-eight freckles seized a small vase of dubious Ming dynasty and threw it with more abandon than accuracy.

"I won't!" she shouted, with satisfaction.

Miss Boyce-Medford, onetime governess and now companion, guide, and mentor to one of the most ungovernable personalities in these United States, ducked, with an expertness born of long and patient practice. Sometimes, given due warning, she caught a far-flung missile; occasionally, she reached and muffed. This bright autumn morning she merely ducked and permitted the vase to shatter against a wall papered in chaste ivory. Unfortunately the vase contained both flowers and water. The wall exhibited an instant stain. Miss Boyce-Medford sighed. "One run, no hits, no errors," she murmured with admirable calm. The accent of her native Sussex still colored her slightly acid tones.

The angular girl, known to stage and screen as Cherry Chester, shrieked with a spontaneous and enchanting laughter. Miss Boyce-Medford, having known this girl for twenty-three years, far too well, was not yet conditioned against her charm. Miss Boyce-Medford's straight, unkissed lips twitched slightly and she shrugged plump shoulders. "It's no laughing matter," she said wearily, "when we leave this place heaven knows what we will have to pay for damage to property." She eyed the ruined wall with resignation.

"We'll pay," agreed Cherry at once. She loped across the room, far too restrained in decoration for her pyrotechnic individuality, and flung herself upon the older woman with self-reproachful fervor.

"Boycie," she said, "I'm a beast. I might have hit you!" Her long green eyes widened, and her generous mouth, guiltless of paint, mobile, mirror of moods, drooped at the corners. "Boycie, if I ever really hurt you I'll kill myself!" she announced tragically.

"I can take it," said Miss Boyce-Medford, in prim, elegantly modulated tones oddly at variance with the phrase. She shook her un-compromisingly gray head, settled her pince-nez upon her high-bridged nose, and freed herself from the smothering embrace. "Sit down," she ordered firmly, "we must discuss this with some semblance of sanity. Your grandmother demands to see you —"

"Damn my grandmother!" said Cherry bitterly. Her green eyes narrowed and snapped. "I never thought she'd demean herself by reading gossip columns," she added woefully.

"Your conduct —" began her companion.

"That for my conduct," interrupted Miss Chester, and lightly sketched a regrettably vulgar gesture. "Can I help it if a completely gaga Egyptian prince takes it upon himself to send me six dozen gardenias every morning? I wouldn't know him if I fell over him tomorrow morning —"

"You've been seen in the Cocoanut Grove with him three times hand running," Miss Boyce-Medford reminded her.

"Pooh! I still wouldn't know him. I've never raised my eyes beyond the emerald and ruby stud in his shirt front. Looks like a traffic light gone haywire."

"Your grandmother —" began Miss Boyce-Medford inexorably.

Miss Chester made a brief remark. In it she mentioned tersely her grandmother's possible early history, her ancestry, and her probable lamentable end. Miss Boyce-Medford's shock of gray hair stood on end.

"Sarah!" she cried, authentically offended.

"Don't call me that," shrieked Cherry, and looked wildly about her. A dog, porcelain in material, pug in portraiture, Victorian in lineage, stood upon an occasional table. Miss Chester's hand stole toward it, grasped it firmly by fat china neck and large blue china bow.

"Drop that," commanded Miss Boyce-Medford sharply, "and stop acting like a motion-picture actress. Enough's enough. We are going east, to see your grandmother."

Miss Chester set down the dog carefully. She rose to her feet. She ran her long fingers through her vivid hair and she stamped her foot. Nature responded instantly. A slight but perceptible earthquake shook Beverly Hills, Hollywood, Los Angeles, Culver City, and environs. It would be reported in the eastern papers as something of a catastrophe. It would be ignored by the California press.

The white walls rocked, china and glass and the prisms of the drawing-room lights tinkled. The pictures on their chaste background were disturbed, and Miss Boyce-Medford turned very pale. She disliked Nature in the raw. Cherry spoke, and laughed, being without fear. "You can't accuse me of that!" she said.

The unnatural tinkling stopped, the walls settled back to their foursquare solidity, Miss Boyce-Medford drew a long breath. She was a courageous woman — only such a woman could have lived with Cherry Chester all these years — and she had common sense. Hence her heart beat fast and the long breath was painful to her. She eyed her charge with something resembling animosity. Cherry was amused by earthquakes, mice, snakes, storms at sea, producers, supervisors, stage managers, young men threatening suicide, and even income tax collectors. Such a nature lacked stability and good judgment.

"Cherry," began Miss Boyce-Medford feebly.

"Don't call me by that ridiculous name," said Cherry casually. "It makes me sick at my stomach."

Miss Boyce-Medford was showing signs of strain. She said, after a moment, with acerbity, "Perhaps you'll answer to 'Hie'?"

"I'd adore to," answered Cherry, grinning.

She was by now sitting upon a large footstool of petit point. She clasped her hands about her slender knees and whistled, half a tone off key. Two satin-sleek dachshunds came from a room beyond to crouch beside her and to regard her with an unexacting devotion. Cherry's red hair was a wilderness about her small and noble head. Her thin face with its pointed chin, its healthy pallor and its freckles, her wide, unpainted mouth, would have been unrecognized by any of her innumerable fans. She photographed like a million dollars. She photographed like a modern houri, all glamour and languor, fire and enchantment. She was, her face washed clean, and her slim body draped in uncreased, slightly soiled white slacks and a turtleneck sweater, a plain young woman with beautiful bones.

She unclasped her hands and scratched the ears of Lohengrin and Elsa, her dachshunds. They crept closer to her. Miss Boyce-Medford, regarding her, thought, not for the first time, how much she looked like a nice boy and how deceptive such an appearance could be. She said briskly, "That interviewer will be here in half an hour —"

"I won't see her!"

"Oh, yes, you will, you've been aloof long enough. The public will stand for it from Garbo. Not from anyone else, except in small doses. This woman is important."

"Oh, all right," said Cherry wearily. Then she snapped into animation. "Am I to have no private life?" she demanded so hotly that

Lohengrin barked and Elsa dutifully echoed him. "Am I not to call my soul my own?"

"Save that for the interview," replied Miss Boyce-Medford sharply. "Of course you can't have any private life. If you'd wanted a private life, why on earth did you select the most public of professions?"

"God knows," said Cherry, and grinned again engagingly. Miss Boyce-Medford's heart, which had been hardened against the girl, softened instantly. She sometimes thought she would end up with angina or some other cardiac disease due to this hardening and softening process which attacked that patient but purely human organ at least a dozen times a day.

Miss Boyce-Medford rose to her full height, which was just five foot two, and advanced on very small, plump feet toward the younger woman. She stood over her in the attitude of a schoolteacher and Cherry looked up at her. Cherry wore a grave mouth and the eyes of an experienced imp. She said nothing, astonishingly.

Miss Boyce-Medford uttered a fact. "Your picture is finished," she said.

"It will gross a couple of millions," murmured Cherry.

"That remains to be seen," said her closest friend. "You and I will leave for the East as soon as possible. We will stop with your grandmother for perhaps two weeks and then we will sail for Europe."

"I've heard all that before," said Cherry. "You will go to England and restore your soul in the bosom of your large family. I will go to Sweden and quarrel furiously with my mother and her latest husband —"

"After that," added Miss Boyce-Medford, "we will meet in Paris, and then return to New York."

"For rehearsals," said Cherry; "damn them!"

Miss Boyce-Medford sat down. She said, "You are the most perverse human being it has ever been given me to know — for my sins."

"I know, darling, but you love me just the same."

"I suppose I do," conceded Miss Boyce-Medford sorrowfully. "Habit is very insidious. After all, I used to spank you." Her small gray eyes gleamed reflectively and she regarded Cherry with a renewed hope.

"No," said Cherry instantly, "you couldn't." She flexed an arm. She had plenty of muscle.

"I suppose not," agreed Miss Boyce-Medford regretfully. She added, "Look here, be sensible. Your grandmother asks very little of you —"

"Only my right eye —"

"And this does not much interrupt your plans. If your grandmother becomes seriously annoyed —"

"You needn't go on," said Cherry. They eyed each other. There were a few things which her public did not know about Cherry Chester. One of them was known only to Cherry, her grandmother, her grandmother's lawyers and Miss Boyce-Medford.

"After all I can earn my living and a pretty good one."

"That," replied Miss Boyce-Medford, "is true — with reservations. You have had only two releases so far. They have been great successes. You have had three flops and one hit on the stage. This play you are contemplating for the spring may be very bad indeed. When you return to take up your picture contract you may have a failure. You can't afford many. No one can. The fact that you have an independent income enables you, at this juncture, more or less to dictate your contract terms. If you were to lose that income — through your obstinacy —"

"Skip it. We'll go east — to Gram's. And her blood — and mine — be on your head." Cherry rose. "I must now go to make myself beautiful," she announced, "and you keep out of this interview, Boycie. I don't want

15

anyone crabbing my act — as a stooge you're not so hot."

"I'll be there," said Boycie, "just in case you start throwing things."

Miss Chester was leaving her rented drawing-room. At the stairs she stopped. She exclaimed, not softly, "Just the same I'll be glad to see the old devil again."

"Who — the interviewer?"

"No, my grandmother," shouted Cherry, and ran up the stairs and gave herself over to the ministrations of Hilda, her almost miraculous maid, who cared for nothing in this world except Cherry, football games, and her savings accounts.

The interviewer arrived, on time. Cherry kept her waiting for twenty-two minutes by an ornate clock. At the end of that period, which was garnished by light conversational pleasantries from Miss Boyce-Medford, she was bidden to the presence.

Cherry lay upon a chaise longue in a slightly darkened boudoir. She wore a negligee, a ravishing concoction of palest apple green and sunset mauve. She was smoking a cigarette in a long holder. Her wild hair had been subdued to lovely ripples, caught at the neck with a tortoise-shell comb. A curling fringe fell over her brow. Her little face was ivory tinted, flushed with delicate color at the cheekbones,

16

her green eyes were jewels in cunningly contrived shadows, and her mouth was a triumph of scarlet. She was, as the interviewer later clicked out upon her trusty typewriter, the most beautiful, the most glowing, the most glamorous creature any worshiper can ever behold. . . .

"I'm so sorry," apologized Cherry in her husky voice, "I've kept you waiting — but somehow the morning has flown by. I rose early and walked alone over the hills. When I came home again I sat down at my desk intending to write letters but I picked up a book — and the first thing I knew, you had been announced!"

Miss Boyce-Medford, from the shadows, snorted very gently. The interviewer, accepting a glass of sherry and a biscuit from the manservant who suddenly and noiselessly appeared, did not hear her, but Cherry did. She turned her glowing head slightly. "Oh, Boycie darling, would you mind asking Hans if he will pick some roses for Miss Manning — the deep pink ones — buds, if possible."

Miss Boyce-Medford rose and departed. She hoped that Miss Manning would find six thorns for every rose with which Cherry presented her.

Miss Manning, looking at Cherry, looking about the room, which its present occupant

17

had had redecorated to suit her aura, was visibly impressed. The room had somehow the sweetness of flowers, the fragility of Venetian glass, the strength of steel, and the tang of the salty sea — and so had Cherry Chester. It was all too good to be true and Miss Manning for one did not believe it. She was an old hand at this game. Yet for the moment she was forced to be credulous. Cherry's subdued voice ran on, her laughter lit the room now and then like a shower of falling silver stars, and her long white hands were graceful and restrained in gesture. Miss Manning, sly soul, endeavored to catch her once or twice for her own private satisfaction. But Cherry was not to be caught. If she spoke of a book, she had read it. While her statements on Love and Marriage and What Constitutes Charm in a Woman were indubitably her own, they were startling, and they were news, and they were copy.

"Marriage," stated Cherry, "should be without background —"

"Background?" asked Miss Manning, dazed.

"I mean," said Cherry, "that if I ever fall in love it must be as one takes a difficult ski jump — into the air — not quite knowing the end, no matter how clever one's judgment or technique. It would not be Cherry Chester who fell in love, it would be just a girl — immortal, fixed in this most treasurable moment of her youth. I would like to fall in love with a man whose very name I did not know, a man who did not know me. We would start on such an equal basis, then. No past — cluttered up with careers and families and traditions — and quite possibly no future. Just the present, magnificent and memorable."

"Suffering cats!" ejaculated Miss Boyce-Medford under her laboring breath. She had returned hastily and stood now in the doorway, unnoticed.

Cherry's voice would have drawn tears from a stone. It was something to remember her by — it was utterly and completely sincere. Three months hence a fan magazine would carry an interview signed by Meribelle Manning. Its title would probably be: *Love is Like a Ski Jump — Says Cherry Chester.*

Miss Manning swam up out of deep waters. She asked, rather timidly for her, "You are leaving us, are you not, Miss Chester, for the East — ?"

"Yes, within a few days. I adore California, Miss Manning. The sunlight runs through my veins like liquid fire, I never have enough of it, but I have certain obligations and I am very tired. I must get away from everything and rest."

"You are sailing for Europe?" asked Miss

19

Manning curiously. She knew all about Cherry Chester's mother, born Sylvia Van Steeden, and thrice married. The first time to Cherry's father, a banker named Brown, and shortly after his death to Rudolph von Waldheim, a baron, and now by the grace of divorce to Gerhard Torkal Erik Something-or-other, a minor prince of Sweden, and she knew all about Mrs. Augustus Jonathan Van Steeden, Cherry's maternal grandmother, who ruled a small, restricted section of New York society and an almost unlimited amount of money with an iron hand and an acidulous tongue.

"Yes," replied Cherry. "But don't ask me when — and don't ask me where I'm going. You see," she explained, smiling, "I might tell you — somehow you're *so* easy to talk to — and I don't want anyone to know. I want to hide and relax and rest. I'm so tired."

It was Miss Manning's cue. She accepted it, gracefully. She murmured something about procuring new publicity photographs from the proper department at the studio, and presently departed. Emerging into the full sunlight, she shook her head and looked fixedly at a magnificent palm. *The girl*, she mused, *is phony. No, she isn't phony, she's real. What the hell is she?* demanded Miss Manning, a forthright person and still under the spell hastened to her modest home and yanked the cover from her typewriter.

"How'm I doing?" asked Cherry of Miss Boyce-Medford.

"Swell. If I recall your last interview, you were all open-air athletics, the true type of American girl. You wore spotless slacks and a pullover and hopped a couple of hedges to prove your fitness. You regarded all men as comrades and scoffed at the thought of romance. You lived for your dogs, your horses, your art, and your passion for fresh air. You never opened a book. Books were vicarious living, you said roundly, you would rather live firsthand. That was last winter after your first picture when you had stolen away to Palm Springs to breathe the divine air of the marvelous desert and to feast your eyes on mountain peaks and stars. Stolen away," added Miss Boyce-Medford, "with three cameramen, a couple of press agents, and four dozen other motion picture escapers from artificiality!"

Cherry swung her legs to the floor. She commented, "I loathe this glorified Mother Hubbard." She ripped most of it from her in a couple of unconsidered gestures. She ran her fingers through her hair again. "Just the same, there's something in what I said —"

"I'm glad you think so. To what are you referring now? . . . Hilda," called Miss Boyce-Medford, "come and get this garment before it's in shreds —"

"What I said about falling in love with a man whose name you didn't know, of whose background you had no idea — any more than he knew your name or background. That's romance," decided Cherry, "that's perfection. Complete. Whole. No tag ends. As new-minted as a just created world."

"Bilge!" said Boycie cruelly, and without refinement. "That lanky Manning woman's gone. I'm here. Marian Boyce-Medford, spinster, aged fifty-two. Stop play-acting and find some form of rag which suits your mood, for we're about to lunch — and personally I'm starved. As for meeting a man without background — I've met very few with background since we came out here. You pays your money and you takes your choice."

"You're inhuman," cried Cherry. She jumped up, and Hilda silently rescued the trailing clouds of glory. She stood there straight and slender and rather tall in silken shorts and a wisp of lace, in gossamer hose and silver mules. She kicked off the mules. One of them hit Elsa, coming in at the door, and Elsa howled dismally.

"Oh, my satin lamb!" cried Cherry, "did I hurt you?" She raced across the floor and gathered the sleek, long animal to her small round breasts. Boycie grinned. She suggested, "Give her a bottle of perfume — or a couple of football tickets; that's what Hilda or I get when we're slow at dodging."

Cherry dropped the dog and stood up. She said, "Hilda, bring me my flannel bathrobe. When do we eat? I hope it's hash!"

CHAPTER TWO

"I LOATHE HANDSOME MEN."

Miss Cherry Chester, redheaded, tempestuous, and social register star of the stage and screen, traveled east as quietly as a boiler factory. The few days preceding her meteoric departure were cataclysmic. The little bungalow — eight master bedrooms and baths — which she had rented from an English star now back in her own country informing all and sundry how comic Hollywood could be, was a welter of tissue papers, trunks, suitcases, orders, countermanded orders, and reorders. Cherry, in blue denim overalls, worked so hard on the first day that Boycie went to bed at teatime with a sick headache, Hilda was moved to rare Scandinavian tears, and Ashtubula Higgins, Miss Chester's remarkable butler, contemplated no less than three times giving notice by telegraph. There was no use delivering it by word of mouth, as Cherry would merely have placed her pink-tipped fingers in her pink-tipped ears and made faces at him.

On the second day, Cherry, wearying of

packing, went riding — with the latest foreign importation, a handsome young man from Riga, who had already been mentioned as the possible lover of one much-married star, the probable lover of a second, unmarried, and the leading man for no less than three ladies operating their photographed charms for three mammoth companies. She lunched with her deadliest rival, a soft-surfaced but inwardly macadamized blonde, and drank milk at a cocktail party for a visiting author in the afternoon. During her absences, broken only by cometlike returns home in order to change her garments, the bungalow was singularly peaceful.

They left at midnight on the *Chief*. Miss Boyce-Medford contemplated her compartment with satisfaction. She could at least lock the door and sleep. Under no circumstances would she share Cherry's drawing-room. The apparently placated Mr. Higgins and the once again cheerful Hilda had suitable and separate quarters elsewhere. The excellent cook — who had once been Mrs. Higgins but who, since divorcing Ashtubula on grounds of incompatibility, had serenely continued to be an important member of Cherry's household — "I'm sure that we'll get along fine if we aren't married, Ashie. As long as I don't have to live with you, I don't mind your being around — besides, what would she do without either of us?" — had remained in California to close the house. With her were the parlormaid and the chauffeur. Later they would motor east in Cherry's car and take up their residence in Cherry's small but complete Park Avenue apartment. There the staff would await the next move on Miss Chester's variable part.

Hilda, of course, was going abroad with her mistress and sat now in her section, the morning after their departure, sorrowfully contemplating the desert and wondering why God had seen fit to create the ocean.

Cherry slept late. The departure had been feverish. Press agent, publicity department, her favorite producer, her most hated director, a couple of supervisors, nineteen of her dearest friends, most of whom hoped that the *Chief* would stage a very small wreck, all the reporters in town, and three cameramen with flashlights. Even now, as she idled with the cup of coffee which a colored porter, chaperoned by Hilda, had brought her, she was smiling gently to think that the multitudinous wires controlled by the press were even now flashing the news from coast to coast that ere long Cherry Chester, beloved of millions, would be restored to the doting arms of her fragile little grandmother, whose millions were beloved by herself.

"Meow," said Cherry suddenly, reflecting upon her grandmother whom she alternately adored and disliked, and Hilda looked anxiously under the couch while Lohengrin and Elsa, baldly smuggled into the drawing-room, barked with an increasing interest.

The trip was without any especially untoward incident. To be sure, at Kansas City it took all Boycie's tact and will power to persuade Cherry into her cinematic mask as the Cherry Chester Fan Club of that fair city would be at the train to gaze upon their idol for fifteen minutes. They were cheated by five, for Cherry, having endured them for six hundred seconds, departed abruptly with her arms full of their roses, and her ears full of their sighs, leaving Boycie to hold down the fort and distribute autographed — by Boycie — pictures while she, eluding bored reporters with magnificent strategy, entertained herself near the cab in converse with the grimy engineer.

Chicago was autumnal. Boycie, her blood somewhat thinned, shivered in the cool breeze from a bright blue lake. Cherry's small nostrils dilated. She said, driving to the Blackstone where she was supposed to rest for the four hours which would elapse until the *Century* departed, "That's what I've missed. Cold. Snow."

27

"There isn't any snow," Boycie reminded her literally.

"Of course not, darling," explained Cherry patiently, "but there will be. Oh," she cried and spread her slender arms and knocked over a couple of handbags, "to be alone on a mountaintop, alone with the snow and the sunlight and the stars."

"At one and the same time?" asked Boycie, sniffing.

"Boycie," said Cherry, "I do love you!" Her green eyes were light with laughter and her wide mouth, painted for such of her public fortunate enough to see her, was curved with laughter. "Boycie, you think I'm an unutterable fool, don't you?"

"No, I don't. I know better. If you were I could cope with you. But you're not. That's the trouble."

Cherry leaned back and looked complacent.

Their temporary suite in the Blackstone was filled with flowers. Higgins at the door and Hilda at the telephone tried with some success to stem the tide of worshipers, representatives of the press, a theatrical gentleman who thought it would be nice if Cherry could make a brief personal appearance in a couple of weeks, two personages from the broadcasting stations, and a couple of doughty insurance salesmen. Finally the ranks were reduced to a motion picture critic who brought orchids and was asked to lunch. He was a young critic, and quite susceptible. He inquired timidly, over tomato juice, served in the suite, "All this adulation, Miss Chester, what does it mean to you?"

"Everything," announced Cherry and smiled at him. He caught his breath and forgot the girl to whom he was engaged, at the moment. He said, gaping, "You really mean that? So many of the stars are — bored. Oh, they recognize the business value of it all but in their hearts they take it for granted and are wearily amused —"

"Only until the fan mail falls off," commented Boycie. She kept a wary eye on her charge. The green eyes were narrowed, the mouth dreamed. Cherry's voice when it came was low, huskier than ever, as thrilling as the sound of bells on a frosty night.

"I'll never take it for granted," she said. "I couldn't. It's the breath of life — my life — all the life I possess. I am not myself, Mr. Tompson. I don't belong to myself. I belong — to them. When they tire of me I shall die, even though I live to be an old, old woman."

Boycie choked on a crumb of Melba toast. She would never become accustomed to it, never in all this world. Was it for this she had been dragged from a quiet English vicarage in order to be governess to a redheaded brat of three whose mother contemplated remarriage?

"Tire of you!" ejaculated Mr. Tompson, breathing out an undying devotion. It wouldn't matter to him for the next few years how bad her pictures were: *Despite an unfortunate paucity of good material, Cherry Chester, the incomparable, the glamorous, rose above a routine story and by sheer force of magnificent acting and perfection of charm held her audience breathless in their seats last night —*

"You're sweet," Cherry murmured, and smiled at him again. The slow smile, the long smile, intimate and secret, for himself alone.

Poor devil, thought Boycie, and asked briskly, "And how has the weather been in Chicago?"

Mr. Tompson dragged his fascinated eyes from an enchanted contemplation of translucent green depths in which it would be very easy to drown. "Eh," he asked abstractedly, "what's that? Oh, the weather! Yes, certainly, it's been fine. We've had almost continuous rain . . ."

When luncheon was over, and Mr. Tompson had taken his departure, Cherry kicked a perfectly good hotel pillow across the room. "How much longer," she demanded crossly, "must I play up to young men not yet dry behind the ears?"

"As long as you continue being a motion picture star," said Boycie and retrieved the pillow. "You know that as well as I do. Moreover, you eat it up. You love it."

"I hate it," said Cherry.

But there weren't as many people to see her off on the *Century*. A mere handful of gapers. Someone had slipped up, somewhere. In her drawing-room she pulled a chrysanthemum to pieces and cried wildly, "I'm slipping — I know it — I might as well give up here and now!"

She flung the petals to the green carpet and turned on Boycie. "Meals in here, as usual. I'm going to bed. I won't get up until we get in. I won't see anybody — not even you. Send me in some soup for dinner."

"I suppose you want the Invisible Man to bring it," said Boycie. Her head ached. She contemplated their meeting with Mrs. Van Steeden with some satisfaction. She thought, *If only Cherry would meet a man as self-willed, as dominant, as vain and as clever as Lucy Van Steeden, I could wash my hands of her with a sigh of relief.*

The drawing-room door stood open. A young man strolled by. He was idiotically handsome. He possessed a perfection of fea-

31

ture which would have caused the Apollo Belvedere to gnash his marble teeth in envy. But there was strength in those features too. He was tall and broad-shouldered, he was slim of hip and thigh and waist. He was spoiled, rich, orphaned, and thirty. And the dark locks which curled upon a Byronic brow in something the early novelists have termed a rich profusion had never, as heaven is my witness, felt the touch of a marcel iron or the torture of the permanenting machine.

He glanced in at the door. Boycie saw him and caught her breath. "Good heavens!" she murmured. Cherry, with her back to the corridor, was contemplating the suburban scenery with gloom. "What is it?" she asked, and turned. But the young man had gone.

"It was," replied Boycie, "the handsomest man I have ever seen in all my life."

Cherry said, "Probably won a contest for teeth or something and is on his way back from Hollywood, *not* having landed the contract. I loathe handsome men."

Boycie sighed, strangely fluttered. "I've an idea this one isn't merely handsome." She resolved to dine, after all, in the diner.

"You're not coming down with something, are you?" asked Cherry anxiously. She walked over and shut the door. She put her long hand on Boycie's brow. "No," she decided, "you feel quite cool."

"Well," said Boycie, after a minute, "perhaps I merely dreamed him — a hangover from my youth."

The young man continued down to his drawing-room. He was in a very bad humor. He rang for the porter. He asked, "What's your name?"

"Al, sir."

"Al. Nice name. Short, to the point. I don't want to be disturbed. Understand? I'll dine in here and you may send me coffee half an hour before we get in tomorrow morning. Send the train secretary to me now, will you? I want to get off some wires at Elkhart."

"Yes, sir," said Al.

When the secretary arrived, notebook in hand, the young man told him his name. The secretary was impressed. "Not *the* Mr. Amberton?" he asked hopefully.

Anthony Amberton smiled. In a gentleman of less charm, a casual observer might have deduced a modicum of complacency. "I'm afraid so," he admitted, sighing. He dictated his wires. He gave the secretary the necessary sum and something lavish over. The secretary ventured, "There's another celebrity on board — Cherry Chester."

"Never heard of her," said Anthony.

"Oh!" The secretary's eyes were wide and

blue. "The motion picture star," he ventured.

"I never go to motion pictures," said Anthony. "I never read about them. They disgust me. The artificiality, the puerility — No," added Anthony, and lighted a cigarette in a gesture almost wickedly graceful, "give me the simple primitive woman, copper colored, with small high breasts and dark liquid eyes, a woman of long silences, expert in love, patient in childbearing . . ."

Flushing, the secretary withdrew. Mr. Amberton, the handsomest, the most publicized, the wealthiest and most startling explorer-writer of his time, smiled slightly, yawned, and reached for his notebook. He now contemplated a book on *Darkest Africa*. He rarely saw his native land. His university days had been spent in England and his preparatory school days in France. The rest of his days and nights had been spent almost anywhere on the face of the globe. His expeditions, financed by himself, were fantastic in the extreme. He traveled by sampan, elephant, camel, airplane, or submarine, as the fancy took him. He had an entourage of almost regal — Indian style — proportions. This entourage he had left behind him in foreign parts on coming reluctantly to the States from the Orient in order to confer with his lawyers on matters pertaining to a slightly diminished income. Fortunately for him, Mr. Amberton's father and grandfather had manufactured certain commodities which were an integral part of existence in most civilized communities. In short, Mr. Amberton's grandfather and father, whose name had been Smith, were the largest manufacturers of plumbing supplies, wholesale and retail, in the country if not in the world.

Samuel A. Smith, the third, had changed his name. He was a farsighted young man and when early in life it was borne upon him that a chance rescuing party finding him in the depths of Africa, Abyssinia, or Bali would be forced to say "Mr. Smith, I believe?" he came to the conclusion that Anthony Amberton would ring with a more romantic force around the world. Besides, it would look well on the covers of his books.

He supposed wearily that once in New York he would have to see his publishers. But he would put down his shapely foot when it came to teas, dinners, and such. He preferred the publicity accruing to the shy, the evasive, and the elusive. His public appearances were, as a rule, purely social, and limited to Paris, Berlin, Budapest, Singapore, London, or Buenos Aires. There was, as he understood society, none whatever in Manhattan. For the little while he must remain in the States he would guard the integrity of his privacy as closely as possible.

"Cherry Chester," he murmured, "how unutterably ridiculous."

Thus Boycie dining in lonely state was not vouchsafed another glimpse of that startling young man, nor did she see him when she, Cherry, Higgins, Hilda, and the dachshunds left the train. For Mr. Amberton, glancing from the corridor windows, came to the conclusion that all that crowd was for him and withdrew at once to his drawing-room until it had made up its collective mind to disperse. When, a little later, his young and vigorous publisher knocked at his door, he asked nonchalantly, "Welcoming committee gone, I hope?" his publisher blushed faintly, an accomplishment given to few publishers.

"I'm afraid I'm all the committee there is, Amberton."

"But that mob — ?"

"Cherry Chester came in on the *Century*, too."

"Oh," said Amberton, "I see. The motion picture actress, I understand. I can't imagine anything more futile. Give me a primitive woman, the slim copper girl, with the high, small breasts —"

"Certainly," murmured his publisher, anxious to please an author whose books sold

36

well into the sixty and seventy-five thousand class, and wondered frantically where in Manhattan such a young woman might be found. He thought fleetingly of the Cotton Club. But he understood that in these days Harlem went to college and read *Anthony Adverse*.

But perhaps Anthony Amberton as well.

He asked, "Hadn't we better get along now? I took a suite for you as you asked. How long will you be here?"

"I've no idea, no longer than is necessary, I hope."

"There are certain people very anxious to meet you. I thought — a luncheon or two, with some of the more important critics? And if you'd be willing to address a book luncheon, a publishers' dinner, and several women's clubs? The women are really vital; they buy the books, you see. And of course, if you'd sign books at one of the department stores — ?"

Mr. Amberton brushed back the curls from his brow. His publisher, regarding him, fascinated, wondered why the gesture did not nauseate him, the beholder. It did not. Mr. Amberton suggested, "Let's talk about that later, shall we?" and smiled upon the other man. And the publisher thought, *By the Lord Harry and this and that — if I could get him on a platform and he'd smile like that at the female customers, we'd sell a hundred thousand.*

"I am," remarked Mr. Amberton, striding along the platform beside his welcoming committee, "a very simple man, at heart. Cities appall me. I am at home only in the speaking silence of deep woods or on the top of some distant mountain close to the stars. Will you believe me when I say that I am afraid of women — civilized women?"

"Sez you!" thought the publisher, who was no fool. He merely thought he thought it. To his horror he discovered that he had thought it, aloud.

Anthony Amberton laughed. He flung back his head and laughed. The publisher looked at him and then he, too, laughed. They stood at the taxi entrance to Grand Central Station and laughed in unison and aloud. The porter who bore Anthony's bags mopped his brow and chuckled.

"We'll get along," decided Anthony.

He had swum the Hellespont, the Panama Canal, and a couple of rivers; he had shot great rapids in birchbark canoes, and had stood on far mountain peaks and proclaimed himself a Cortez — not too stout. He had grappled with lions, panthers, tigers, lynx, cobras, bushmasters, fer-de-lances, prehistoric lizards, and mosquitoes. He had lived as a native, among lost tribes. He had kissed a duchess and slapped a lady with royal blood in her veins. He had taken part in three revolutions and once he shot the incoming president of a new republic in the right leg, by error. He had thought the gentleman the outgoing president. However, they remained the best of friends. He was completely at home with machine guns, rifles, revolvers, shotguns, krisses, daggers, poniards, machetes, and seventeen different forms of poison. He had lived with a cannibal tribe and partaken unblenching, of their most prized fodder. He knew all about voodoo. He had had eight savage mistresses of varying shades of color. And he had left no stone of incident in his exciting life unturned in cold print. He was, in fact, quite a person.

In the taxi, as they rode toward his hotel, he said thoughtfully to his publisher, who was completely aware of his real name and his sober, industrious ancestry, "Perhaps it is because my father's fortune was made in — ah — certain rather practical commodities that I was fated to roam those parts of the world in which bathtubs and other alleged necessities of existence have no place."

I bet, thought the publisher, while registering proper interest and agreement, *that he carries 'em with him — portable, and possibly in platinum.*

Passing a street in the Fifties, Mr. Amberton glanced carelessly from his window and perceived a large crowd gathered in front of the house on the corner. Several stalwart cops, afoot and ahorse, held them back. Photographers flourished their black boxes, which can carry such a charge of flattery or the reverse, and a small truck on which was perched a newsreel camera ambled snortingly past.

"What on earth?" asked Anthony, indicating.

The publisher glanced out. "Oh, that's Lucy Van Steeden's house. She's Cherry Chester's grandmother. Marvelous woman, the Van Steeden. She wrote her memoirs a year or so ago. I had them in the office. Amazing. But quite unpublishable. We would have been knee-deep in libel suits in no time."

Anthony shrugged. "It's a curious commentary on civilization, so called — especially American civilization," he remarked, "that the stupid eyes of the populace are forever riveted to the ordinary spectacle of some fairly personable young woman — personable only because of her dressmaker, her hairdresser, and her cosmetician — merely because she is fortunate enough to photograph well, while the camera records her stereotyped gestures and the sound apparatus her voice uttering the platitudes whipped together for her by some overpaid scenarist. Yet the scientist toils in his laboratory and discovers the secrets of life and of death, and the world passes by his unnoticed door, neither knowing nor caring."

"Quite," agreed the publisher. He thought, *He talks like a book. His books.*

"Nevertheless," he added, "I'd like to see the meeting between Cherry Chester and the Van Steeden. The family is filthy rich, and the old lady holds the purse strings. They say she keeps an eagle eye on her granddaughter's doings. The mother is married to a minor Swedish prince — Gyllencrona — it's her third marriage. She's rarely in this country."

Anthony yawned. "Comic place, America," he observed; and the publisher thought, *If I hit him — But he's bigger than I am — and besides, he's selling like hot cakes.* He remembered that Mr. Amberton had held a couple of boxing and fencing records at Oxford. And was an excellent shot. Wounded elephants, mother tigresses, or patriotic publishers — what did it matter? He swallowed twice and said, "Isn't it?"

Meantime, in the house on the corner of Fifth Avenue and Fifty-something Street, Lucy Van Steeden was stamping a very small foot. "Somebody send those howling lunatics away. No, I will *not* see any members of the press. Why God has seen fit to endow me with a public woman for a granddaughter only He in His wisdom can fathom. . . . Come here, Sarah!"

Not too meekly, Cherry came.

Her grandmother looked at her. She said, "You've been in this house for half an hour and it is now bedlam. Pull down the shades. Put crepe on the door. Send for Dr. Martin. My nerves are completely shattered. Go upstairs to your room and wash off that disgusting paint!"

Cherry blinked and a whole strip of eyelashes fell off. Her own lashes were short and thick and dark and rayed out like those of a Chinese doll. Her grandmother shrieked. The sound was positively profane. "Will you stop dropping eyelashes all over my carpets? Go this instant, and scrub your face. When you can confront me looking like a human being and unlike one of those dolls in a Coney Island shooting-gallery, I'll talk to you. But not until then, Sarah Brown."

Outraged, Cherry Chester, whose name was Sarah Brown, left the room. And Lucy Van Steeden closed one rakish black eye and looked at Marian Boyce-Medford. "She'll do," she said, "but no high horses around here. I'm the only one with a stable in this house. She'll have to remember that. Look here, Boycie, is there anything in this Egyptian prince business?"

CHAPTER THREE

AN ANTIQUE AMONG ANTIQUES

"No," said Boycie.

Mrs. Van Steeden sat down upon a chair. Her imperious hand motioned Miss Boyce-Medford to do likewise. Boycie sat. She had no choice. Mrs. Van Steeden regarded her granddaughter's companion with narrowed eyes. "I hope not, for her sake. But you'd lie for her, steal for her, commit murder for her if necessary. You spoil her — inexcusably. I thought, when Sylvia left her on my hands, that in engaging you I was guaranteeing her future. Now look what's happened to her!"

Boycie's head was bloody but unbowed. She raised it, abruptly, even higher and her gray crest gave her the look of an aging, plump, but still vocal cockatoo. "Nothing's happened to her," she said roundly. "Underneath this veneer —"

"Veneer!" said Mrs. Van Steeden and snorted genteelly. "A Van Steeden — for she's half that, thank heaven, with *veneer!*" Her eyes consulted her furniture for consolation. There was no veneer about the furniture. It stood in the smaller of the Van Steeden drawing-rooms as solid as Gibraltar's rock. The drawing-room was solid also. It had not altered with the times. Like the late Queen Victoria, Mrs. Van Steeden disliked change and disliked also the giving away of objects which had become endeared to her by long association. Lucy Van Steeden's Manhattan house was the envy of antique, junk, and curio dealers. It was completely filled with *objets d'art* and *objets* not at all *d'art*. It had whatnots and gimcracks, bric-a-brac, shells in which the ocean roared, tea chests left by ancestors who had sailed to China, ormolu, steel engravings, Currier and Ives, Corots, Whistlers, Sargents, chromos, lithographs, The Stag at Bay, photographs, some of crowned heads and some of heads which should have been crowned, and some of heads which had been dropped by nurses. It was also full of furniture, maple, mahogany, walnut, carved, plain, comfortable, and uncomfortable. There were Morris chairs and pampas grass, Chippendale, Queen Anne, several relics of the Louis', Sheraton, Duncan Phyfe, Adam mantels, crystal chandeliers, green student lamps, tidies, Brussels lace and velvet draperies. There were even gas fixtures which had been somewhat insanely converted into electricity. There were large vases and

small vases and thousands of simpering shep-
herdesses, and a boat in a bottle and a complete set of doll's furniture made out of gilded
wire. Nothing in this house had been
changed, except the bathrooms. The bathrooms were completely Smith and Company.
But for the rest Mrs. Van Steeden did not al-
ter, she merely added. Boycie, looking around
her, wondered, not for the first time, what a
good old-fashioned California tremor would
do to the Van Steeden mansion. It had often
occurred to her that if Cherry should take it
into her head, and hand, to throw things she
might go completely berserk in the presence
of so much handsome material.

Velvet, chenille, fringe, china, glass, pot-
tery, footstools, fire screens, pouffes. Two
pug dogs. The house was a nightmare.

Boycie said gently, "Cherry —"

"Her name is Sarah!"

"I'm sorry, I forget. Sarah's a very fine person, Mrs. Van Steeden. A generous, warm-
hearted, kind —"

"I'm not engaging a domestic!"

Boycie gave up in despair. "She can't help it
if the men are attracted to her. She's a very alluring creature —"

"Alluring!" Mrs. Van Steeden looked
slightly ill. "I thought we'd done with allurement in the person of my daughter Sylvia.

Where Sylvia derives her insatiable —"

She broke off. She knew perfectly well whence Sylvia's characteristics, to say nothing of Sylvia herself, had been derived. Mrs. Van Steeden's late and unlamented husband had been of the very gay Edwardian type. For him the era of gaslight and hansom cabs, stage doors and little slippers filled with vintage champagne had been created. Or so he had thought. He had made the most of all his opportunities and importunings.

Mrs. Van Steeden put her feet on a petit point hassock and clucked to a pug. "Are those ridiculous foreign dogs of Sarah's safely locked away?" she inquired sharply. Boycie nodded. Mrs. Van Steeden relaxed.

"I've a cable from Sylvia. She's gone off somewhere with that Swedish person. She doesn't want Sarah to meet her for another two months. I don't wish her to either. I wish her to stay with me until at least after Christmas."

Boycie sighed. This meant, of course, that the sailing would be delayed and that her own plans must be changed. Mrs. Van Steeden continued, "We will spend the holidays as usual, at Riverview."

Boycie's sigh was deeper. Riverview was a large frame house overlooking the Hudson. Mrs. Van Steeden still preserved the original grant from the Indians, or perhaps from Henry Hudson himself, to the acres and acres of wooded estate. The house was, alas, of a more recent vintage. It evoked memories of General Grant. It was gingerbreaded and gabled and mansarded and porticoed, and inside it was a replica of the Manhattan house. It was an entirely terrible place.

A manservant came in. He was incredibly old. He bore with him two very small glasses of a sherry dryer than cowboy wit and a couple of biscuits which may or may not have been meant for the pugs. Mrs. Van Steeden put out a white, veined, aged yet surprisingly strong hand for a glass and graciously conveyed to her guest that the other glass was hers. The glass was fragile in the extreme and Boycie lifted it gingerly to her unenthusiastic lips. She glanced over the rim at her hostess. She thought, *She's completely period.*

Lucy Van Steeden was a small, thin woman. She looked her years which were many. But her wrinkled skin was pink and white and satin soft. She had believed in soap and water for a very long time. There was a dusting of rice powder on her very thin, very high-bridged nose. Her eyes were still extraordinarily black. Her hair was very white, if sparse. She wore it high and in a fringe, in the mode once adored by female royalty and now coming once more into fashion. Since her husband's death she had worn black or white, dove gray or lavender. She wore these colors in silks, brocades, satins, velvets, and moires. She had her dresses made for her and they each possessed at least a thousand hooks and eyes, slips and plackets. Around her throat she had bound a black velvet ribbon with a pearl slide. She wore the Van Steeden minor pearls by daylight. Sometimes at night the major rope came out of the safe and with it a few of the diamonds, rubies, or what have you. She had almost everything. Today, in black, with rose diamonds in old, old settings on fingers and wrists, she lacked only a prime minister.

"What's keeping the girl?" she demanded.

Cherry was upstairs in the suite allotted herself, her dogs, and her companion. She was making faces at herself in the mirror. Hilda, standing by with the simplest of wool frocks, regarded her with stoic sympathy. What, in her mind, Hilda called Cherry's grandmother — in round Norwegian — doesn't bear repeating or print. She was very sorry for Cherry.

Cherry asked, "Am I plain enough, Hilda?"

"Very plain," agreed Hilda, after a moment.

The red hair was slicked back of the little

ears, the waves battered to a semblance of smoothness. There was no paint upon the high-cheekboned face and the beautiful mouth was the pale pink nature had intended. The false eyelashes lay abandoned upon the dresser.

Cherry sailed at Hilda, embraced Elsa, the dachshund, patted Lohengrin, who slumbered in a basket near by, and went on downstairs. She stood presently in front of her grandmother with her hands folded. She was demure and she was meek. Boycie's heart quickened with apprehension. Something would happen. It was the lull before the storm. "Will I do?" asked Cherry.

Mrs. Van Steeden put up a gold *lorgnon* and surveyed her grandchild. She snapped it shut, dropped it to dangle from its gold and diamond chain, and nodded. She said, "Sit down. Here — on the hassock."

Cherry sat. Her grandmother remarked, "You're thinner."

"It's the camera," explained Cherry.

"The camera — what camera? Don't tell me those oafs have not gone," began Mrs. Van Steeden in rising anxiety.

"They've gone," Boycie assured her. She rose and walked to the windows, held aside the lace and velvet, and peered. "Yes," she reported, "no one's there."

"Good," approved Mrs. Van Steeden. "Now please explain, Cherry, carefully. I don't understand this jargon of yours."

Cherry said patiently, "The camera adds ten pounds. I mean, one looks ten pounds heavier on the screen. Hence we all have to keep thin."

"You look starved," said her grandmother. "A picked chicken. Pindling. Peaked. We'll fatten you up."

Cherry shuddered and looked appealingly at Boycie, who turned her head aside. *I'll get even with you for that,* thought Cherry, sensing disloyalty or hidden laughter. Meantime her grandmother continued.

"I really don't understand. Of course, I've never seen a motion picture."

It was a lie and Cherry knew it. Her grandmother had seen both her pictures. But appearances must be kept up.

"And it is amazing to me how the public — Really, Sarah, you are very plain. Good bones. Race. An excellent skin if it weren't for your deplorable freckles. But as for looks — Your mother," remarked Mrs. Van Steeden, "is far handsomer. Not," she added casually, "that I care for the type."

Cherry laughed. She flung her long arms about her grandmother's old, sharp knees. She said, "You're a humbug. You know you think I'm beautiful — a credit to all the Van Steedens."

Her grandmother pushed her away. A reluctant smile jerked at the corners of her soft thin lips. She said, "Don't try to cozen me. What's all this I hear about an Egyptian prince?"

Cherry said, "Mustn't believe all you hear. He was rather nice. Asked me to marry him."

"What?" shrieked her grandmother.

"I didn't," said Cherry hastily. "I refused. Don't worry, Gram, none of it makes sense. They all want to marry you, or else —"

"Or else what?" inquired her grandmother.

"Dear me," said Cherry, "and you a woman of the world! Skip it."

Boycie said hastily, "I assure you, dear Mrs. Van Steeden, that the child hardly knew Prince Nubar."

"Pasha," murmured Cherry.

"Hardly knew him, yet he proposed marriage?"

"Just an old Egyptian custom," said Cherry casually, "and Cleopatra is supposed to have had red hair. Myself I think it was by grace of henna."

"What has Cleopatra to do with it?" asked her grandmother.

"Nothing," said Cherry, adding tentatively,

"by Anukis and Ptah!" and Boycie shuddered while Mrs. Van Steeden asked sharply, "By — what? Is it possible that you are becoming profane?"

"Anything is possible," agreed Cherry, "but I was just invoking a couple of Egyptian gods." She smiled at her grandmother, and, reluctantly, her grandmother smiled back. Cherry said softly, "Honest, Lucy, I can take care of myself."

Mrs. Van Steeden permitted the impertinent use of her Christian name to pass unrebuked and Cherry added, "Or if I can't there's always Boycie."

Boycie did not look flattered. Mrs. Van Steeden said, "Sarah, you know how deeply I resent this persistence of yours to continue on the stage and in the motion pictures against my wish. I have not altered my mind on the matter —"

No, she had not. She no longer stormed, a frigid storm with words like small, sharp pieces of ice, of hail, cutting, flaying; she no longer threatened. But she would never be reconciled. Cherry, looking at her with green and thoughtful eyes, realized that. She'd said to Boycie often, "She'll get over it, after a while." But she would not get over it. Lucy Van Steeden had been born in an era when actresses were not received although they were received now, and welcomed, in any society except Lucy Van Steeden's; they were still, to her, public persons, created for the fickle amusement of those who paid to see them put through their paces. They might be, it was even said that many were, honest women, in the old sense of the word, even admirable, but that guarantee was no card of admission to the Van Steeden house.

Lucy Van Steeden had twice in her life loved intensely. The first person she had loved was her husband, whom she had married at eighteen. He had destroyed her love because he had destroyed her respect for him. She was not aware that there are women to whom love and respect are not necessarily teammates. The second person was her granddaughter. She was fond of her daughter Sylvia, with impatience and with her unreasoning blood. But Cherry she loved.

Cherry had lived with her for a good many years; here in this great overcrowded house, and at Riverview, and in hotels in Europe, and that Cherry had been a lunatic child, with red hair flying and terrible tempers and of an unconquerable sweetness. Then her mother had taken her and Boycie. But after that Cherry had come home again, a slim girl with very green eyes and a thousand rebellious moods. At that time she was eighteen and determined to go on the stage. Mrs. Van Steeden had forbidden it. Sylvia had written to forbid it also, but weakly. A daughter on the stage would entertain her, if the truth be known, and moreover she was by then in love with Gyllencrona and she had always been incapable of harboring more than one major emotion at a time.

But Boycie had advised, "Let her have her way, Mrs. Van Steeden. She'll tire of it . . ."

Cherry had her way, but not until, with her stage all set and her hair down, and her face made whiter than usual with powder, she had taken poison. She hadn't taken very much and she was careful to announce immediately that she had taken it; and there had been immediate doctors sworn to silence, and all the usual rather undignified aftermath. But although Lucy Van Steeden, furious, made her pronouncement: "I don't believe it . . . not enough to harm her . . . dramatizing herself — I won't be coerced . . . !" she had been very much shaken. So Sarah Brown had become Cherry Chester.

England first, with Boycie on guard, and several months of walking on in a Shakespearean revival. Then a small part in a modern play; then a better one. Finally America, and the press agents rubbing their hands: Cherry Chester, granddaughter of — daughter of —

"I'll thank you to leave my name out of it!" Mrs. Van Steeden had cried furiously. "Have you no shame?"

Now Cherry asked softly, "Grandmother, haven't I convinced you yet? My career —"

"Fiddlesticks!" said Lucy.

She rose so suddenly that she almost upset the hassock and the girl upon it. She said, "Your career isn't worth that." She snapped her thin fingers. "You have made a certain *réclame*. I cannot judge your worth as an actress for I have never seen you play. You have an aptitude for aping others, you can speak lines given you by a playwright. I have seen certain photographs —"

"Stills," said Cherry.

"How absurd. Yes. You look utterly unlike yourself in them. As you do — I assume," she said hastily — "on the screen. Fools pay you a salary out of all proportion, and other fools go to the theater in order to recompense your lunatic employers for that salary."

"I have thousands of fan mail letters a week."

"Fan mail!" Her grandmother glared at her. "From your recent letters it appears to me that you believe me reconciled to all this spurious excitement — and notoriety. I am not. You spoke of a career. There is only one career to which a well-bred, well-born woman

56

is entitled. That is the career of wife and mother. I have told you what I am willing to settle on you should you, by any fortunate chance, happen to marry with my approval. And of what will happen also if you become involved in anything even remotely resembling a scandal, married or unmarried."

Her small narrow jaw snapped shut. Boycie regarded her, fascinated. Cherry yawned slightly. She knew this all by heart. One breath of scandal and not only would her private income cease, and at once, but the Van Steeden will would be changed. Sylvia was no longer in that will. Her mother had settled a certain sum upon her, on her third marriage, and that would have to serve her for the rest of her life. But Sylvia had the Brown money. Unfortunately for Cherry, Mr. Brown had died while still in the first, almost apoplectic flush of infatuation for the slender and golden-haired Sylvia. And Cherry, christened Sarah, had been but a small, unconsidered atom. Therefore the Brown fortune had descended to Mrs. Brown with no strings to it. It was doubtful, as her habit was for expensive husbands, whether at Sylvia's death there would be any Brown money left.

And as far as that went, the Van Steeden women lived, it seemed, forever.

Mrs. Van Steeden said, "It is time for luncheon." She regarded Cherry and Boycie. She did not add "wash your hands and face" but the implication was there. She said, "I have asked a few old friends to dine with us — and your cousin Horace, who is just back from Europe."

In their adjoining rooms:

"Horace!" cried Cherry furiously, "fish face! Harvard. Football. Wall Street. Clipping coupons. He makes me sick. She's been trying to marry him off to me since I was three and he was ten."

"He's very eligible," Boycie reminded her.

"He's a stuffed shirt. He reminds me of baked eggplant. I can't stand him," said Cherry, and flung a cake of soap upon the bathroom floor.

Boycie appeared in the doorway. She suggested, "It might be wise to be a little — kinder to him."

Cherry looked at her in the mirror. Boycie shrank. The expression was of pure ferocity. She said however, mildly, "What's Gram thinking of? The idiot's my cousin. Think of the superidiots we might be expected to produce!"

"I'd rather not, if you don't mind; and he's your third cousin," said Boycie, "remember that — or second, once removed."

"He couldn't be removed too far to suit me. Horace Van Steeden," said Cherry savagely.

"Come, you're a little unfair. He's rather good-looking, and not too unintelligent, and sound as a bell —"

"Did you ever hear of bells cracking?" asked Cherry. She laughed suddenly. "Never mind, it won't be long now — When are we sailing, exactly?"

The news was broken to her gently. It was now November. They wouldn't sail until, say, January.

"Hell!" said Cherry, and flung a toothbruth glass on the floor. It shattered beautifully. Elsa pricked up interested ears and Hilda, unpacking, smiled. Now it was becoming more like home.

"Quite," murmured Boycie, perfectly convinced.

CHAPTER FOUR

LOVELY, IN A CURIOUS WAY

Horace Van Steeden presented the Van Steeden flunky with his hat, stick, gloves, and overcoat, cast a satisfied glance at himself in the mirror, and went into the drawing-room to pay his respects to his elderly relative, the head of his house. He was a large, blond young man, as scrubbed and shining as a prize pig and with the small alert eyes of such an animal. His fair hair was neatly brushed. He had enormous shoulders and, regrettably, a slight tendency toward a thickened waistline. Cherry in a corner of the room observed him with malice.

"Paunch and Judy!" she muttered, as he advanced toward her and bowed over her hand.

Her wardrobe always included Van Steeden frocks, worn only in the company of her grandmother. Tonight's was black velvet. The *décolletage* was modest, the sleeves were long. Really, thought Horace, murmuring his delight over her hand, the girl was very plain. He failed to understand it — he had heard

60

that the camera never lied. But Munchausen was a George Washington beside whatever magic apparatus had caught and fixed the shadow of Miss Chester upon the screen. Horace had seen her. He had even nudged the man beside him and asked hoarsely, "Who'd believe it?"

Horace was quite aware that Lucy Van Steeden desired that a marriage between himself and her granddaughter be announced. He, for one, was not at all averse. Plain or not, his third cousin was a dangerously attractive young woman. One heard stories about her. Secretly Horace purchased all the motion picture magazines and read with astonishment sundry statements attributed to Miss Chester. Nowadays it gave a man a certain cachet to be married to a woman in the public eye. He would not even object if she continued on the stage and screen after their marriage. But, of course, the old lady would raise the devil.

Horace's twig of the family tree was affluent. But nothing to be compared with the other branch. Moreover, with things in the present desperate state, due to causes he thought of as Communism, Socialism, Reds, and What-is-the-country-coming-to when a man may not earn a dishonest living, it would be as well to have the bulk of the Van Steeden fortune as a sort of anchor to windward. Unfortunately he and Cherry had never got on very well. They met only at rare intervals. Once, during the making of her first picture, he chanced to be in Los Angeles and so, dutifully, "looked her up." But Cherry had not been in a mood for relatives that day. She had just reduced her supervisor to unmanly tears and had broken the violin of a musician across her knee because the music played for her big scene had been, she said, "off key." So when Horace arrived at her hotel she had no use for him. "Send him away," she demanded, from her bungalow in the hotel grounds. "No. I don't care if he is my cousin. . . . I haven't any cousins . . . No. I won't see him. . . ." And she had all but torn the telephone from its moorings.

Horace was looked upon with suspicion. The management said smoothly, "I am sorry, Mr. — er — Van Steeden, but Miss Chester does not seem to know you!"

"That," said Horace, "is absurd." A little later he went into action. Up and at 'em, Harvard. He arrived by stealth at the bungalow and knocked. A window opened. Cherry regarded him balefully. "Go away," said Cherry, and threw a thermos of iced water at him.

He had ducked and been ducked. He had shouted, and twenty years slipped from his massive shoulders, "I'll tell Cousin Lucy!"

"Tell and be damned," said Miss Chester, and slammed the window with a finality which cracked the glass.

Boycie had said, "My dear!"

"He won't tell," said Cherry. "Gram hates what she calls lack of enterprise. He'd be ashamed to tell."

He hadn't told.

"You're looking as charming as ever," said Horace, and smirked upon her.

Cherry said, "You're a liar, Horace, old bean," and gave him her most radiant and malicious smile. They stood together by the mantel and Lucy regarded them through her *lorgnon* with satisfaction. Dinner was announced. "Horace," said his hostess, "your arm."

He hastened to present it. She hardly reached to his shoulder but she towered inches above him in dignity. Boycie and Cherry followed presently into the paneled room hung with grim portraits of hideous ancestors who had been colonial governors, or merely British scapegoats or Dutch opportunists. The rest of the company settled itself sedately. Elderly ladies covered with the sort of bugles which never blow reveille; and elderly gentlemen with white whiskers and bloodshot eyes, still discreetly roving.

A family gathering.

"I shall go mad!" announced Cherry at eleven o'clock that night. The gathering had dispersed, and she now sat cross-legged on Boycie's bed in green pajamas.

"I think not," said Boycie, yawning.

"Oh, yes, I shall. I escaped from this once —"

"My dear, you say that every year."

"I know," admitted Cherry. She contemplated the long weeks ahead. "if — if you don't get me out of this, Boycie," she menaced, "I'll break out in some kind of a rash act. Wait and see!"

Apprehensively Boycie waited. Nothing happened. Christmas came and went and the holiday week spent at Riverview was memorable for its dullness. Horace spent it with them; and as there was no snow and the mild weather held, he took Cherry for walks and sat with her in the ramshackle gazebo overlooking the river, and proposed to her solemnly in homeopathic doses. And regularly she refused him.

Home-grown turkeys, homemade mincemeat, imported plum pudding, and very old brandy, Burgundy laid down by a dead Van Steeden. Relatives. Neighbors. Much too much to eat; and an odor of Christmas greens and ancestors. Cherry tore her hair. She wailed, "I can't stand it!"

Boycie said soothingly, "You must. It won't be for long."

"I've been dead and buried for over a month. I'm beginning to haunt myself, I tell you!" She thought longingly of a great steamer and a white deck and passengers whispering as she walked by — "That's Cherry Chester!" She thought of the wind in the canyons and the palms stirring and the lights in the Cocoanut Grove and the music at the Trocadero. She thought of Palm Springs and the desert sun. She thought of a dark man with a regrettable wife and a very British way of casual seduction. She thought of Hans working in the garden she had leased and which was no longer her own; she thought of the flat on Park Avenue where Higgins and the ex-Mrs. Higgins, the parlormaid and the chauffeur waited.

"No," her grandmother had said, "of course I won't let you go. I am a very old woman, Sarah, you owe me a little of your company. What would people say, my own granddaughter living in a rented apartment with the Van Steeden house standing empty?"

She'd give the million dollars Lucy might leave her to walk down Olivero Street again; or to drop in at the Vendome for lunch; or to dine at a Brown Derby.

"She has refused me again," said Horace to his father's cousin.

"Be patient." Lucy, who took to embroidery in her idle moments as a lesser woman might take to drink, set a stitch in her interminable tapestry and looked at him through her glasses. "She is very young —"

"Not so very —"

"Young enough not to know her own mind. All this trivial adulation has turned her head. She will welcome, one day, a good man's love."

Horace's chest swelled. He remembered that. He repeated it to Cherry a little later.

"A good man's love —" he said, among other things.

Cherry regarded him, it seemed, with sympathy. Her pointed chin was cupped in her pink palm. There were other palms, but not those of her garden, in Beverly Hills. She and Horace sat together in the underwater atmosphere of the Riverview conservatory. She asked timidly, "Are you really a good man, Horace?"

Horace started. He remembered the apartment on Riverside Drive and the flaxen-haired lady of the chorus. He had run true to old-fashioned form. He even preferred it if the truth were known. He looked at Cherry's very slim lines without desire. Just for the moment he regretted that the apartment was no longer his; nor yet the lady. But as for desire — when Cherry wished, she had a way with her, and there was about her a glamour not entirely composed of grandma's gilt.

He replied, "I — I'm a man of the world, Sarah. There have been episodes — you'll understand — your recent life —"

"Horace!" she gasped, and to his startled gaze she all but swooned. "Horace, I can't believe it of you!"

"My dear," cried Horace, consoling, "it was over long ago. I assure you you have no need for jealousy. I —"

"Leave me," commanded Cherry hoarsely. "Leave me, I implore you." A couple of generations vanished. She was a lady with hock bottle shoulders weeping over the cruder lusts of brutal man. Aghast, Horace left. He looked for Boycie; he found her, and whispered, distracted. "She — she needs you."

"Who needs me?" inquired Boycie, suspicious.

"Sarah — I have wounded her — deeply, in the conservatory."

Boycie, amazed, but moved to mirth by his sentence construction, went briskly to the overheated and dank bulge of glass which formed a curious excrescence upon the house called Riverview. She found Cherry curled up in a wicker chair having, it appeared, a convulsion.

"In heaven's name!" said Boycie severely.

Cherry raised her face. It was streaming with tears. Laughter shook her. She said weakly, "Boycie, can you believe it, but Cousin Horace has once had an affair. He confessed it to me, as ever was, not ten minutes ago by the clock in the stomach of Venus in yonder drawing-room."

Boycie laughed too. She sat down, after a minute, and said, "It isn't very kind of you, Cherry —"

"You mean," asked Cherry, solemnly, "that I Lead Him On?"

"I'm afraid you do."

"Good," said Cherry viciously, "and where I'll lead him will be nobody's business."

Horace returned to New York without his third cousin's promise. And yet were not the green eyes softer than usual as she gave him her slim and narrow hand in farewell, and did he not feel in answer to his manly pressure a faint response? When he had departed Cherry tenderly straightened out her slender fingers. "I should have them insured along with my legs," she mourned.

On the next evening, their last in Riverview, Cherry was summoned to the presence after the household had retired. Mrs. Van Steeden lay in her high carved bed. Her nightgown was finest handkerchief linen, long sleeved and high at the throat. She wore over it a quilted satin bed jacket of mauve. And she drank chocolate from a gold-encrusted porcelain cup of Sèvres. Her maid, who was probably older than the Flood, tottered about the room putting things in order. Mrs. Van Steeden set down the cup and dismissed her. Then she beckoned Cherry closer. Her look said that she did not approve of pajamas, but her lips were silent on the subject.

Cherry sat down beside the bed.

"Horace," announced her grandmother unnecessarily, "has gone home."

As no reply occurred to her, Cherry made none.

"You heard what I said," her grandmother inquired sharply.

"Why, yes," admitted Cherry, longing for a cigarette, "I heard. But I thought it purely rhetorical."

Mrs. Van Steeden smiled slightly. She reached for a tortoise-shell box at her bedside and extracted a scented object composed of tobacco and paper. She offered one to Cherry. "You may smoke. I know you do so, in your own rooms. I have smoked since my marriage — but never in public. It relaxes the nerves."

Cherry lighted her grandmother's cigarette and then her own. She coughed slightly. The thing was execrable. Mrs. Van Steeden stated quietly, "It is my desire that you and Horace marry."

"But I don't love him," argued Cherry.

The old lady shrugged slightly. "That doesn't matter. You will probably become fond of him. That does matter. It has been my observation over a long period of time that the ardent love matches do not always create a steady flame of happiness."

Her fingers holding the cigarette trembled slightly.

"Horace," she continued, "has good blood. And he will make you a good husband. He is not, I grant you, exciting, but then so few men are nowadays." She sighed faintly. "He will be reliable and he will be honest —"

"I'm not hiring a butler!" said Cherry angrily.

The black eyes twinkled. Mrs. Van Steeden remembered a remark of her own to Miss Boyce-Medford not so long ago. This girl was very like her in many ways. Perhaps that is why she so doted upon her, vanity being the last of the passions to die.

"I have no intention of forcing you, even if I could. I am aware that you are of age. I am quite aware that for some absurd reason, incomprehensible to me, you are able to — make a living. But — I simply ask you not to be too hasty in your decisions. I am aware," she added, as Cherry was silent, "that Horace is a rather dull young man. But dullness in a husband can be counted among the major virtues. That is all. You may go. You may kiss me good night."

Cherry's cool soft lips touched lightly the wrinkled cheek which smelled faintly of lavender water and talcum. Then, as she turned, "If you will hand me a Kempis?" suggested her grandmother.

Cherry gave her the book from the bedside table. "And tell Matty that she may take away my cup," added Mrs. Van Steeden.

Cherry fled. Encountering Matty hovering by the door, she delivered her message. Matty said, crossly, with the latitude accorded the very old servant, "I hope to goodness you haven't crossed her in anything, Miss Sarah, her stomach is that easy upset these days," and went on into the room. Cherry, bursting into Boycie's gloomy sanctum, flung herself upon a very uncomfortable chaise longue.

"She'll have me married yet — !" she cried.

Boycie looked up from her book. It was *David Harum*, the most modern novel she had been able to find in the Riverview library.

"Marry whom?"

71

"Horace, of course. Don't sit there like a judge. You make me nervous. She'll write Sylvia," said Cherry, speaking thus disrespectfully of her mother, "and she'll put the screws on her. All the time we're abroad Sylvia will be at me. She'll weep and she'll rage and she'll — oh, you know Sylvia!"

"Yes, indeed," said Boycie thoughtfully.

"I've half a mind not to go abroad," said Cherry. "If I could find a place where I'd be alone — oh, don't look like that, Boycie, I didn't mean you. Anyway you have to go, you owe it to yourself to get away from me for a while. But if I could find a place where people didn't know me, where Grandmother and her Horace couldn't pursue me. He will, I tell you. He as much as told me that he's thinking of running over again while I'm there — isn't it just like Horace to run over some three thousand miles of Atlantic? If Sylvia could help pull this off she'd be in solid with Gram for the rest of her days. She knows that. Look here, Boycie, something's got to be done about this."

"Go to bed," suggested Boycie, "and sleep on it. I've never seen you as upset."

"I know. But I've never seen her more determined," replied Cherry, moaning slightly. She rose and went to the door. There she looked back, darkly, very slender in the pajamas, the red hair ruffled about her head, a rakish halo. "I've never been drunk in my life," she said, "but I wish I were — this minute."

On the following day they returned to New York. The next few weeks were sodden with dullness. No reporters darkened the Van Steeden door. There was an edict: "As long as you remain with me, Sarah, you are to live an entirely private life." No gay and casual friends from the literary and theatrical circles in New York, no visiting cinema stars so much as saw Cherry Chester. She lived a completely incognito existence. Now and then she fled to walk in the park or to taxi madly around the teeming streets. But never alone. There was always Boycie, faithful shadow, by her side. "Not that I want to," Boycie apologized, "but you know she'll think you're up to something."

It had been established that she and Boycie would sail during the third week in January. Shortly after the middle of the month, with her packing done, Cherry, wandering disconsolately about the house, was ordered to her grandmother's small study. In this white paneled room Mrs. Van Steeden sat at her desk and wrote out her checks and received her lawyers and her men of business, her housekeeper, her cook, her butler, and others of her staff. She asked, looking up from the letter she was writing in her fine, angular hand:

"Cherry, will you do me a favor? I promised to see Nettie today and bring her some things — if you would go in my stead? Mr. Anderson is coming this afternoon."

Mr. Anderson was the lawyer. He was senior partner of Anderson, Anderson, Anderson, and Abrahamson.

Cherry had reached the door when her grandmother spoke again. She said, "Take the carriage. You know I disapprove of taxis."

Mrs. Van Steeden had one of the last of the stables in Manhattan. Sighing, Cherry ordered the brougham. The coachman was older than time but the vehicle was as polished as a jewel and the horses, if a trifle plump, were smart and shining. Lucy Van Steeden had never owned an automobile and never would. On the rare occasions when she was forced to ride in one she sat with her lips pinched together and a look of hatred on her face. She loathed the odor of gasoline. The odor of horseflesh was, at least, in nature.

Cherry was accustomed to the carriage — the various carriages — and the horses. In a way, it was amusing. It would make, she reflected, an excellent publicity picture and then reflected again that even if she could manage a miracle, she was not sufficiently titivated for publicity.

She drove to Nettie's, with a box and a basket. Nettie was an ancient crone who had once been the family seamstress. Once a month Mrs. Van Steeden called upon her, drank a cup of very weak tea, passed the time of day, and departed, leaving behind her a box of elegant and, it seemed, scarcely worn garments, a basket of table delicacies, and a check. Nettie lived in the East Thirties in a house which had once been fashionable and was now given over to roomers. She had known Cherry since that young woman's childhood.

Stately and dignified, the horses drew Cherry and her grandmother's carriage through the traffic. Policemen touched their caps and grinned and taxi drivers not inured stared in amazement. People looked from the sidewalk and said, "My dear, how quaint!" And inside this equipage Cherry smoked a cigarette and yawned.

Arriving at Nettie's and while climbing the dark stairs leading to her fourth floor habitation, Cherry wondered if she would ever be Cherry again. For now she was merely little Sarah Brown, come to call upon an old retainer. She was long-legged and wore pigtails and her face was scrubbed to a pink shininess.

At eighty-six Nettie lived happily and exclusively in the past. It is quite in order to suppose that she knew dimly of Cherry's rather disturbing fame but it did not trouble her overmuch. She saw the girl perhaps once annually and the rather doddering landlady and the still more decrepit lodgers knew that Nettie was visited occasionally by the granddaughter of her former employer. More than that they did not know. Which accounts for blank walls and closed doors as Cherry progressed upward and onward.

There was tepid tea and the usual rather pathetic deprecation, "You shouldn't have brought me so much, Miss Sarah," an exchange of courtesies and a — for Cherry — patient hearkening to long stories. "Miss Sarah, will you ever forget the time you cut up your grandmother's velvet drapes and made a crown for yourself out of a cardboard hatbox and begged me to sew some jet on it? 'I'm a queen, Nettie,' you said, 'and this is my carnation.' You meant coronation, of course," said Nettie, her thin hands fluttering and her failing eyes lit with laughter.

A little later Cherry fled down the stairs as if pursued by evil. To grow old, to be alone, to depend on casual charity, to live in memory, to be gallant withal — she was quick to tears, her throat ached. She wanted to forget Nettie, her chronic cold in the head, her icy hands. And she wanted to remember her. She thought, as she stepped into the carriage, *Some day I'll be old.*

No! No! She wouldn't be, she couldn't be! Or if ever she was, if that practical joker Time must be up to his sly and disgusting tricks with her, she must have a marvelous old age — surrounded with memories of triumphs and not of failures. And she must not be alone.

She consoled herself with thinking that elderly ladies with bank accounts are never alone. But bank accounts dwindle and sometimes —

That did not bear thinking about, she decided.

She looked from the carriage windows. She had given orders to be driven home through the shopping-districts. Presently they were passing a big department store and Cherry looked out, her attention arrested. There were policemen and there was a long queue of waiting, struggling women. Something was happening within the store — a bargain day, perhaps?

She leaned back and then forward again as the horses were forced to halt for lights. A young man was making his way through the crowd and women were screaming and putting out their hands to stop him. He was a hatless young man. He had a wild white face.

Even at this moment Cherry was aware of his most unusual appearance.

Somehow he had escaped the pursuers, if pursued he was. Cherry, flicking cigarette ash from her window, was astonished to find him there beside them at the curb. He held a handkerchief to one eye. He glared at her with the other. He asked, aggrieved, and loudly:

"Why in thunder did you do that?"

Cherry, at the window said, "I'm so sorry."

She wasn't particularly. It didn't matter much to her whether or not her blowing ashes flew into a strange young man's eyes. Why did he have to get in the way of her ashes? was her immediate reaction.

A couple of women were elbowing toward them, pushing through the usual crowd of shoppers. They were calling, waving their arms. They bore little books and big books. They looked determined.

"Good God in heaven!" exclaimed the young man. He dropped the handkerchief, tore open the door of Mrs. Van Steeden's exclusive and shining equipage, and stepped in. The lights changed, the horses moved on, but Cherry was aware that there might be agitation on the box. She thrust her red head from the window and yelled, "It's all right, Peters."

Peters nodded resignedly, touched his hat, and they paced on.

Cherry smiled at the young man. He was, she saw, very handsome, now that he no longer exhibited that tortured expression upon his regular features. He was a big young man with curly dark hair.

She waited for him to recognize her and be overcome. He didn't. Or so it seemed. Neither was he overcome. He merely mopped his brow with another and cleaner handkerchief and muttered distractedly to himself.

Cherry thought, *After all, I'm not made up and I don't look like my pictures, and —*

The young man said gloomily, "Very good of you, I'm sure. If you'll just drop me off — farther on a bit."

Cherry said severely, "I should hand you over to the police. What did you steal?"

He didn't look like a shoplifter. But, crowd and cops and women with blood in their eyes? All the earmarks of minor crime, she decided.

"Steal?" repeated the young man blankly. Then he turned and looked at her fully, it seemed, for the first time, and laughed. He said, "Oh — you thought — I see — but I haven't stolen anything."

He wasn't convincing. Yet he didn't look like a petty thief. Any larceny he might be impelled to commit would surely be on a larger scale. Still times were parlous — and he had a shabby air. The suit he wore — for he had no overcoat — was well cut but showed signs of wear. Buttons were missing from his coat. His tie was askew. His collar was wilted.

Cherry put her hand in her purse. She withdrew it and a bill. The bill was legal tender for twenty American dollars. She said, more Sarah Brown than Cherry Chester, "Here. I don't know what you've done and I don't care but — this will see you through, for a little while."

She thought, Miss Chester again, *What marvelous publicity!* But no one would ever know — unless some day at the right time she said something rather casually and someone overhearing might prick up ears and send in a little item where it would do the most good: *One thrilling thing about Cherry Chester is that her most bountiful charities spring from the impulse of her heart and are never publicized.*

The young man gazed at the twenty dollars. He asked incredulously, "You really think — But that's sweet of you. You — you don't *really* know who I am?"

Cherry replied coldly, perceiving that charity had not begun at home, "No, I can't say that I do —"

He peered at her, interested. "And you don't care?"

"No," admitted Cherry. "I don't. But you

can't be anybody much, or I would have recognized you."

The young man sank back against the lavish upholstery. For the first time he took everything in; the fact that he was actually riding in a private carriage with a slender redheaded girl who had no pretensions to looks but whose speaking voice had personality.

He said, outraged, "If you speak English —"

He meant read. Cherry giggled. Suddenly she was enjoying herself. She replied, "Not very well."

She had, he heard at once, a slight but fascinating accent. He shook his head and blinked. Surely she hadn't had it before? But then he had been occupied with his own thoughts. He shuddered and cussed himself and his publisher and his public. The fact that Anthony Amberton was to sign books in the book section of one of America's largest shops had not gone by unnoticed. It could scarcely have done so, blazoned as it had been in the daily press. Anthony had expected an audience, and one willing to part with two-fifty apiece for the privilege of owning an Amberton autograph. But he hadn't expected about a thousand avid urban and suburban ladies who cried out for romance, if vicariously; who tore buttons from his coat; and who beseiged him with grasping hands and

81

desperate eyes, fat and thin, old and young, blond and dark. He had been overcome by the pressure and weight and stupendous staying power of femininity in the mass. He had been also overcome by odors of face powder, perfume, lipstick, and the hot sweat of adulation. He had even welcomed for once an insult. One small girl dragged to the bookshop by her determined mother — whose husband weighed two hundred and six pounds and always snored after dinner — had cried out shrilly, "But it's only an ole man. I wanna go home — what we hafta stay and look at an ole man for? I thought he was Shirley Temple!"

He asked doubtfully, "You aren't an American?"

"Yes," said Cherry, "I am. But I was brought up in Europe." She rolled her r's faintly.

He said, "This is a horrible city, New York. I'm going to get out of it. Where no one knows me. Where I can be alone."

This matched an earlier mood. Cherry stared at him. She said slowly, "I — too —"

"You?" said Anthony. He looked at her more closely. Her wide mouth drooped, the green eyes were tragic. Cherry said, "I am very lonely," in a tone which took his heart by storm.

He asked again, "You — ? But you're quite lovely, in a curious way. You could be very lovely. Is this your carriage?" he demanded practically.

"It belongs to my people," said Cherry. Her lips quivered. She added, "They do not understand me."

She was enjoying herself very much. Having adopted a role from sheer mischief, she now threw herself into it. She read her lines as if she believed them. She thought of the young man at her side as a thief, compelled to dishonesty by circumstances. She had not been hoodwinked by his denial, his mysterious hints of a personality known the world round. Not she. Of course, he wanted to get away and be alone — where the law couldn't find him! Meantime, he didn't know who she was, that much was patent. One day, picking up a newspaper or a magazine, one day dropping into a motion picture theater, he would see her face, camera featured, and would wonder — where have I seen? No, it can't be! But it must be — the girl in the carriage!

She said slowly, "They are trying to marry me to a man I detest."

Amberton spoke earnestly, "In this day and age! My dear girl, you're free, white, and twenty-one — or aren't you?"

She didn't look twenty-one, he thought;

but white she indubitably was. He added, "Get out — get a job. I never heard of anything more absurd."

Cherry said mournfully, "He has a great deal of money."

"Money!" shouted Anthony. He was outraged. "They'd sell you?" he demanded. "But, my child, these are antediluvian ideas."

"You don't know my family," she sighed. "If I could get away from them — and think — and be alone somehow, on a mountaintop, alone with the stars."

Anthony caught his breath. Here was a young woman who talked his language. He leaned forward and took her hands suddenly in his. He had nice hands, very strong. Cherry, her own lying passive in his clasp, was aware of that strength and was aware also of a slight disturbance of her blood. She thought, amazed, *This isn't happening; not to me —*

"See here," he said, "I must see you, talk to you."

Cherry said, "You can't."

No one ever said you can't to Anthony Amberton. Nor had he as yet encountered a door closed to him. He began to tell her so with indignation, but thought better of it. No. Let her remain in ignorance. It was idyllic, this way. "I'm going away — very soon — far away from the clamor and the fever of this restless city. Come with me. No, don't speak. There must be a way. I must see you again. Free, untroubled by people, yourself — speaking to me from your heart under an open sky. I don't want to know your name, or where you live — I shall not tell you mine. If Fate decrees that we come together once more it will be as if we were the first created man and woman on the earth — nameless — free." He added anxiously, "You are free, are you not?"

Cherry said, "Yes — I'm free — that is, I'm not married. Not yet."

"Nor," he told her quickly, "am I." She sighed, whether with relief or nor he could not tell. He looked out the window, glanced at his wrist — his watch was gone. He yelped with anguish.

"Someone," he announced bitterly, "stole my watch."

Cherry said, "It's five o'clock."

And indeed it was dusk on the streets and the great lamps had flowered into their monstrous blossoms of yellow and it was almost night in the carriage.

He said, "I've an appointment. If —"

But the carriage was stopping again, for a light, on Fifth Avenue. And Anthony put his hand on the door. He said, "This has been an experience very like a dream. If you come, I'll

85

know that it's real —"

He had gone. The door slammed. Cherry said, putting her head out of the window, "Come where?" She shouted, but he had gone. She could see him in the crowd, head and shoulders above most men, hatless, walking swiftly — and without an overcoat — like a young god.

"Well," cried Cherry and sank down against the upholstery, "I'll be damned!"

The twenty dollars lay on the seat beside her. And something else. A card. She picked it up and smiled, ironically. His card, of course. He talked about — I shall be nameless — and left his card. A shoplifter with an address. Raffles, robbed of his wrist watch.

She took it between the thumb and first finger of each hand and tore it. She tore it in half. It was large for a visiting-card. It had no smooth slipperiness nor did her sensitive touch reveal to her the slightest obtrusiveness of engraving. It was so dark in the carriage. She could not read visiting-cards. She ceased to tear and put the two pieces in her purse.

Much later, having delivered Nettie's various messages to her grandmother and having withstood a rather searching cross-examination — "But you have been gone a considerable length of time, my dear." "I know, but I drove through the shopping-district for a breath of air" — she escaped from Mrs. Van Steeden and from Boycie, who regarded her with something resembling suspicion, and went to her room. Once there she delayed a little. She took off her hat, she brushed her hair, she removed the plain expensive tweeds and shrugged herself into a belted robe of heavy silk. And then she took the two pieces of the card from her purse and fitted them together.

She stared; and stared again.

Here was the address of her mountaintop.

The card was plain, it was cheap, it was printed. It advertised the winter rates of a *homelike farmhouse, with good beds, home cooking and all winter sports* situated in New Hampshire. *Accommodations for a few during the winter season,* it read further.

After a long time Cherry crept to the telephone in her bedroom. She looked in a directory, she gave a number, and waited to ask a question in a low and cautious tone. One never knew when Boycie might come in and when Grandmother might take it into her head to lift the instrument off its cradle downstairs.

"Information," came the bored reply, after a couple of long eternities in which worlds were made and remade, people lived and loved and died, and several new revolutions got well under way.

Hanging up, Cherry went over and sat down on her bed. One took, it seemed, the *State of Maine* express and changed at Portland in the morning and was picked up and carried from there to one's destination.

She thought, *I didn't want to go abroad anyway.*

There would be a way. There must be a way. She'd find one and take it. She was tired of being Cherry Chester, she told herself valiantly, the public's Cherry Chester. She was tired of being her grandmother's Sarah Brown. She'd be herself — for a day, or a week, or forever. You live only once. She had a right to adventure and a rendezvous with a shoplifter.

She'd keep that engagement, by hook or with crook.

Chapter Five

DESTINATION: ROMANCE

Boycie was dog-tired. She felt like the successful candidate for a marathon crown at the end of a grueling day. But everything was at last in order. Even the fog, which for the past few days had threatened all shipping and delayed sailings, had lifted. Bright blue and a chilly, but heartening gold were the colors worn by the day of their sailing. Last minute alterations in plans had been made, of course, by the rattlebrained Sylvia but now, barring a brainstorm beneath her yellow hair, their itinerary had been arranged. They would sail direct to Southampton. Boycie would thereafter thankfully deliver her charge to Sylvia and Sylvia's husband in London and would then very gratefully betake herself to a village in which she would be assured rest, quiet, peace, and nothing at all improper but the sanitary system. Cherry would racket around Europe with her mother and stepfather, spending some time at Cannes. For Sylvia had decided that the rigors of a Swedish winter were simply past her powers of endurance. In the spring Boycie would meet them in Paris, be present at the tearful leavetaking — for Sylvia cried very prettily — and then return with Cherry to New York for rehearsals of the play. That was that. The rest was on the knees of the gods. But as the Hollywood contract renewal was signed and sealed, the autumn would see Cherry on her way west again.

The boat sailed at noon. Mrs. Van Steeden was not going to see them off. She loathed seeing people off almost as much as she did meeting them. Besides, Cherry's departure would be attended with fantastic demonstrations. She could not always bide amid Victorian furniture. Her brief conventual period of retirement was over and once more she must step out into the full glare of the spotlight.

Mrs. Van Steeden bade her grandchild farewell in the white paneled study. She offered her a cheek to kiss and some advice to ponder. "Good-by, Sarah," she said. "Don't make any more of a fool of yourself than is strictly necessary. One of your weaker qualities is an ability to adapt yourself to your company. This makes for popularity but not for character. Your mother is an idiot. This husband of hers — I've only seen him twice — is attractive. But meek. She leads him by his rather long nose. Cable, if you wish, but don't write. My eyesight is not as good as it was, and your penmanship is execrable."

Cherry murmured, "But when I had a secretary —"

Mrs. Van Steeden interrupted sharply, "I'm glad you did not see fit to bring her with you —"

"She was only by-the-day," deprecated Cherry.

"You never dictated your letters to me or to her," said her grandmother. "You said 'write my grandmother —' and she wrote. I have never read such specimens of utter vacuity. 'Dear grandmother, the roses are blooming in my garden and the weather is very fine.' " She snorted, with vitality. She put her thin veined hand on Cherry's. "Good-by, my dear," she said gently, and battled with the ache in her throat. She despised saying good-by. Each time she spoke the word it brought her a little, and coldly, closer to the eventual farewell.

Then she said, "And if I may be permitted a conservative observation, you look completely absurd."

Boycie, popping in at the door, stated, rather distractedly, "We must go," and added mechanically, overhearing the last sentence, "She really can't help it, Mrs. Van Steeden."

An ambiguous defense. Yet Cherry couldn't help it. She would face cameras, both still and in motion, reporters, admirers, and whatnot. She would be photographed at the rail of the ship, mostly glittering smile and lovely legs.

She was wearing lavish orchids, plentiful lipstick, foundation cream over the freckles, and under the powder, spectacular eyelashes, and generous layers of eyeshadow. She was also wearing very smart tweeds, a mink coat, and a pert hat. She was unrecognizable as Sarah Brown. But almost identifiable as Cherry Chester.

Boycie thought, *She's been remarkably silent and amiable and docile for the past few days.* The thought fretted her. It boded no good. For no matter what she had advised, suggested, or announced, Cherry would reply, "Of *course*, Boycie darling."

The boat was to sail at noon, but they went aboard early "because," explained Cherry, "I'll have to see such quantities of people, and I'd like them to all clear off and leave me alone to rest a little before we actually sail." This seemed reasonable enough although fairly unlike Cherry. Boycie looked at her sharply but Cherry's eyes were as green and clear as forest pools. *Humph!* thought Boycie.

Horace had come to bid them a temporary

Godspeed. He still adhered to his original idea of running over. To be sure, this notice had been met with what appeared scant encouragement but Cousin Lucy had sustained him. "She doesn't know her own mind, Horace. Be patient — she's really very fond of you."

Cousin Horace came in a large car which, as it happened, was to purr majestically toward the North River bearing Hilda and the Higgins family. Hilda was sailing with her mistress, and the Higginses, who would occupy the apartment in her protracted absence, were coming to see them off. Horace, Cherry, and Boycie went in Cherry's car. It was a very nice car indeed. "I can't see," argued Horace, a practical man, "how you could let it eat its head off in the garage all the time you were in town. You don't suppose for a moment it wasn't used, do you?" he inquired loudly. At which the chauffeur shot a look of pure hatred into the mirror; and then relaxed as he heard Cherry's reply.

"No," she said, "to your last question as Robinson has my permission to take the car out. And I didn't use it because of Gram. She hates cars and if it pleased her to have me go gay nineties behind spanking horses, it was all right with me," she added, and smiled secretly.

At the pier Horace was buffeted this way and that. Gentlemen of the press, schoolgirls, idle young men, males hiding behind cameras. His dignity suffered greatly. On the boat itself things were no better. They were, in fact, a good deal worse. Autograph seekers with passes to the ship, reporters without notebooks — *Funny,* thought Horace, *I thought they always carried notebooks* — and two or three ladies from motion picture magazines. Cherry appalled him by the ease with which she handled all and sundry. Her suite with its small private deck was filled with flowers, wires, baskets of fruit, bottles of beverages, pots of caviar, boxes of candy, and other delicacies.

"Nuts!" announced Boycie, surveying all these. And Cherry, talking animatedly to a reporter, started. To be sure her last few words had been, she decided instantly, rather on the goofy side, but even so — ! She turned in astonishment to perceive that Boycie was merely exhibiting trophies of the chase to Horace.

"Is there anything," asked a reporter, "in the rumor that you and Mr. Van Steeden — ?"

"Oh dear," interrupted Cherry, sighing, "why bring that up?" She smiled at the reporter who instantly became her slave, and made a very comic little grimace. "We are the very best of friends," she explained softly and untruthfully, "and have been ever since we were children together. I was, of course, much younger than Horace," she added hastily.

She smiled again and thought of a fat, perspiring little Horace, a number of years her senior, pulling her red pigtails and kicking her in the shins. She also remembered how once she had induced him to smoke one of her stepfather's cigars with results disastrous to Horace and her grandmother's best Aubusson carpet.

Cherry glanced at her watch. It still lacked forty-five minutes to sailing-time. She began to shoo her visitors with sweeping gestures of her long arms and expressive hands. "Please," she begged pathetically. "I'm *so* tired."

They shooed amiably. And Boycie a moment later found her charge in her own cabin where Hilda was busy unpacking, and spreading the famous silk Chester sheets upon the bed and putting at its foot the equally notorious throw of ermine. "Has Horace gone?"

"Not yet — what are you up to?"

"Nothing. My head aches. Truly it does, Boycie." Cherry turned pleading eyes upon the older woman and indeed she did look rather badly, with two high spots of authentic color on her cheekbones and her eyes shining and desperate as with fever. "Get rid of him — take him on deck, see him safely off the boat — and, look, Boycie, there's a Miss Petersen from one of the movie mags somewhere about. I had a special delivery about her. Can't think why she hasn't been shown down here. Find her if you can — but get rid of everybody else and —" Here, to Boycie's astonishment, Cherry flung her arms around her and kissed her. She said emotionally, "You are a lamb," and then released her.

Boycie, shaking her head, went back to the living-room. "Cherry has a headache," she reported to Horace, "she's going to lie down."

Horace tiptoed to the door with exaggerated care. Cherry said, on the threshold, "I haven't typhoid or anything." She gave him a cool, firm hand. "Good-by," she said.

"Sarah, I can't let you go like this," said Horace passionately.

"But you must." She disengaged her hand and smiled. "I'll be seein' you," she promised. The door shut. Horace, with Boycie beside him, made his way out of the suite. He said enthusiastically — for him, "Look here, Miss Boyce-Medford, that's a promise, isn't it? I mean, that she means — or doesn't she?"

"Who am I to interpret her for you? She so rarely knows what she means herself."

He delayed her a little at the gangplank with

96

his burbled farewells. When she finally got rid of him she was accosted by several people whom she knew, and by others who knew her for Cherry Chester's companion. She made Cherry's excuses with a glibness born of long practice. And then she took her way through various lounges and salons with a page boy in tow in search of a Miss Petersen who proved to be nonexistent. It wasn't until they had actually cast off from the piers and the little tug was fussily snorting about and getting them under way that Boycie went back to the suite.

"Well," she announced cheerily, opening the door, "we're off, at last. I wish I could tell you how much my feet hurt."

Silence greeted her. The room was full of flowers and candy and telegrams and what-not, as it had been before; but of nothing else. Boycie, a frown creasing her brows, went to the door of Cherry's bedroom. It stood wide open. There was a steamer trunk, and some luggage. And no Cherry. No Hilda, either.

She's gone up on deck again, thought Boycie, annoyed. *Very like her . . . funny I missed her. No, not so funny.* This was a big boat and a popular one.

She sat down on Cherry's bed and Cherry's note promptly stared up at her from the pillows.

Boycie darling: Don't be angry. I've run away. Hilda helped me. I've changed and taken the bag I'd already packed for this excursion. I've got plenty of money and my passport. I'm going away, to a farmhouse I've heard of in the mountains, for a little while. Not for long. Please don't worry. I'll join you later, and let you know my plans ahead. When I do, it will be entirely incognito. The papers mustn't get hold of this. They'd make a fuss and Gram would have a convulsion. She isn't to know either. When you land cable her we arrived safely. She won't expect to hear from me directly for a while. Show this letter to Sylvia. She'll understand. Give her and Gerhard my love. And you try to understand. I want to be alone. I don't want to be Cherry Chester. I don't want to be Lucy Van Steeden's granddaughter. Just myself for a little while. Don't scold Hilda. She couldn't help herself. When you land, ship her to Norway for a vacation. She can join us later. Everything's been arranged. Don't worry. I'll cable you — and I do love you, Boycie. Stand by me, as you always have.

Boycie sat limply on the bed. Her eyebrows worked agitation. Her throat worked also. She had all sorts of mad impulses. Captain, stop the ship! She'd swim ashore. She'd get police, state troopers, reporters, radio cars —

No, she wouldn't. She'd never failed that redheaded girl; she wouldn't now. And Cherry had never failed her. Not really. Boycie didn't know what it was all about. She forgot her longing for her home, her deep-rooted, silent nostalgia, and wished herself back in New York at the apartment with the divorced Higgins in attendance, where Elsa and Lohengrin, brushed and well-fed, were established to await the return of their owner. She wished herself anywhere but aboard a ship heading as rapidly as possible for the Narrows and Sandy Hook.

If I could lay my hand on her, she thought grimly, and waited, dark as an empty theater, for a subdued Hilda to creep in, anticipatory of her scolding.

Hilda came. Boycie transfixed her with an austere eye. "How could you have lent your-self to anything so insane, Hilda?" she demanded.

Hilda shrugged. "Miss Cherry said —" she began.

Boycie sighed with weariness. "Yes, of course. So you said, all right. You'd give her your head if she wanted it, wouldn't you?"

"I would, just," said Hilda, making hash of her J.

"So would I. Look here, Hilda, what are we to do about reporters and things? After all, she's down on the passenger list and although we can keep up the fable that she's having her meals in her rooms — But how can we do even that," she asked despairingly, "with stewards and such popping in and out?"

"I go to bed," offered Hilda.

Hilda didn't look in the least like Cherry. But she was fair-skinned and not uncomely. Boycie said, "You can land in her clothes — and —"

No. It wouldn't do. She'd wait. When inquiries came, as they would come, she would say merely that Miss Chester had decided not to sail after all, at the very last minute — and would follow later on another boat. What the papers would make of it, she dared not think.

After a while she decided, aloud, "We'll stall as long as possible. Yes, you go to bed, Hilda. I'll have your meals brought in here to the living-room, I'll take them in to you myself. I'll huddle you in her mink coat and put a veil around your head and tell the press at Southampton that you're ill, you've been ill all the way over. And heaven help us —" she said wildly.

Before the gangplank was pulled up and shortly after Horace had taken his departure,

100

Cherry slipped away from the boat and into the crowds at the pier. No one noticed her. Or if people had looked at her more than once all they would have seen was a tall, slim young woman in a rather shabby serge suit, a little short in the skirt — for Hilda was shorter than Miss Chester — worn under a gray tweed topcoat collared in modest fur, and with good gloves, well-cut shoes, and a nondescript hat. She had a frank and freckled countenance guiltless of powder, paint, or pomade. She had short thick black eyelashes which curled against the windowpane glass of large horn-rimmed spectacles. She walked briskly, and now and again smiled to herself, and she carried a suitcase, and a flat brown handbag.

It was noon. The *State of Maine* express would not leave until nine. Cherry taxied over to the station and checked her bag. Miss S. Brown. Then she bought her tickets. No drawing-room for S. Brown, who believed in doing things up that color. A lower, merely.

After this she disappeared into the crowds and vanished from the sight of man, lost in subways and department stores.

She rather liked shopping for things and paying cash. She had never done so before. This was fun. Luncheon in a store restaurant was fun. Woolly sweaters and ski pants and woolen socks and a pair of skates and shoes,

101

and thick mittens and warm underwear and silly knitted caps. Staggering under the last of the bundles she went to the luggage department and bought another suitcase. With that she went to the restroom and packed.

When she checked the second suitcase the man at the station counter looked at her with amazement but his suspicions died aborning. Nice plain girl with queer-colored eyes and a frank, pleasant smile. Cherry fled. There was still so much time to kill. She decided to murder it in the movies. She spent an hour or two in a large gilded temple of cinema watching a woman she detested weep and suffer on the screen. After that she drank some tea. Then she went to a small motion picture house which for the past year had been doing revivals of old pictures. She knew that her second picture was being shown. For ten cents she was enabled to sit in the balcony, smoke a cigarette, and criticize herself severely. But it took all her will power not to turn around, torn between rage and pleasure, when the girl in back of her remarked, yawning, "I don't think she's so much, do you?" and the young man with the girl replied, "I think she's swell, Lottie, she's got what it takes!"

Lottie sulked and Cherry sulked.

She was back in the station by seven. She ate her dinner there, watching the indifferent people about her eating and gabbing. She bought all the evening papers and read about her sailing. She looked at her photographs with decided distaste. She paid her check, over-tipped an astonished attendant and went out to the telegraph office and arranged for a wireless. It read, *Am all right everything fine carry on don't worry love Sarah* and was addressed, not to Miss Boyce-Medford, lest the wireless operator aboard ship turn Sherlock, but to Hilda Johnsen. It did not occur to Cherry that Hilda Johnsen might no longer exist as such. Hilda, however, was having the time of her hard-working life. She had never before lain in bed for longer than six hours at a stretch, not since her innocent babyhood.

And the wire would reach Boycie, of that Cherry was certain.

When the train was made up Cherry and her suitcases boarded it. She spoke briefly to the porter who assured her that her berth was ready and then she went, with one suitcase, to the ladies' dressing-room. A little later, in pajamas and robe and slippers she crawled into bed. A man snored all night, not far from her, in the strange intimacy of sleeping-cars. A child cried. A woman, newly widowed and afraid, wept. And in the drawing-room Important Men drank highballs, played Canfield, told the usual stories, and said nothing of any importance whatever. In another a bride and groom looked at one another with hope, panic, and a certain astonishing but unsung courage.

There had been snow in New England. Cherry, waking very early, looked from the windows and saw it lie white and glistening and almost untrodden. At one small station a team of horses waited by the gates. Their breath smoked upon the clear and frosty air. The sun was gay and yellow and distant. Later on her way she would see children with bright red sleds toil up small hills and shoot down them again, laughing. And where the trees grew thickly there was snow like a benison upon their branches.

There were villages, and churches with tall white spires, and farmhouses on roads lonely save for the steel passing of the rails. Chimneys were like high red hats, sending forth blue smoke, and gables were like eyebrows over the bright curtained eyes of windows. Cherry's mood was as cool and innocent and quiet as the snow. She thought, *I'd like to live in such a little house, the garden white in winter and very green in summer.* She even convinced herself.

When they reached Portland it was still early and there was some time before her train left. Cherry made the transfer and boarded the train and with it crossed, presently, the state line. There were the White Mountains, their eastern range, the color of their name. And in not too long a time they came to the station which in her heart she called, romantically, *Adventure*.

It had a more prosaic name. It was near Plymouth. The village was a small one, and it was like numberless villages Cherry had seen from her train windows earlier. The air was mountain clear and cold, the lone cab driver waiting at the depot wore a shaggy fur coat and a coonskin cap and smoked a blackened pipe.

There had been a heavy snowfall here but the roads were comparatively clear and the ancient cab lurched in the ruts. Its driver nodded when Cherry told him her destination. He volunteered the information that the Simpsons hadn't many city folks this season. Only one man. "Queer cuss," said the driver reflectively.

Cherry asked, beating her hands together for warmth, and feeling her heart quicken, "Is he a young man, driver?"

"Lemuel," said the driver, "Lemuel's the name — Lem for short. Dunno — well, yes, I guess I'd call him young. It all depends on your age. I'm fifty. Judging by appearances I'd say he's twenty years younger than me.

Probably seem like Methuselah to you, miss," he said cheerfully; and added, "I didn't catch the name."

"Brown," said Cherry.

"His name," said Lemuel, "is Smith. The other boarder."

Smith. Cherry shrank back a little and huddled in her borrowed coat for comfort. Smith. But — why not? Brown and Smith were good names, they were substantial, they were impersonal somehow, and they were real.

The road ascended steadily. Here was the Simpson farm, which would accommodate a few in winter and more in summer. A long road lined with sugar maples led to it. Back of it and beyond there were hills, high and rolling. At the foot a meadow all blossoming in white and a little circular pool, the ice frozen clear and black and hard, and newly swept of snow. There were fences about the pastures, and here was a red farmhouse with many chimneys, all smoking, and a collie that ran out and barked and rolled in the snow.

"Here we are," reported Lem-for-short, superfluously.

CHAPTER SIX

HER DREAM COMING TRUE

The door opened, the collie, following a sharp suggestion, ceased to bark. Mrs. Simpson regarded Lem, the suitcases, and Cherry with true New England reticence. No glow of welcome illuminated her features.

Cherry asked, feeling inexpressibly young and unwontedly shy, "Mrs. Simpson? I wonder if you have room for me, for a few days?"

"Yes and no," responded Mrs. Simpson, pulling her red sweater about her sparse chest, "that is to say, I have a room, but you may not like it. I don't believe you wrote for accommodations," she said severely.

"No," admitted Cherry, "I didn't. I — that is, a friend told me about your place and I wanted a rest so — I came away unexpectedly," she added, gropingly and with considerable truth. She smiled tentatively. "Please," she begged with some return to her natural wiles, "please don't send me away!"

"I wouldn't turn a dog out," said Mrs. Simpson darkly, "not without at least feeding him. Come in," she said to Lem. "What are you standing there gaping for?"

Lem hoisted the bags. Mrs. Simpson held open the door. They followed her in.

Cherry, on the way upstairs, looked about her, peered over rails and through half-open doors. She saw no one. Yet Lem had said — She asked, when at last she stood in a pleasant and many-windowed room overlooking the hills, "I'm not the only guest, am I?"

"No," said Mrs. Simpson briefly, "you're not." She wrapped her arms about herself, in the manner of a contortionist. Baffled, Cherry turned to Lem. "How much do I owe you?" she began.

"A dollar-fifty," said Mrs. Simpson briskly, "and don't let him charge you a mite more!"

Lem gripped his pipe and shuffled his feet. He looked abashed. "Shucks, Mitty, I wasn't agoing to —"

"That's what you say," said Mrs. Simpson.

Cherry gave him two dollars. He regarded her with gratitude but Mrs. Simpson's eyes showed disrespect. Lem departed, after a sprightly word or two about the weather. Mrs. Simpson said, "Breakfast eight, dinner twelve-thirty, supper half past six." She went over to the bed and punched it. "Like your pillows hard or soft?" she asked.

"Hard," replied Cherry. She walked to a

window. She said, "It's beautiful here — so peaceful —"

"That's what you think," said Mrs. Simpson glumly. "Been two murders and a couple of robberies in the vicinity in the last six years. Scandal too. Not that I'm one to talk scandal. Comes of young folks riding around in cars, drinking and card playing and going to the movies. This place is teetotal," she announced.

"That's all right with me," Cherry told her, laughing. "It's good of you to put me up. I — Is there a young man named Smith staying with you?" she inquired, breathing deeply after the manner of a swimmer taking a plunge in cold water.

"Smith?" repeated Mrs. Simpson, as if she had never heard the name. "Oh. Why didn't you say you were Mr. Smith's cousin he was expecting?"

So he had expected her! Cherry wondered how soon she could get a train out. She said, carefully, "I wasn't sure I could come — and I didn't know whether he'd stay on or not."

"Quiet young man, gives no trouble. Good appetite. Spends his evenings writing. I think," said Mrs. Simpson, "it's a book. He said when he first came up here that he wanted to be alone. But his cousin might follow him for a few days. He didn't tell me your name."

"Brown," said Cherry, "Sarah Brown."

"You *are* his cousin?" asked Mrs. Simpson slowly.

"Why, yes," said Cherry, feeling slightly mad. "I am — that is, distantly — we — we haven't seen each other for years. I — ran into him the other day and he told me —"

Mrs. Simpson nodded. Apparently accounts tallied. She mentioned her very reasonable rates in a brisk and matter-of-fact tone. She added, "Maybe you'd like to lay down and rest a little. It's two hours to dinner. You'll hear the bell. There's two others besides you and Mr. Smith. Miss Hambridge, she's a schoolteacher with a nervous breakdown, and Mr. Hill. He's a retired gentleman, he comes here every winter for two weeks and every summer for four."

At the door she said, "The bathroom's down the hall to the right. And you can have all the hot water you want in here." She indicated the washstand, complete with pitcher, toothbrush mug, snowy towels, and soap dish. "The telephone's downstairs in the sitting-room. You pay me for all calls. There's skis and sleds if you want to use 'em, in the woodshed. And a toboggan."

"Is Mr. Smith — ?" began Cherry.

"No, he ain't," interrupted Mrs. Simpson. Remarkable woman, no one ever had to finish a sentence for her. "He's out walking. Great hand to walk. He might do worse. Keeps him healthy."

Cherry, when the door had closed behind her hostess, unpacked her bags. The room was big, it was light and sunny. It had gray paper scattered with roses tied with silver ribbons. There were roses on the water pitcher too. Yards of tatting edged the bureau and washstand and night table covers. The bedspread was heavy, white, knitted. There was a bolster. There was a squat lamp and a bridge type lamp and two chairs, one with rockers and one straight. The room was spotlessly clean, even the rag rugs showed no signs of wear. On the walls were two pictures which were evidently framed magazine covers.

Half an hour later Cherry made her way downstairs. Not a soul seemed to be about save an elderly woman reading a newspaper in the living-room. A room beyond was probably the dining-room, while on the other side of the hall what was evidently the best parlor brooded behind drawn blinds. There was a smell of very good cooking.

Cherry, in her green ski suit, stout laced boots, and ski cap, floundered off the road and into the snow. She had elected a path

111

leading off behind the house. The collie pranced after her, his plumed tail waving. He was good company. She spoke to him earnestly. She said, "I shouldn't have come, should I, pup? After all, if he was so sure of himself — !"

She made snowballs and threw them, her mittened hands clumsy. Her hair escaped from the tight woolen cap and curled about her broad forehead. Her cheeks were flushed with color. She said to the barking dog, "Perhaps I can go back — without him seeing me — if there's a train —"

But she was hungry, she was free, she was happy. She wouldn't go back. She retraced her steps toward the house, peered in the woodshed, and dragged out a bright red sled. With the collie at her heels she toiled up a small hill and shot down it again. That was fun. On the third trip something happened and Cherry and the sled parted company with great abruptness. Head down in a snowbank, her slim legs waving wildly in the air, she choked and sputtered and tried to roll over.

Someone plucked her deftly from the snowbank and set her upon her feet. This was Mr. Amberton, *né* Smith, the popular explorer. He wore a mackinaw, a heavy sweater, and remarkable pants. He wore no hat. He was laughing at her. He said, *"I knew you'd come!"*

Cherry stamped some of the snow from her person. She rubbed her sleeve across her face and eyes and sneezed violently. She looked at him with hatred. He had no right to be so perfectly at ease, so self-confident. She said, at once, "I wish I hadn't —"

"No, you don't. Here, let me take that." He took the sled rope and began walking up the hill. He said, "There's room for two aboard. I'm glad you came."

"I —" She stopped, halfway up the hill. "I didn't come," she argued, "to see you. I came because — I was tired, I wanted to get away." She remembered her accent in the nick of time. It thickened a little. "I wanted to be alone," she said tragically.

"So you came to a place where you thought you'd meet me?" He put his free hand under her arm. "Come, don't fight against it. It's real, we're together —"

She asked abruptly, "Is your name really Smith?"

"Yes," said Anthony Amberton, "it is. Yet that isn't the name by which most people know me. But I don't want to tell you that. It would spoil things."

Blue sky and feather-white clouds drifting across it, white snow, blue in the shadows, chimney smoke and black trees etched against the heavens on the crest of the hills, and here and there the living green of firs. An air so pure it hurt the lungs and a sun so dazzling that one turned one's eyes away. Cherry asked, "Are you so sure there's anything to spoil?"

"Yes. So are you," replied Anthony, known as a masterful man. He halted on the top of a hill. "Sit down, behind me. Put your arms around my waist. Let's go!"

It was somehow better than flying, this brief escape with the air as sharp as knives on your face, and the suggestion of laughing danger, cold, disaster. "Like it?" he asked, when they had reached the bottom.

"I love it," she said.

Later he said, "You've probably been hedged about with artificiality all your life. There's nothing manufactured about this. Sky and a hilltop and a pleasure as simple as childhood. Yes, I knew you'd come. I knew we'd meet, just here, stripped of conventionality."

"It — it sounds rather chilly."

He laughed at her. "On the contrary, it's as warm as life." He hugged her arm close to his side. "You're rather lovely. I've told you that before. I'll tell you again, a hundred times."

When they returned to the house Mrs.

Simpson said unnecessarily, "So you found your cousin, Miss Brown?" and Cherry nodded. Going into the dining-room Anthony whispered to her, "Is your name really Brown?"

"Yes," said Cherry, "but it's not the name by which most people know me. I shan't tell you that. It would spoil things."

They were quits.

Miss Hambridge's nervous breakdown did not preclude her from attendance at the table where, as she said, she picked at her food. She picked to advantage until her plate was quite clean. She was a fat woman, with mild, china-blue eyes and a plethora of conversation centering, for the most part, about her three major and her four minor operations. She was enchanted at the arrival of new guests for she had about exhausted her surgical sessions and the symptoms of her breakdown — "spots before my eyes and the most dreadful crying-spells" — with her present audience.

Mr. Hill was a spare man, who had retired from the feed business some five years previously. He had large, staring false teeth of an ancient vintage set in rubber gums of an extraordinary ruby red. He possessed two sterling virtues: he was amiable and without curiosity. When Cherry and Anthony were escorted by Mrs. Simpson to the square table at which the other guests and Mr. Simpson were already seated and the introductions were made, Mr. Hill vouchsafed but three remarks. He was glad to meet them, he came from Boston, and he hoped their stay would be pleasant.

Simpson, a large man with graying, straw-colored hair, was a pleasant host, and a master carver. It was evident to Cherry, however, that Mitty was the master mind in this informal household.

Miss Hambridge, who came from New Haven, was a woman who liked to be well informed. Schoolteaching had done this to her, perhaps. Her china-blue eyes darted ceaselessly from Cherry to Anthony. Twice she murmured, "I'm sure I've seen you before — somewhere, Mr. Smith." Cherry's heart, which had quickened at the first words, steadied, only to resume its accelerated pace when Miss Hambridge added, on the second occasion, "And you too, Miss Brown."

Cherry said lightly, "Oh, I've the sort of face duplicated by thousands all over the United States." Anthony grinned at her. Mr. Hill was not interested. He champed away at a magnificent New England boiled dinner, more concerned with the behavior of his dental work than with anything else. Mrs. Simpson piled plates high and spoke sharply

116

to the hired girl. And Simpson relaxed over his trencher.

Cherry spoke of her foray into the wood-shed and her rides upon the bright red sled; Anthony of his morning walk. But Miss Hambridge was not to be deflected. She commented upon the kinship existing between these two interesting young people; she probed for details of family life. Cherry, throwing caution to the winds, improvised wildly. She reminded herself of an entire group of hard-bitten, cigar-chewing script writers seated around a commissary table serving up large chunks of mangled story to one another. Before the boiled dinner gave place to apple pie and large cups of coffee blacker than a brunette cat on a moonless night, she had informed all and sundry that she had no living relatives — "except my cousin," she added hastily as Anthony kicked right sharply her very shapely shin; that she had been brought up abroad, and escaped from several revolutions, and that she knew but little of her native land.

Her slight accent became more marked; excellent actress that she was, she put soul, heart, drama, and sentiment into her recital. Mrs. Simpson, the unemotional Mitty, was moved to remark feebly, "Well, I declare!" while Miss Hambridge's eyes were suddenly suffused and looked like marbles under water. Even Mr. Hill clucked a little with sympathy and then looked alarmed. The dental work had given its all to the boiled dinner and clucking was dangerous. Simpson looked with solemn eyes upon his latest paying guests and declared vaguely that something or other was too darned bad.

Dinner was over. Ostentatiously Anthony reached for a toothpick. They left the dining-room, Simpson disappeared and Mitty went off into the kitchen. Miss Hambridge and Mr. Hill departed to their separate rooms for their separate naps. And in the cluttered living-room Anthony looked at Cherry. "I suspect you're a liar," he said.

Cherry tossed her head, a spirited gesture, straight from a Victorian novel. It suited the room, which was furnished with some slight overflow of second-best horsehair from the parlor. "And if I am?" she asked him.

He accepted the challenge. "It wouldn't matter. Not if you had robbed, murdered — anything goes. You're here. You came. That's enough." He regarded her with male triumph which he did not trouble to conceal. He announced, "We're going for a sleigh ride. I telephoned —"

"You hadn't time."

"Yes, I had plenty of time. The sleigh will

be here any minute. Wrap up well."

The vehicle proved to be a cutter, complete with buffalo robes. A younger version of Lem drove it to the house and delivered it to Anthony's experienced hand. He said dolefully, "The mare's apt to be a mite skittish, she's been eating her head off. Her name's Susan."

He watched them climb in and then went into the house. Evidently he resigned himself to wait in warmth and comfort until the skittish Susan returned.

There were roads untouched by the snowplow. These roads Anthony took. Susan was gay. She skittered around corners and the runners shrieked on the snow. Cherry shrieked once, too. Anthony asked, smiling, "Frightened?"

"No," she said stoutly. Frightened? Once she had nearly drowned in a swimming sequence and once a boat had capsized without reference to script and once, in her first picture, there'd been a lion.

"That's good. You're never to be frightened with me. I'll take you into tougher spots than these and we'll turn narrower corners."

He was smiling at her. Now she was really frightened. This — stranger! This unknown! This conceited creature! This probable crook! What did he mean? She wouldn't ask, wouldn't give him the satisfaction. She inquired, instead, "Do you always go without a hat — in zero weather?"

"It's not zero," he contradicted. "Please be accurate. So few women are. In cold climates, no; in hot climates, yes. It's fourteen above."

"I think you're crazy," she murmured.

"About you," he agreed, and guided Susan deftly. The wind sang past Cherry's cheeks, the blood sang in her veins. She was very close to Anthony, the buffalo robe tucked about them. "And why, heaven knows," he added.

"Why?" asked Cherry, with ripening indignation.

"Yes, why? You're not especially good-looking." He looked at her coolly with eyes which were not dark as she had thought, but hazel. "Good shape, if a bit on the thin side. Good bones. Freckles. I hate freckles. A woman should have the dark golden skin of a peach or the fair skin of a camellia, satin, untroubled even by the passage of the blood. You have red hair. I detest red hair. Red-headed women are bad-tempered and stubborn and willful. You have green eyes. I cannot imagine a color less becoming to femininity. It is all right in the cat family. You have long narrow hands and feet. You have a disturbing voice. Moreover, I do not like civilized women."

She gasped. "What sort of women *do* you like, may I ask?"

"You may," he said graciously. "I like simple women, primitive women, women who have no thought beyond food and sleep and the needs of children and the brutal, the exciting needs of men."

Cherry cried, choking with rage, "How absurd!"

"You *would* say that!" He gave Susan her head. They slid smoothly over the dazzling white. They passed lonely houses, they saw little children playing, and they looked through the windows of a square frame schoolhouse and saw older youngsters, their young heads bent over books. The hills marched beside them and the sky was very blue.

"Anyone would," she countered. "I don't believe it. You don't, either."

"Yet you came," he exulted. "I told you to come — and you came! If that wasn't instinct — primitive — It doesn't matter about your civilized trappings. I discard them," he said magnificently, and Cherry shivered with apprehension. For one awful moment she thought that he might, by brute force. At fourteen above! "Beneath those trappings, you are — you could be — all woman."

He spoke sharply to Susan, who tossed a

pretty head upon a bay neck, also in the Victorian manner, while her breath smoked upon the frosty air. They paced, a trifle more sedately. Anthony said, after a moment, and tragically, "I have been exiled for many years."

He paused. Cherry's mind was a pretty gray squirrel in a red-gold cage, revolving this way and that. Exiled. A shoplifter? Prison? Or was this some grand duke of a Versailles-Treaty-forgotten-country, educated, say, in England? The coloring of his words was surely British.

She opened her mouth to speak. Anthony forestalled her. The pause was purely rhetorical. He continued, preferring to forget, temporarily, that his exile had been self-elected, and broken by dazzling appearances in Mayfair, on the Rue de la Paix and other places hardly desert islands. "I have lost touch with civilization. I do not understand modern woman, her lack of generosity, her evasions, her greed, not for love, but for power. You remember the day I opened the door of your carriage? Of course, you remember it. It was the beginning. On that day you saw me escaping —"

Cherry was breathless. She reflected — escaping — ? on a breathless murmur.

"From women," said Anthony firmly, "from the importunities of women who saw in me a symbol — the symbol of a life none of them would dare to live. You," he informed her, "would dare. When I saw you first, in the upholstered gloom of that curious anachronism, a horse-drawn carriage, when I saw your strange eyes and your wide mouth and your reined vitality —"

Speaking of reins, he held Susan's far too lightly, for he had forgotten Susan. Susan was female. She did not like being ignored. She literally bounded off the beaten track, and with a superb gesture of carelessness she tipped the cutter upon one runner and eased its occupants, buffalo robe and all, into a snowbank. Then she stood quite still quivering slightly.

"My God!" exclaimed Anthony with dignified exasperation.

He kicked himself free of the smothering and musty fur. He seized Cherry and stood her upon her feet. There was snow in his dark Byronic hair, and Cherry's knitted toque had fallen off and lay upon the ground. Her hair was lovely in the sunlight and her eyes were very green. She cried, "You are an idiot, why can't you look where we're going!"

He shook her, and the snow fell about her in a sudden white storm. He shook her again. Then when she shrieked out at him and beat her hands against his adamant chest — for she did not like to be shaken — he kissed her. Before he kissed her he murmured — for now and again he was utterly himself — "Shake well before using."

His mouth was hard and cold against her own frosty lips. But here was a flame and a warmth and a singing of the pulses. Cherry freed herself as Susan stamped the ground and started away, thinking perhaps that she had heard a command, and in starting dragged the overturned cutter with her.

"Oh," cried Cherry, "the horse — the sleigh." She added, grinning a little, for after all she didn't know his Christian name, *"Mr. Smith!"*

Anthony stared at her. Then without regard for Susan he seized her and kissed her again. "That for you, Miss Brown," he muttered and went to stand by Susan's head, to coerce her into docility with coaxing words and light deft caressing. "Here," he called to Cherry, "come here. Take hold of the bridle." He went around, put his hands to the light vehicle, and heaved. The cutter was now upright on its runners. Presently it was back in the road again. They were in it and turning homeward.

Cherry said reflectively, "I don't know you. I don't even know your first name. I think you're a crook. I should be very angry at you."

"Because I kissed you? Nonsense, you're not angry. You're interested and excited and glad."

Cherry looked at him with rancor. "I *do* dislike you," she said slowly.

"Good," cried Anthony heartily. "There's nothing more conducive to a really marvelous love affair than a little hatred. For this is a love affair, you know. We both know."

He added, "And my name is — Samuel."

"No," said Cherry, "I won't have it!"

"Yes, you'll have it," he told her. "And me. That's what you came up here for, isn't it? Me."

Cherry said, in a small voice, "I don't know. I wish I hadn't come." She thought of Boycie tossing on the wide blue waves, and in a de luxe suite. She thought of trunks filled with feminine fripperies. She thought of the reporters, at the distant piers — well, they wouldn't be there yet but they would be soon — and of the photographers and of her suite in the big London hotel and of Sylvia and Gerhard anxiously awaiting her arrival; Sylvia all golden curls and large gray eyes, saying over and over again, "My Baby!" with gestures of her scented arms; and Gerhard, a dark man, pulling a small mustache and beaming with masculine indulgence at this feminine demonstration. She thought of Lucy

Van Steeden alone in a vast house. Her mouth quivered. She said again, "I wish I hadn't come."

Anthony asked, all tenderness, "My darling, have I frightened you? But don't you know love should always be like this? Without the artificial preliminaries — a magnificent, thoughtless coming together. No past, no future, merely the present."

Where had she heard that before? She stared at him. Here was a strange man and a mountaintop. Her interview was coming true. Her lips shook again and then trembled into a smile. She said, "Perhaps you're right."

He added, frowning at the landscape, "I don't believe in marriage, you know. Not for men like myself."

CHAPTER SEVEN

NO AVERAGE WOMAN

Cherry blinked. She felt somewhat as if she had been slapped in the face. A new experience. Groggily she recovered and found that she was very angry indeed. What did she care what he thought about marriage? Who had said anything about marriage? This was skipping the preliminaries with a vengeance. She argued sweetly: "Oh, neither do I — not for a woman like myself."

"What?" cried Anthony. "You don't believe in marriage!" He looked at her, perfectly aghast. "Why, that's ridiculous. Who's been filling your head with such half-baked notions? Marriage," intoned Anthony, "is not perfect. But until we devise a better plan — for a woman, marriage is the only possible security."

Cherry gaped at him. Then she closed her mouth with a snap. She said, "I thought you said —"

"Oh, in regard to myself." He laughed at her tolerantly. "I was only speaking, of course, not severally but specifically. For

the average man and average woman however —"

"I," interrupted Cherry superbly, "am not
an average woman."

"What makes you think so?" he inquired
coolly.

"Would you," she asked slowly, spacing her
words, "have fallen in love with an average
woman?"

"No," said Anthony. He frowned and
looked away. "No," he said again more
firmly. He stole a glance at her. She rocked
with laughter. She said demurely, "What's
sauce for the gander —"

Sauce indeed. He wished he could shake
her again. Hard. Kiss her again. Harder. But
Susan had become more skittish than ever,
sensing the turn of the road toward home.

"What's your name?" asked Anthony
abruptly.

"Sarah," replied Cherry demurely.

"Hideous! Sarah, what about this man —
the man your people are — by the way, I
thought you told us at dinner that you had no
people," he added suspiciously.

"Oh, that was at dinner," said Cherry
lightly. "Yes, I've people. Lots of them, fathers, mothers, stepfathers, stepmothers,
grandparents, uncles, aunts, cousins —"

"What a liar you are, Sarah Brown!"

"Yes," agreed Cherry simply.

Anthony went on, "This man — you spoke to me about him that day in New York. Was he also a — a figment of your imagination?"

"Dear me, no," said Cherry, "not at all." She laughed silently. Horace, more solid than the Empire State Building, a figment of the imagination! She said rapidly, rolling every r, "He is, I assure you, a very real person. Rich, very rich. Handsome — an Adonis. Young. Desperately in love with me — but desperately."

"Then," asked Anthony gloomily, "why don't you marry him?"

She cried, in triumph, "But, my friend, like you, I do not believe in marriage."

Anthony was in a couple of quandaries. He looked at her, looked away. Innocence was on her brow and laughter on her lips. Yet she had come to a strange place to meet a strange man with no more than a printed card to guide her. And she didn't believe in marriage. He didn't believe in marriage — for himself. Could he believe in it for her? Could he advise her, could he urge her to marry this — this sickly Adonis with possibly millions, who loved her to desperation?

He prided himself on knowing women; on placing quickly and accurately those who Would and those who Wouldn't. What place had Sarah Brown in this — call it — category? She didn't believe in marriage, she had come here to meet him, a stranger, her past as veiled in mystery, her future likewise. All these signs pointed one way — she *Would.*

For him? Or not just for him?

He was scarlet with rage, and his heart seethed in his side. He said casually, "I suppose you've had a great many affairs?"

Cherry gasped. She recovered herself. Shades of Lucy Van Steeden! She replied, after a minute, "Oh, as to that — I suppose you have — too?"

The "too" defeated him. He growled, "Am I less than a man?" and glared at her. They had arrived at the farmhouse. Susan slithered to a halt. Susan's caretaker appeared at the door. He said cheerfully, "We was thinkin' of sendin' out a searchin' party."

He helped Cherry to alight. Reaching the ground she looked back at Anthony and replied to his question, "You expect me to reply to that on such short acquaintance?" and went without haste into the house.

Anthony put his hand in his pocket and paid Susan's keeper. He strode into the house without a word. The young man looked at the bills in his palm. He scratched his head. There was no accounting for city folks.

Personally, and offhand, he'd say that this

boarder of the Simpsons had not enjoyed his ride.

Cherry reached the top of the stairs and Mrs. Simpson met her in the hall. She asked, "Have a nice time?" and Cherry nodded. Mrs. Simpson declared pleasantly, "There's plenty of hot water."

Nice woman, Mitty. A little later Cherry lay, a little cramped, in the Simpson tub and soaked luxuriously. She thought, *I wish I'd brought an evening gown.* She pictured Miss Hambridge's expression and the agitation of Mr. Hill's teeth if she swept down to supper in apple green satin or gold lamé or frosted white. She giggled. She thought, *I'd like to see his face . . . evening gown, titivation, fingerwave, eyelashes . . . enter Cherry Chester, star of stage and screen.*

But she couldn't, of course, even if she had the materials with her. She was Sarah Brown. To the end of this episode, Sarah Brown. She would go out of his life as she had entered it. She sniffed a little, and sat up in the soapy water and regarded, with disfavor, the rather melancholy bathroom. No long mirrors to reflect the rose-white limbs, no painted walls with swimming fish and scarlet lobsters disporting themselves above a sunken tub, no long glass shelves of bath salts and dusting-powder and scented oils, no reading contraption. Just a tub and bleak white walls.

She scrubbed herself. She thought, *So he doesn't believe in marriage. Who the hell asked him to?*

Wrapped in white wool robe and in bath slippers of heelless straw, she went back to her room and lay down on the bed and pulled a patchwork quilt over her. She'd go away, of course. She'd tell Mrs. Simpson that she just remembered an appointment. That didn't make sense, but it would have to serve — and she'd go away. Tomorrow. She'd never see him again. Conceited, impossible, utterly beneath her notice. She sat up suddenly. Perhaps this was a plot. Perhaps he had recognized her, back there in town. Perhaps this was a kidnaping. Perhaps they were all in it. She began to think of them as a gang, Mr. Smith, dark, smooth, experienced, Mr. and Mrs. Simpson, suddenly sinister, even Miss Hambridge, the stooge, with her phony breakdown — she probably knew all about chloroform and gags — and Mr. Hill and his too, too erratic dental work.

Cherry shivered.

A little later — after a short sudden sleep in which she dreamed that she was being held captive in a snowbank with Susan, a business-like holster strapped around her fat middle, menacing her with a large gun and neighing at

her, "Put up your hands and make it snappy!"
— she awoke in a cold sweat and with her
heart pounding. This would never do. She
rose and dressed, fishing from the closet a
simple wool dress of a curious blue which
made her eyes the color of undersea water. It
was so simple that it had cost a fortune. But
they wouldn't know that — provided they
didn't know already.

She had brought very little with her: Hilda's
suit and coat, the new warm things for skiing
and skating, underthings, and three easily
packed frocks. She brushed her hair severely
and looked once at the lipstick which was in
her hand bag. Then she set it aside. No lipstick, Miss Brown.

She went down to supper.

Supper was friendly. Supper was cold
baked ham and hot biscuits and waffles with
Vermont syrup and gallons of milk or coffee
and preserves and pickles and potato salad.
And Cherry was ravenous. She thought of her
figure and sighed as she passed her plate for
more. Anthony was already in the dining-
room when she entered. He greeted her with a
cool smile.

"It's a good thing I'm staying here only a
short time," said Cherry brightly to Mrs.
Simpson, "I'd put on pounds and pounds."

"That's right," said Simpson kindly — he

was a little hard of hearing, "we'll have to fatten you up, won't we, Mitty?"

"Mercy, no," said Cherry faintly, and Miss Hambridge nodded gloomily. "You on a diet too, my dear?" she inquired. "It's awful, isn't it? Sometimes I think I'll faint away from hunger." And so saying, she passed her plate and looked without satiety upon the second bountiful helping.

"Nothing the matter with my stomach," announced Mr. Hill suddenly. "I don't change my weight from one year's end to the next. It's these teeth," he explained.

Anthony spoke gently. He smiled at the rotund Miss Hambridge and then looked loweringly at Cherry. "A woman," he declared, and helped himself to a very large pickle, "should be as God intended her to be — a woman. Not a slat."

Cherry quivered and said nothing. She spoke but once more during that portion of the meal and that was to say, "No, thank you," to the potato salad.

After supper she turned over the pages of old magazines in the living-room. She shut them hastily when she came upon a photograph of herself in *Vanity Fair* — elected to the hall of fame for this and that reason, the screen, the stage, the relatives. She pushed the magazine aside. She said, "Well —" tentatively.

Mrs. Simpson, knitting busily in a corner, looked up at her. She asked, "Don't you suppose you and Mr. Smith would care to go to the movies in Plymouth? Hank will drive you. He has to go to a club meeting."

"No," replied Cherry hastily, "I think not. I — I don't like motion pictures."

"Oh," cried Miss Hambridge reproachfully, "don't you? How strange. I'm crazy about them. Have you ever seen Greta Garbo?" she asked kindly.

"Yes," said Cherry, "I've seen her."

Anthony, reading a paper a couple of days old, looked up at them and then back again at his paper. Mr. Hill excused himself and went on upstairs. Simpson rose, preparing to drive to Plymouth. Miss Hambridge continued: "She's very sweet, I think. I wish they wouldn't make her play such parts. Not nice women. She's a lovely girl, really, I'm sure. And this new actress — she's only been in two pictures so far, the new one isn't out yet — Cherry Chester. Have you seen her?"

"No," said Cherry loudly.

"I have," said Anthony suddenly and Cherry almost fainted. "We were on the same train coming from Chicago." He laughed shortly. "Absurd," he said.

Cherry's heart cut didos. She stared at him. On the same train. She remembered standing

135

at the window of her drawing-room and hearing Boycie babble something about the handsomest man she had ever seen. She wondered — was it possible? She thought it was. A murrain on him, he was entirely too good-looking.

Miss Hambridge was fluttered. "Oh, please tell us, what is she like, Mr. Smith," she urged; "did you really see her close up? I'm sure I would have just about fainted — I mean — is she like she is on the screen? What did she wear? Tell us all about it."

"Yes, do, Sammy," said Cherry sweetly.

He transfixed her with a look. He said carelessly, "As a matter of fact I didn't see her, really. I only heard the commotion attendant upon her arrival. I wasn't interested. She's just another synthetic blonde, with a flair for publicity." He returned to his paper. No one looked at Cherry. Mrs. Simpson wasn't concerned and Miss Hambridge was struggling with a bitter disappointment. Cherry had a white line around her lips and nostrils. Instinctively she looked around her for something to throw. Then she relaxed. But he'd pay for this, she thought threateningly.

Anthony said easily, "If there's one thing more useless on the face of the earth than a motion picture actress, it is probably a motion picture actor." He began to put the paper aside. Then he whistled. "Speaking of Miss

Chester," he said, "here she is on the front page. Sails for Europe. Press at pier. Here's a picture."

He tossed the sheet to Miss Hambridge, who sat near him. She seized it and peered at it, pulled a gold chain from her ample bosom and set glasses upon her nose. "It doesn't look a bit like her," she complained.

Cherry rose and walked over. Now or never. She leaned over the older woman's shoulder. She remarked, "She's rather pretty, isn't she?"

She said it with relief. For the picture was a trifle smudged. There were her own lovely legs and there was a smile, and there were furs, and that was all. It looked like anybody, sailing for Europe.

"Pretty," repeated Anthony. He rose. "Pretty!" he said again. He laughed. He looked at Cherry. He said, "Put on something, Sarah. Let's go out for a bit, it's a grand night."

She thought, *I won't go. He can't make me. Perhaps when I get outside he'll wrap me in a rug and spirit me away —*

She went upstairs and put on a sweater and over it Hilda's modest coat. She pulled a cap about her hair and drew galoshes on her feet. When she came downstairs again Miss Hambridge had vanished. And Anthony was at the door. "You took forever," he commented.

She walked past him without speaking and out on the veranda. It was wide, and it ran right around the house. It had been swept of snow. Anthony drew his arm through her own and they began to pace side by side. He said, "You're angry at me."

"No. Why should I be angry?"

"You know why. Don't try and make me believe that I mean nothing to you. I'm angry at you too."

She laughed. "That bothers me a lot!"

They turned the corner. On this side of the porch no window was lighted downstairs. They stood there, sheltered from the wind. Beyond them the moonlight was silver on the snow and the trees dark and strange against the sky. He took her in his arms.

"Don't try to get away. I'm in love with you," he said, as in wonder. "I don't know who you are, I don't care. I want you. You belong to me. You know it. Stop struggling. It's of no use. You're just a thin girl with red hair and green eyes. You aren't remarkable in any way. You have the veneer I hate. You are probably rather stupid. But you are a miracle just the same. Mine. Kiss me," he said, and it was a command.

It was rather like a dream. She put her slender arms about his neck and kissed him.

A moment later she broke away from him. Her unfastened galoshes flapped against her pretty ankles. Her running steps were loud on the boards of the porch. And then the door slammed shut.

Anthony stood where he was. After a long time he drew a cigarette case from his pocket and took out a cigarette, and tapped it against the metal. The metal was cold. His ungloved hands were cold. They shook rather noticeably — but not from the temperature. He lighted the cigarette and drew a deep breath.

This was New England. This was the Simpson farm. His publisher had told him about it. "Decent beds, good food, simplicity — just what you say you're looking for. You'll finish that first draft there in no time. Strict. No drinking, no monkeyshines. So if you're looking for that sort of thing —"

He hadn't been.

He did not go upstairs until much later. He killed time alone in the living-room, glancing at old books. He should be finishing that chapter, making corrections on the others in his neat black handwriting which was so like printing. But he wasn't in the mood. He felt keyed up. Not frightened but exhilarated, as he had felt before when facing danger. Of course, most of the danger he had experienced had been in deliberation and with plenty of protection safely hidden beyond the camera's eye, so to speak. But this was rather different. He said to himself, *You're a fool. She's — why, of course, she is —*

He turned out the living-room lights and went quietly up the stairs. He knew where her room was. It was two beyond his own at the end of the passage. He stood there by the door wondering if Mrs. Simpson would take it into her head to come by from her distant quarters, or whether her husband would return at this moment from Plymouth. He hoped Miss Hambridge would not be seized with the colic and that Mr. Hill slept soundly.

He knocked, very softly, on Cherry's door. After a moment she replied. "Who's there?"

"It's —" He swallowed. He couldn't bring himself to say "Sammy." He could have killed her for that. "It's I," he said grammatically. "I must talk to you."

"Tomorrow," said Cherry. She yawned ostentatiously. "Tomorrow."

He put his hand on the doorknob. The door was locked. He went away aggrieved. That sort of girl, was she? A leader-on? Yet he was curiously relieved; he was angry and he was relieved. He thought, *It doesn't mean anything — just an opening gambit.*

Cherry lay in her wide bed and laughed.

Then she turned over on her side and wept. That sort of man, was he? And he didn't believe in marriage. Well, neither did she but that didn't mean —

She'd be even with him.

In the morning, after a sudden and very sound sleep, she appeared all ready for cold weather except for her outer garments. She hailed Anthony across the breakfast table. "Didn't you promise to take me tobogganing?"

He said ungraciously, "I've some work to do."

"I see," said Cherry. "Well, another time, then. Oh, I forgot, there won't be any other time. I really must start back to town tomorrow."

"Why?" asked Anthony.

They were not alone at the table. But they might as well have been. She replied lightly. "I've changed my mind about that engagement I spoke to you about — the other day."

"I wish you luck." He said it so bitterly that Miss Hambridge swallowed a morsel of popover down her Sunday throat and almost choked to death, thus creating a diversion.

Cherry put on her outer things in the hall and set out. She found the little red sled and the collie pup. Both accompanied her up the hill and down again, but when she reached the top of her third trip there was Anthony, waiting for her.

"Why wouldn't you let me in last night?" he demanded.

She looked at him level-eyed. She asked in her turn, "Did you really expect me to?"

"No," he said, "I didn't, damn it!" He kicked at the unoffending snow. "I — I didn't know what to expect."

Cherry took a deep breath. "Get this straight," she ordered, and neither noticed that there was no accent. "I came here to see you. I admit it. Out of curiosity. I wanted to know what kind of man you were. Oh, not the labels, they don't matter. Well, I've found out and I'm returning to New York."

Anthony stared at her. Then he shouted with pure anger. "Putting me in a tough spot, aren't you?" he demanded. "Just what did you think *I'd* think if you followed me here?"

She said, after a moment, "You didn't suggest in the carriage that day that I meet you for reasons you have since figured out to your own satisfaction — but not to mine."

He said, sullenly, "I suppose you're trying to tell me that you're not — I mean that you are —"

She cried furiously, "I'm not trying to tell

you anything!" and turned away and started down the hill.

He raced after her. The collie, thinking this was some grand new game, barked wildly and ran after them both, and his own tail, impartially. He was a very young collie and willing to believe the best.

The red sled sat where it was, deserted and forgotten.

Anthony caught her at the foot of the hill. He held her hands down and away from her sides. She turned and twisted. It did her no good. He said savagely, "You're going to marry this other man?"

"What business is it of yours?"

"You're not going to marry him. You're going to marry me," he told her.

Her hands relaxed in his clasp. She said, sweetly, "Thank you. But I wouldn't marry you if you were the last man on earth."

"Oh, yes, you would," denied Anthony, grinning suddenly; "you and about a million other women. I'd have my choice, I fancy. You'd be my Tuesday wife."

"Why Tuesday?"

"I don't know," said Anthony. "You're going to marry me without knowing anything about me. I can't take the time to dance attendance on you now. Flowers, theater tickets, night clubs, nonsense."

She said, "Go back and get that sled. And I'm not going to marry you. I think you're mad!"

"I agree with you perfectly," said Anthony unhappily.

Chapter Eight

PASSIONATE WOMAN

He turned and left her. She watched him striding toward the house. She wouldn't follow him, not she. He'd come back. She sat down in the snow. The collie came up to her and sniffed inquiringly. He couldn't know that her knees had turned to water and that her heart danced in her breast. She took the pup in her arms and buried her cool flushed face in his long wet coat. She said, "He wanted to marry me. Isn't that priceless?"

Why was she crying?

She rose after a time. Sitting in the snow with your arms full of affectionate collie wore on your nerves after a while. Anthony hadn't come back. She trudged up the hill for the sled, whizzed down it again. A car, Simpson's Ford, drove out of the barn and stopped at the house. Someone came out and got in. Cherry shaded her eyes with her hand against the dazzle of snow on snow. Anthony. She knew Anthony by the set of his shoulders and his remarkable height, and the dark, hatless head. Was he carrying anything? Was he running away?

The fun had gone out of sliding downhill. After the car had driven away she went back to the house. She put her chariot in the wood-shed and went in, stamping the snow from her feet. Mrs. Simpson was bustling about the living-room, with a duster. "Never saw a hired girl worth her salt," she was muttering.

"Did Mr. Smith drive out a minute ago?"

"Yes. I thought maybe you was with him," said Mrs. Simpson. "He asked Hank to take him over to Plymouth on an errand."

Cherry went on upstairs. The rest of the morning stretched ahead of her, dull and bor-ing. She went down again to ask Mrs. Simpson for some writing-paper. Provided with a pad and envelopes and several stamps, she went back upstairs. She took off her ski things and settled down to write, curled up on the bed. She'd write Boycie, and she'd catch the first boat and radio from it, when it docked. She'd mail the letter herself.

The letter didn't write easily. She made several false starts, tore them up, and began again. She tore that up too. She lay full length on the bed and stared at the ceiling, her arms crossed behind her head. *You might as well come clean with yourself, Sarah Brown. You're in love with this impossible man and you know it. You don't know who he is, beyond a name that might be anybody's. You don't know what he does for a living, whether he's a baker, butcher, businessman, thief, Indian, for that matter. Dark enough to be. You don't know that he hasn't a dozen wives already. But you're in love with him. You don't even care that he doesn't venerate you as Cherry Chester. You don't want him to. Nor do you want to be Sarah Brown, with the Van Steeden millions back of you. You want to be yourself, a woman, nameless, weeping and laughing and trembling in his arms.*

Anthony, driving back from Plymouth, thought, *I'm probably insane. I know I am. Yet she needn't know. This hasn't committed me to anything. I can get out of here on the first train. She hasn't the remotest idea who I am. If she had she might start something. How do I know who she is? And perhaps she does know who I am — perhaps she was in the terrible shop that day, with the carriage waiting and everything staged, even to the cigarette ash, risking that I'd come out that way. Perhaps this means blackmail and publicity of a singularly unpleasant kind. I don't care.*

He was in love with her. For the life of him he couldn't discover why. That is why he knew he was in love. Without reason; unreasonably.

He swore. Simpson, driving steadily, looked at him with astonishment. Anthony apologized, "Don't mind me, Simpson, I'm a little haywire this morning."

He never intended to marry. Or if he had ever thought of marriage he had thought of it as something well ahead of him in the future. In the future, at forty, say, or forty-five, he might consider it. An attractive woman, not too young and with an assured social position. They'd travel. He'd write a little. And settle down.

You'd never settle down with this redheaded girl beside you.

He began to think of her, a comrade, a lover, a gay companion on his treks and safaris and excursions and alarums. In breeches and shirt with a kepi tilted over her green eyes. Tireless. Learning to take her trick at the wheel — provided it was a sailing ship — or her turn at the watch — if it wasn't. Bossing the black boys around. Riding. Sitting cross-legged on the ground watching them break camp. And at night, in the tent, with the stars and the arched black sky and the cry of some distant animal, coming into his arms, a soft flame, a surrendering glory —

He shook himself. Nonsense. He couldn't take a woman with him. Not that his journeys were the acme of discomfort. They weren't. Now and then there were certain inconveniences, of course. But his money bought as much comfort as was possible in the circumstances. But taking a woman — *Mr. and Mrs. Anthony Amberton off for the jungle* —

No, half his popularity with his readers, with the women who paid to hear him lecture, was due to the fact that he was not married. A bachelor. Free.

If he took Sarah Brown with him she'd very soon become aware of his occasional romancing. Provided she would read his books. Of course, she'd read them. She'd laugh at him. She was no fool, worse luck. He'd said she was probably very stupid. She wasn't. He knew that.

Not that he lied about his explorations. He merely touched them up a little, merely enlarged upon the dangers. Most explorers did, he consoled himself.

Of course, he couldn't take her with him.

They'd have a marvelous time, he thought, his heart quickening. He thought how after they were married in the little town he'd just left he would take her in his arms and kiss her deeply and tell her, "Darling, I've something to tell you. You're Mrs. Samuel Smith . . . Oh, you knew that, did you? Well, here's something you didn't know. You're Mrs. Anthony Amberton, too. You have Anthony Amberton's name and Samuel Smith's money. You're a bigamist!"

She must have heard of him. What would she do? Would she cry or laugh, would she faint or shriek?

His errand in Plymouth accomplished, he felt pretty self-confident. Five days. They had five days. They had to have five days. In five days he could fly around the world, conquer a woman.

At dinner she said politely, "I hope you enjoyed your ride, Sammy."

Sammy again! He answered, and attacked chicken and dumplings with relish. "Yes, it was quite successful. I had an errand to do — a very important errand. I'll tell you about it later."

After dinner she asked him, "Well?"

They were walking. The collie was at their heels. There was a path through a little thicket, the evergreens burning their cool green flame. The sun was obscured and before they had gone very far the first snowflakes drifted down.

"Well what, darling?" he asked impudently.

"What were you going to tell me?"

"Oh, that. Not now. Some time — between now and the next five days. Perhaps later, perhaps sooner."

She said, "I won't be here five more days."

"Yes," said Anthony, "I think you will." He

stopped and set his back against a tree. He opened his arms. The collie sat down and looked at them with his intelligent golden eyes. He waited. He thought, *What curious people.*

"Come here," ordered Anthony and the dog rose. But he had not meant the dog.

"I won't."

She came. His arms were around her, the rough material of his mackinaw rasped her fine skin. He counted the freckles, touching each with a gloved finger. "Freckle-face," he taunted, "redhead —"

"Shut up!"

"No, don't move. I like you here. Close." He kissed her. After a moment she opened her eyes. "We're both crazy," she wailed.

"I know it. I love you, Sarah Brown. You love me. Admit it."

She said, and wept to say it, "I do love you. I don't know why. I don't *want* to love you. I don't know the least thing about you."

"Does that matter?"

"No," she replied after reflection.

"I don't know the least thing about you, either. That does not matter. Once or twice I thought it did. It doesn't; not any more. You may have had a hundred lovers —"

"I haven't," she cried, and flushed pure scarlet, "not one. Not one!"

151

"Oh," said Anthony. That was, he knew, the truth. He could not mistake it. He forgot that he was Anthony Amberton who could have almost any woman he wanted, because of his legend. He forgot a lot of things. He was simply a young man in love. He kissed her again and held her cradled. He said, "Life's going to be pretty grand. You know that, don't you? Isn't this the way things should be — just you — and me — alone, no past, no —"

He stopped. Idyls had no future. This was real, it wasn't an idyl. He said, "No past. But a present *and* a future. You've got to marry me, Sarah Brown."

"No," she said, and struggled away from him. "Can't it be like this," she asked him breathless, "an — an interlude? And then good-by and never seeing each other again?"

"That *was* my idea," he admitted. "It isn't any more. Do you think I'd let you go back to that comic carriage and the rich young man and all the relatives you've been lying about? Not now. We belong together."

"No, I don't want to belong to anyone."

"Darling," he said, "you must. I — I felt that way, too — once. For a long time. Not any longer. Can't you see?"

"No," she said again, and her lashes were briefly wet and then stiff with miniature icicles. "See," she said, half crying, "I'm — freezing."

He drew her back to him and kissed her and put his lips to the eyelids and the stiffened lashes. He said, "You're very lovely. You'll marry me — soon —"

"No —"

"You don't want me for a husband?" he asked her.

"No —"

"Then — for a lover?"

"I don't know." Cherry shrugged herself free of him again. "I do," she said rather wildly, "and I don't."

No, she didn't. She thought of her grandmother and shuddered. She thought of never seeing Samuel Smith again and cried out with pure grief. She walked away from him. He said, when he had caught up with her, "I'll not let you go. Every day for five days I'll ask you. Give me five days, Sarah Brown — five days out of your life."

She asked, "Why five?"

"Never mind. . . . I'll race you out of the woods," he challenged.

He beat her, by a length. When she reached him, breathless, he had her in his arms again with no strength to struggle. Intoxicate her with embraces, drug her with kisses, woo her with touch and word, and then — let her go, shove your hands in your pockets, whistle, be indifferent, quarrel with her, make her angry — she's lovelier when she's angry.

That was the way it went. Day in and day out. There was an evening when at sunset they put on their skates and with their hands clasped skimmed over the thick black ice of the little pond. And one night by moonlight they went there and skated and the Simpsons came down from the house and Mr. Hill and even Miss Hambridge, bundled up like a million dollar baby, and there was a fire of brushwood at the edge of the pond and frankfurters roasted on a long fork, and great mugs of hot cider.

On the fifth day it snowed and they walked in it, and the wind tore their words from their mouths and the snow melted on their warm cheeks and blew into their eyes and blinded them. And when they were back indoors again and Mrs. Simpson brought them strong tea and sugary toast to the living-room, Anthony said, "It looks like a blizzard. We won't be able to get away from here very soon, Sarah."

She had been saying for three days that she must go. She was afraid to look at a paper. Surely they would have found out, by now? Boycie must have landed. Someone would have discovered her absence. If it were headlined — She thought of Lucy Van Steeden. Could Boycie's ingenuity keep the truth from her?

That night they were alone downstairs. The others had gone to bed. They were playing Canfield in a corner of the living-room. Mrs. Simpson had not approved. And these were Anthony's cards, the two rather shabby decks. "It's just double solitaire," explained Cherry, smiling, "and no stakes."

"Well," said Mrs. Simpson, "I suppose it's all right. Turn out the lights when you come up, will you?"

In her own room she said to Simpson dubiously, "I declare I don't know what to think. They seem pretty fond of one another for cousins. But I've kept my eyes and ears open and I haven't seen anything to really upset a person —"

"If I beat you, will you marry me?" asked Anthony.

Red on black. Black on red. He beat her, well enough. Thirteen cards to her eleven. She cried, "You cheated, I know you did!"

"What of it?"

"A man who would cheat at cards!"

"I would," he said, "for your sake. I'd cheat at anything. Today's the fifth day, Sarah Brown."

"And after today?"

"After today," he said, "I'm going away. You'll never see me again. You'll never hear from me."

"I'll survive," she told him.

They were quite alone. The wind was eerie in the chimney and the snow hissed on the pane. The wind was singing in the eaves and the snow fell from the branches. There was no moon and there were no stars.

"No," he said, "you won't, not really. You had your chance. To be a woman. To accept your destiny, to embrace it. And you wouldn't. That chance will never come again."

"There are other men," she reminded him.

"They don't count," he said carelessly.

He rose. He picked her up in his arms and carried her to the worn sofa there across the room where no light had been turned on. It sagged beneath their weight. He held her across his knees, her head in the bend of his arm. He raised her to kiss her. They were silent a long time. And then she wept suddenly and turned and put her arms about his neck and held him, close.

He was quiet, waiting for her to speak. But she did not speak. She could not. She was herself, at this moment. She had no name, nor wanted any.

"Love me?"

She moved her head a little. Her tears were wet on his cheek. He asked, "Then why fight against me, Sarah Brown?"

She said simply, "I don't want to marry you. I'm afraid. And I can't — I *won't* have you any other way."

He laughed a very little. He said, and pulled her up against him, "Afraid? You'll be afraid a hundred times a day with me. And like it." He kissed her again.

She said, after a while, "It's late. I — I must go —"

"Do you want to?"

"No. That's why I must."

He let her go and rose as she stood there, and faced her. He was so much taller. She had to look up. He said, "You'll marry me? If you won't — I swear to you I'll leave tomorrow — and you'll never set eyes on me again."

His face was very dark and his eyes were angry. This was because he loved her very much and because, being male, he hated her also, as she was taking his freedom from him, that bright freedom he had always cherished. And because if she married him he would be defenseless, himself and his vanities and his artifices and his smooth lying to himself and the poses it had so long amused him to assume that they had become part of him.

And looking at him her small face was dark

157

also and her eyes were angry. This was because she loved him very much and, being female, hated him also because he had already taken from her her freedom, the bright freedom she had won and cherished and because, if he forced her to marry him, she would be defenseless, herself and her vanities and her artifices and her smooth lying to herself and the poses it had so long amused her to assume that they had become a part of her.

He took a seal ring from his little finger. It was not particularly attractive, being a common bloodstone carved with a crest. He put it loosely on her lax finger. Then he caught and held her.

"We'll be married," he said, "tomorrow."

She had not said yes. She had not said no. He let her go and she went quickly from the room. He heard her running up the stairs. He thought he heard her sob. He smiled a little. Then he sat down on the old sofa again and mechanically lighted a cigarette. He knew he dared not go up those stairs. Not yet. Not yet.

He thought, *When I tell her* —

Standing at the mirror in her room she stared at her reflection. She thought, *When I tell him!* Was she really going to do this? She couldn't. If Boycie were here — Boycie wouldn't let her. She'd scold her, lock her up. But Boycie was thousands of miles away.

★ ★ ★

She was late to breakfast. They had almost finished when she came down. She came shyly. She couldn't remember really feeling shy since her childhood. She was afraid to look at Anthony. And there was sunlight in the room. It had ceased to snow in the night and the world was very clean and new.

"Oh," said Anthony, rising. "I was just telling our good host and hostess, Sarah, that we will be leaving them today. But I haven't told them why."

"Wait," said Cherry, stammering. "I mean, perhaps —"

He wouldn't let her even attempt to change her mind or his announcement. "We're going to be married."

"I knew it," said Mrs. Simpson, while Miss Hambridge fluttered faintly, and exuded sentimentality to the point of rising from her chair and hurrying around the table to embrace Cherry. And Mr. Hill beamed upon them both.

"When?" cried Miss Hambridge. "Oh, isn't it too, too romantic. Just like a motion picture!"

Mitty Simpson folded her hands under her apron and told the hired girl to get going with fresh coffee. She then said disapprovingly, "I don't hold with marriages between cousins."

159

"We're very distant cousins," explained Anthony, "three times removed in fact. You see," he hurried on, "we've misled you a little. We've been engaged — a long time. And then — well, you know how things are, we quarreled. And I came up here and Sarah —"

"Oh," said Cherry almost inaudibly. Her eyes blazed. He would do that! She had a vision of herself rushing after him to New Hampshire, begging forgiveness for something that never happened. He would make just such a song of it!

"We want you all to come to the wedding," he told them, "in Plymouth. Today. Then, we're going on —"

He'd been thinking about that. The Simpson farmhouse wasn't the exact setting for a honeymoon, not with Miss Hambridge and her nervous collapse — and other drawbacks.

"You can't get married today," said Mrs. Simpson, and Cherry wondered whether to laugh or cry. "There's laws in New Hampshire. You have to file your intention to marry five days previous to getting your license."

Five days.

"I did file it," said Anthony simply.

"Here," said Mrs. Simpson, looking at Cherry's white face. "Where's that coffee? I

160

declare, such goings-on."

After a while everyone had left them alone. Cherry drank her coffee. The hired girl lurked in the kitchen with the door a little open. She wasn't going to miss anything if she could help it.

"You were so sure of me," said Cherry.

"I was," he told her, "and of myself. Look, you can't let me down now," he told her, his hand over her own.

She had thought it was rather like a dream, last night. But today was another day, with sunlight pouring in. She would remember sunlight on china and silver and honey-in-the-comb as long as she lived.

They were married that afternoon in a white parsonage, in Plymouth. The Simpsons were witnesses, and Miss Hambridge wept throughout the ceremony and even Mr. Hill was moved. And everyone kissed the bride. The license was a proper one, and delivered duly to the minister before the ceremony, having been issued by the clerk. It read, Samuel Smith, bachelor, and Sarah Brown, spinster —

No longer.

Because of the insistence of the Simpsons they returned to the farmhouse for an improvised wedding supper. And what a supper that was! And entirely on the house. They were guests, but no longer paying guests. Anthony had settled their bills. "Your bills are mine now," he said in his lordly way to Cherry when she demurred, and she had laughed a little, wondering what he would say when he saw some of them. She thought, *Poor darling, perhaps he hasn't much money. Writers haven't as a rule. I've never asked him what he writes. I suppose I can get him a job at the studio.*

That was when she gasped and once more turned so pale that those about her thought she would faint. She had forgotten all about the studio. There was a marriage clause in the new contract. She'd forgotten that too. Well, it didn't matter of course, but if — if Lucy Van Steeden knew — when Boycie knew — *Oh,* she thought despairingly, *they mustn't know.* She'd tell Anthony the truth about herself tomorrow. Not until tomorrow. For this one night let them be passionate strangers, without labels.

Tomorrow she would tell him, would persuade him they would have to keep it secret until she had seen her grandmother, no, Boycie first, for her advice, then Lucy — until she had talked to studio officials.

"What's wrong?" asked Anthony quickly.

"Nothing. Tired, I guess," she said, trying to smile.

An instant polite murmur rose, and everyone avoided looking at everyone else. It was nearly ten o'clock.

They drove into town. Hank took them. They went, with their suitcases to a hotel. They registered: *Samuel Smith and wife.* There weren't many people in the lobby. But one man, hearing Cherry laugh, as they left the desk, looked after her curiously and sat in his wicker chair and frowned at a large overfull ash tray. And after a while he rose and consulted the register, still frowning.

Anthony had taken two rooms and a bath, large rooms which communicated. Cherry, looking about her, said, "I feel — pretty darned funny."

Anthony asked, "Why?" lazily. He was unlocking the suitcases. He looked up and asked, "Why?" again.

"It's the first time I've ever been married."

"It's the last time." He came and put his arms about her. "The first, the last — I'll not even leave you a widow. You'd be a damned attractive widow. Now I've something to tell you."

"Tomorrow," she begged; "wait till tomorrow. I've something to tell you too."

"Tell me now."

"No —"

He kissed her. He said, walking into the next room, "I'll take this one. I like its looks."

He left the door open.

CHAPTER NINE

CHERRY BLOSSOMS

Cherry closed the door — part way. She looked about the hotel bedroom, shook her head, sighed a little, smiled. She'd never thought much about marriage. She had supposed she would marry some day, and, according to the mood she was in when she considered it, she had dreamed, vaguely and alternately, of a church wedding, with the organ making its sonorous appeal, the prettiest bridesmaids in town, herself in satin and orange blossoms — Lucy Van Steeden in a front pew and Sylvia weeping on Boycie's shoulder; or of a romantic elopement by plane, probably to New Mexico.

But the face of the man at her side had remained a pleasant blank. And she'd never been in love.

Oh, a little — a very little — a quick attraction like sunlight glancing, or a love which expressed itself in light, provocative words — and went no further. But now —

Cherry shivered. She heard Anthony moving about his room beyond her half-shut

164

door, beyond the bathroom. He walked lightly, quickly. He walked very lightly for a big man. Like a cat. Like a burglar. She went to the door and called through it. She asked, "You aren't really a shoplifter, are you?"

"Would you mind?" he asked her, laughing.

"No," she said, "I suppose not."

Tomorrow perhaps, but not tonight. She laughed suddenly and went with a new briskness to her unpacking. Standing there above the suitcase he had unstrapped and unlocked for her, she frowned, her fingers on her flushed cheek.

She had brought so little with her. And nothing at all that one could call a trousseau, not by the wildest stretch of the imagination. The very utilitarian boyish pajamas of balbriggan, the severe warm robe of white wool with its knotted girdle and high collar.

She began to laugh helplessly. How on earth would she ever be able to convince him that she was who she was? Not a sweeping eyelash to her name! Only powder, her lightest, her most invisible; and the lipstick in her handbag.

A little later, in the woolen robe, she went into the bathroom. She moved swiftly to the communicating door and closed it. When she emerged again she wore the shining scrubbed look of a baby. Swiftly she brushed a veil of powder over that appalling simplicity and made up her mouth. She drew a dampened comb through her hair and pressed it into loose soft waves. She leaned on the dresser, her palms flat on the glass top, and stared into the mirror. Her eyes were very young and questioning. She thought, *I'm not afraid — I'm not.* But she was.

Then she shook her head at herself and the red hair belled out against her cheeks and half concealed her face. She flung it back. She thought, feeling alone and lost and frightened and expectant, *There must be something —*

She went over to the bag Hilda had packed for her and rummaged in it. Of course. She'd forgotten. Hilda had put in the new perfume without consulting her. It was a noble bottle, created just for her — for anyone else who had $40 with which to buy it — by the prince among perfumers. It was called *Cherry Blossom.*

There were no cherry blossoms in it. It had a very heavy, very clinging base of gardenias, skillfully blended with a hint of amber and more than a hint of orange blossoms. She unscrewed the cap and rubbed a drop on the back of her hand, and sniffed, her eyes closed. It was really a lovely fragrance — as alluring as the woman you've never met — a very Lilith of a perfume. It was like moonlight on a hundred bushes each set with the white stars of gardenia blossoms, it was like a warm wind blowing through an orange grove in flower.

Cherry smiled. She took off the cap and put on the clever atomizer. She sprayed her shining hair, the white wool of her robe, the sober balbriggan of her pajamas. She thought gratefully of the man — a man she hardly knew — who had sent her this glorious perfume in a huge box of forced spring flowers, to the boat. She danced across the room, suddenly feeling secure again, surrounded by fragrance, the smooth scarlet of salve on her curving lips, her hair released from duress, and sprayed, smiling, the sedate white pillows of the hotel beds.

Anthony knocked as she set the atomizer down on the bureau. He said, "I may come in?" making it less a question than a statement, and came, at once, looking absurdly attractive in the brocade dressing-gown belted about his slender waist. He had brushed that curly dark head into some semblance of neatness but it was so much wasted effort for he said at once, ruffling it with an agitated hand, "You look — marvelous." He advanced a step toward her, another step, and then stopped. A very curious expression replaced the one with which but a second before he had been regarding her and which she had remarked with a most delicious trepidation.

Cherry ran lightly across the space between them and with a gesture wholly histrionic — for she had employed it before on stage and screen, praying that her leading man had no urge for garlic — she flung herself into his arms — but with no thought of cameras. His arms, however, appeared as incapable as those of Milo's Venus. Cherry, who had been relaxed and secure, now slid to the floor. She stared up at him from that astonishing position.

"What in hell have you got on?" demanded Anthony. He was quite pale.

Cherry rose to her feet. She said sharply, "What's the matter with you? Got on — what do you mean?"

"Scent," he said thickly, and his nostrils quivered like those of a bird dog. "Perfume. I can't *stand* it. I — open the windows!" he ordered.

She had never heard of such a thing. She thought he had gone mad. She did not know that while a thousand men are pleasantly stirred by fine, subtly blended perfume, on warm flesh, the thousand-and-oneth man is sickened by it. Anthony Amberton in his wanderings around the patient globe had endured primitive odors — and without a quiver. But perfume turned him inside out. Women who had loved him and whom, temporarily, he had permitted to love him, had learned this. They had, every last one of them, surrendered, without a word of complaint, all their glass bottles, their Lalique containers, their satin and tasseled boxes. They had banished these far from Anthony's sensitive nose — and had had the consolation of knowing that when the romance was over they could at least mourn it in darkened rooms steeped with forbidden fragrance.

Cherry did not move. She stood and stared at him. Anthony said, growing sicker, "Well, why don't you *do* something? What's the idea of standing around like — like a petrified forest? Can't you see that I'm *suffering?*"

He dashed past her to the windows. There were three of them. Cross ventilation. He opened them all, to their widest. And the very frosty air of New Hampshire entered in.

Cherry shivered. She wrapped her long arms about herself. She said acidly, "Do you expect me to stand here and freeze to death because you've got a complex or something?"

She thought, *Perhaps it was some woman he knew and loved — and still loves — perhaps she used a scent like this and he can't stand it.* Her chin went up. It quivered a little but she soon had it under control. She suggested, "Perhaps you'd better go back to your room — and stay there."

She was really very lovely. Anthony looked at her and was completely aware of her charm and her utter desirability. He loved her to distraction. But ardor and nausea are not teammates. The spirit was willing but the flesh was very weak. He made a supreme effort and came toward her. He said softly, "Darling, I'm so terribly sorry. Idiotic of me. But I can't help it. I should have told you. But — I never dreamed — All this time you've never used —" He grew whiter. Cherry Blossoms on retentive wool and on the thick short masses of Cherry's red hair was something overpowering. He pushed her away from him. He said, gasping, "Look here, I'll go into the other room. You'll have to wash that off — change, bathe — anything —" He staggered away from her calling upon every ounce of his considerable will power. If he could get away at once, lie flat — in a room untainted by this horrible, devastating fragrance he'd be all right. He passed the twin beds with the prim night table between them. Another wave of perfume rose to smite him amidships. He said, with a ghastly attempt at a smile, "So — sorry —"

The bathroom door slammed. Cherry was alone.

Alone with the tides of fragrance rising about her from her white woolen robe and with her scented red hair swaying about her incredulous and horrified face.

He — It wasn't possible! A strong man. A young man and a healthy man. A man standing over six feet tall with a pair of shoulders on him like an ox. She had never heard of anything so ridiculous. There must be another woman mixed up in it somewhere, one whom he could not forget. Or — another explanation reached her swift and transfixing as an arrow, and no more painless. It was herself. An excuse. Play-acting. He had repented of his unconsidered bargain. She — she was *repulsive* to him. He hated her. Anything for an excuse!

Anthony spoke to her weakly from behind the closed bathroom door. "I'm all right now, I think. But I'll have to ask you to come into my room — after — after you've washed that stuff off."

He heard something crash. He hadn't the remotest idea what it was. He couldn't see through a bathroom door although he had often remarked that he could see through a stone wall as well as the next man. What had crashed was forty dollars' — less a fraction — worth of Cherry Blossom perfume. And the room became not one orange grove but a hundred, and not one hundred gardenia bushes but a thousand. It stole, that fragrance, through keyholes and under doors and was a stench in the reviving nostrils of Miss Chester's bridegroom.

He heard something slam, once, twice, thrice. This was Cherry closing her windows. He went into his own room and cast himself down on a bed. He was as light and empty as a discarded carton. He thought, *Poor youngster* — He thought further, *In a minute she'll come in and I'll tell her how sorry I am and it will be all right*. He thought, *What a darling she* — He thought no further. Emotional and psychological and physiological strain had proved just a little too much. Nature has a way of combating too much of anything. In grief her remedy is tears. But in this case it was sleep. Anthony Amberton, the great explorer, Samuel Smith, the recent bridegroom, fell suddenly and soundly and quite explicably, asleep.

Cherry was packing. She was also dressing. Likewise she was swearing. Her brain was a streamline, steel projectile hurtling through space, now and then seeing as it passed the lights of way stations at which it had no time to stop. An act! Because he was ashamed of her. Because he was afraid. Because he was repentant. Probably had a wife and six children in Peoria.

But she had found him out. She'd think it

all out after a while, but meantime she had to get away.

Plymouth. The Pilgrim Fathers had — No, this was New Hampshire. Another Plymouth. Plymouth Rock. That was a hen, wasn't it? Red? White? How in heaven's name had she ever got into Plymouth? How would she get *out?* What a place! To reach it from New York you went via Portland. What time was it?

It was very nearly midnight.

Trains? Of course, there would be a train. This was the United States, wasn't it? There had to be trains.

How would she explain at the desk?

She wouldn't. Let him explain. In the morning. She didn't care. She was accustomed to having her own way. Her own way led out of Plymouth, alone.

She was dressed. She was packed. The room was heavy with perfume. The beautiful bottle lay shattered on the floor. *Like my dreams,* she thought.

Silent picture. Subtitle. *Dreams which shattered like colored glass, their faint fragrance lingering on the air.* It wasn't very faint. It was far from faint. It was lusty, it was persuasive. Cherry sobbed. The tears were on her cheeks. She brushed them away. Another subtitle. *Thank heaven, it is not too late.*

She left the room with exaggerated care and

reached, still practically on tiptoe, the lobby.

The night clerk looked at her in amazement. This was the bride. This was the Talk of the Town. This was Mrs. Samuel Smith who after her wedding supper at the Simpson farmhouse had come to spend her bridal night under this sheltering roof. He goggled. He waved his hands, feebly. He hadn't realized she was so good-looking. Waving red hair, curling tendrils. That hat wasn't so hot, and her clothes weren't much — but —

Lipstick and eyes bright with determination and surrounded by a most marvelous fragrance. The night clerk, a susceptible young man, closed his eyes and all but swooned, just as Anthony had closed his eyes and all but swooned, but for an entirely different reason.

Cherry said sharply, "I have to get to New York — at once. As soon as possible."

The night clerk had banjo eyes. They were now open to their fullest extent. They Eddicantored. They rolled. They all but fell out of his bewildered head.

"But — but —" he stammered, "*Mr.* Smith —" He looked toward the elevators. No Mr. Smith was in sight.

"He will follow," said Cherry briefly. "I — I have had very bad news. I must —"

"But there isn't a train," he said, and painstakingly explained the coach connections with Portland.

He added helpfully, as Cherry's color heightened and her foot tapped on the floor, "How about Boston?"

What a man! You said, "I want to go to New York," and he said, "Sorry, how about Boston?"

"Boston?" repeated Cherry. She, too, looked toward the elevators. No, no Mr. Smith. He wouldn't come after her. He would be enraptured when he discovered presently that she had gone. Perhaps he had discovered it already. She hoped he was happy. She hoped the aroma from the shattered bottle in her room would choke him.

"There was a train," admitted the clerk, but it had left at six-something.

"A car," decided Cherry brilliantly. "I can hire a car, can't I — to take me to Portland — I get a train there?"

"You could," said the clerk cautiously. "It's a hundred and fourteen miles — by rail. Boston's a hundred and twenty-four."

She said, "I'll go to Boston."

From Boston she could entrain for New York. For that matter she could fly, she could go by boat. She could walk, if she had to. But he — that brute upstairs — assumed her from New York in the first instance. If he did try to follow her, how Boston would confuse him.

She stopped tapping her foot. She smiled upon the clerk dazzlingly, softly, alluring, as no bride should smile at a man who is not her husband. She apologized, "I'm so upset — please forgive me. I didn't mean New York. I meant Boston — all the time. Could you get me a car and a driver? At once?"

The clerk thought, *Where have I seen her before?* He knew that he had seen her. Just such a smile — but where? Or did it just remind him of someone infinitely more lovely and a million miles more distant than Mrs. Samuel Smith, who carried two nondescript suitcases, who leaned on his desk, whose eyes bespoke his aid and chivalry, and whose tweed coat was respectable but not elegant?

She was repeating, "Could I get a car, at once?"

Well, it was rather late. But he did know a man who had a private car. For hire. Might come pretty expensive.

"That's all right," said Cherry in her most regal manner, a Hetty Green with big ideas and grown openhanded. The clerk's eyes snapped back into his head. He inquired, devoured with curiosity, "But Mr. Smith — ?"

"Mr. Smith?" said Cherry as if she had never heard the name before. "Oh, you mean Mr. *Smith*. I — he can't come with me. He isn't well." She stopped and looked suddenly as malicious as a Persian kitten confronting a catnip mouse. "If — if he hasn't called downstairs by, say, seven tomorrow morning," she said, "I wonder if the house doctor —"

The clerk became more and more confounded. He reached groggily for the telephone and was connected with the near-by garage. He spoke briefly into it. "Party wants to drive to Boston — in a hurry," he said.

"Oh," said Cherry when he had hung up, "how long before — I mean — I must hurry — you see," she said softly, confidentially, leaning across the desk and spurred by wild mischief, "you see" — and here her eyes filled with tears — "it's my little boy — he's terribly ill."

The clerk quivered. She'd been married — this afternoon. These modern girls! He recovered. A widow, of course, a young widow. Only a beloved child by a former marriage — ill-considered, runaway at, say, sixteen could move a lovely and loving woman to desert her groom on her wedding night. But what of this Smith? Was he really ill or did he sulk in his lonely tent? Had they quarreled over the child? Had he cast her from him? The clerk's narrow chest swelled. This Smith was, indubitably, a louse. He, Harold X. Mannerly, would live up to his traditions and his name.

A little later Cherry conferred with the sober and middle-aged driver of the private car. He shuffled from one foot to the other. No, he wouldn't go so far as to say that he wouldn't take her. But Boston was a good ways off. No, m'am, it was a state road and would be cleared all right. Leastways, he thought so. But —

Yes'm, he was a careful driver and accustomed to night driving. He was on night trick anyway at the garage. But —

"I'll pay you a hundred dollars," said Cherry sharply.

The driver goggled, the clerk clutched at the edge of the desk. The driver said, nearly tearing his scalp apart in an effort to scratch some sanity into his slow-moving mind, "Well, that'll be all right I guess. Plus gas."

At the door Cherry turned back and ran to the desk. She put down several bills. "I don't know the rates."

The clerk told her the rates. "But — Mr. Smith — ?"

Cherry smiled. "He'll be checking out in the morning," she told Mr. Mannerly.

There wasn't any sense to that.

Outside, the car waited, a solid arrangement of gears and such. Comfortable too. Cherry got in. The driver put in her bags. It was now something after midnight and the moon was sinking toward the west. But its light lay upon the roads and the snowbanks beyond. Magical, that light, soft and silver and enchanted and utterly false. In the hired car Cherry wept stormily. She thought, *I've got to plan.* But she could not plan. Later, perhaps, when she had rested, when she had bathed and slept and eaten.

There was very little traffic this time of night and this time of year. Four hours saw them in Boston.

Cherry went to the Copley-Plaza. She was white with fatigue, she had cried herself into disfigurement. There wasn't a trace of powder left, or of lipstick. No one would have recognized her. No one did.

She slept until after ten o'clock in the morning. Then she woke. She woke from very troubled dreams. She ached as if she had influenza. Her head was killing her. It hurt to move, it hurt to the touch. She longed for Hilda and her trained soothing hands. She longed for Boycie. She longed for California and a rose garden, for Park Avenue and Mrs. Higgins and Ashtubula himself. She longed even for the Van Steeden mansion, its stolid security and for her grandmother. If Horace had entered now she would have greeted him with gratitude.

She reached for the telephone and ordered newspapers, orange juice, and coffee. But then it came upon her that she was hungry. Very hungry. She added ham and eggs and hot biscuits to her order. Then she crawled out of bed and went gingerly into the bathroom and ran a steaming bath.

When she was back in bed and the breakfast came, and the newspapers, she felt a little better. But she set down the glass of orange juice as her eyes fell on a headline. This was a New York paper at which she was glaring. This morning's. It was a tabloid, a convenient and pictorial affair.

Where is Cherry Chester? ran the headlines.

The coffee cooled, the eggs congealed, the ham curled up for comfort and warmth. Cherry read and read. She picked up the telephone and asked for more papers.

The papers were not convinced. This might be a publicity stunt. But it was news.

It appeared that Miss Chester had ostensibly sailed for Europe. The press had seen her off. But she had not landed at Southampton. On the ship it had been presumed that she was ill or resting. She was not seen at meals, on the public decks, in the lounges. Someone, muffled in a mink coat and veiled, had been observed in a deck chair on the private deck, but not closely. And all Miss Chester's meals had been sent into the living-room of her suite and her companion, Miss Boyce-Medford, had taken them herself into the bedroom.

But it appeared that this invalid person was none other than Miss Chester's personal maid.

Cherry dropped the papers. She hadn't thought of that. She hadn't figured what Boycie would do. She had her own passport with her, safely zippered inside a large pocket in her handbag. And Hilda had her own. Naturally Hilda couldn't disembark as Miss Chester. Even if she had had Cherry's passport there would have been one too few in the Chester party on landing — before landing, even, when the medical inspectors came aboard.

She picked up the papers again. Cherry Chester had vanished. There wasn't a trace of her. No one knew — or admitted they knew — anything. Miss Boyce-Medford when interviewed in England had by telephone and cable announced merely that Miss Chester had decided not to sail at the last moment and had gone away for a rest. There was nothing at which to be alarmed. Everything was perfectly in order. Miss Chester would follow on a later boat. Here were all her trunks and luggage for proof. Of course, she would follow. But Miss Boyce-Medford did not know when.

In London Cherry's mother had refused

herself to interviewers. The princess was not to be seen; nor yet the prince. They sent down word through their secretaries that they wished the reporters would kindly go elsewhere. There was no mystery — none at all. Miss Boyce-Medford had explained.

In New York Mrs. Van Steeden's door was closed upon the inquiring reporters' large feet. Her butler was old but he was plenty tough. Naturally, Madame Van Steeden had been informed of her granddaughter's plans. There was no cause for alarm. Thank you so much. Good-by and good riddance.

In California movie magnates tore their hair, the press and the publicity departments were, for once, speechless. What was the big idea? Was she off her head? But by no means try to kill the story. Keep it going. It was priceless. "Honest to God, I don't know a thing about it," groaned the star's special press-contact man, "I'd tell you if I did, Herman — but I don't know a damned thing."

The studio had offered a reward. The Egyptian prince had offered a reward. The amateur detectives got in the producer's graying hair.

The New York producer who was to put on Cherry's play in the spring said to his press agent, "This means an eight weeks' advance sellout if she'll only stay away long enough. Where the hell is she, Bill?"

"How the hell do I know?" inquired the press agent.

Where is Cherry Chester?

A columnist said brightly, "Maybe she's killed herself!" It was suggested that they start dragging rivers and oceans, haunting morgues. In two days which elapsed after Boycie's landing, Cherry had "been seen" in twenty cities and almost identified on half a dozen unpleasant slabs.

A broken heart, wrote one of the better known sob sisters. *No one has ever realized that for three years Cherry Chester has been secretly in love with a married man whose invalid wife has refused him a divorce.*

Out in Hollywood six married men whose wives were invalided through temperament, alimony disagreement, hay fever, or spite, looked sheepishly if triumphantly at their men friends whose wives were far too healthy.

"Holy smoke!" cried Cherry, hurling the papers from her and upsetting the orange juice. Yet she might have known this would happen. She had known it. But she hadn't quite realized the extent to which it would happen.

She must get in touch with Boycie and with her grandmother, at once. She put her hand on the phone. A transatlantic call, a New

York call, a cable blank. Easy as ABC. No, not as easy. Reporters would come running, they would invade this room within half an hour, they might easily retrace her steps — they might —

She had to get back to New York. To the Van Steeden house. She would be safe there.

She'd wire Higgins to tell her grandmother. But they'd know who Higgins was, at the telegraph desk, that is, if they read the papers.

She drank her coffee. Dressed. Packed. She telephoned downstairs. Was there a plane leaving for New York? No, not at once. But she had to leave at once. Please call the field and hire a plane, said Miss Brown.

Before she left she telegraphed to her grandmother's lawyer. He was so many people's lawyer. No one would think of him. The girl who took the message looked — and was utterly indifferent.

Please telephone grandmother I am on my way home by plane. S. Brown.

Bags. Bellboys. Bill. Taxi. Flying-field. Consultation. Exchange of money. And the plane taxiing down the field and rising easily and lightly into the air. The pilot smiled at her. He was a dark young man, rather good-looking. A smudged carbon copy of the man she'd left behind her.

Good-by, Samuel Smith.

CHAPTER TEN

STRANGE HONEYMOON

Anthony woke. He stretched away his drowsiness. He tried to remember. Yet he couldn't remember anything worth remembering. He spoke tentatively. He said, "Darling —"

The light was still on but it was morning. Still rather on the dark side at something past six-thirty but nevertheless morning. This was an unfamiliar room in an hotel in Plymouth, New Hampshire. It was, save for Anthony and the necessary furniture, quite empty.

She hadn't come. Of course, she hadn't. And he had slept — all through the night. Soundly. He recalled the victorious perfume and frowned. He sat up. He felt all right. He felt like a million dollars.

Or had she come to the door and knocked and he had not answered? Or had she come in without knocking and found him sleeping? He shuddered. He hoped fervently that she had not done that. Or that if she had — did he by any chance snore? Did he sleep with his mouth open?

No one who had ever been in a position to

know had taxed him with these unfortunate habits.

She was, he decided, asleep in the next room. Worn out. With tears, and with, he trusted, disappointment. What a way in which to begin a married life! But she had been hopelessly stupid, stubborn, idiotic, completely without comprehension. Hadn't he explained to her clearly and kindly that perfume made him ill? All he had asked her to do was to air the room, wash herself, and spend the rest of the night in his own unpolluted quarters.

He should be very angry with her. He was very angry at her. She — and her cursed scent — had caused him to appear a fool in his own eyes as well as in hers. Unforgivable! He had lost face, and considerably more than face.

But what an inexplicable woman! She hadn't used the faintest hint of bottled fragrance during that divine, disturbing, insane week at the Simpsons'. Naturally he had not thought to explain the taboo.

He rose and put on dressing-gown and slippers. He stole, very softly, into the bathroom. He brushed his teeth and performed the civilized gestures. He put his hand on the knob of her door. He turned it. It was not locked. It had not been locked save for a brief interval around midnight. Of that interval, wrapped in

186

merciful slumber, he had known nothing.

He would go into her room. He would wake her, very gently. He would take her in his arms. He would ask, "Darling, you've forgiven me?" He would be utterly gentle and completely magnanimous.

He walked in. The room was empty. He trod on glass and stepped back, profane. He looked about. He sniffed. That cursed stuff was still most apparent. He couldn't stay here very long.

The bureau drawers gaped wide open. Likewise the closet door. Not a sign of her, of her clothes, of anything. She had gone.

He went back into his bedroom and sat down upon the bed and took his head in his hands. He had surrendered his freedom to her — and she had left him. He had endowed her with two magnificent names: one, which she could read upon all the fixtures in the utilitarian room between their own, and one which she could read in the daily press and on the covers of sought-after books. These names he had given her and she had left him. Well, she'd come back.

Perhaps she hadn't left him. Perhaps she'd merely gone downstairs — perhaps —

There was a knock at his door. He thought, *She has come back. She has repented.* That was it. She had packed and vacated merely in or-

187

der to frighten him. Perhaps she'd been having breakfast — *at this hour?* he asked himself, astonished. It was now seven.

"Come in," he said plaintively.

The door was locked. The doorknob rattled. "Come the other way," called Anthony, and hastily climbed into bed, shedding the robe, kicking off the slippers, "through your room."

A man's voice inquired, amazed, "I *beg* your pardon?"

Anthony leaped from the bed. Pajamaed, his hair in great disorder, he unlocked the door and flung it open. A man stood there; little and round and smiling. He carried a black bag. A process server? A — a reporter. What in heaven's name? Anthony could not guess that here was the stork, in person, but only on occasion. This was not one of the occasions.

"I am Dr. Elman, the house physician," announced the little man. "Mrs. Smith thought —"

"*Mrs. Smith —*"

With agitated hands Anthony dragged the gentleman into the room. "Where is she?" he cried wildly.

The doctor looked bewildered. "I don't know, I'm sure," he replied mildly. "I had an early call from the desk. The night clerk had left a message. You were not feeling well, he said, and if you had not called downstairs by seven, I was to come right up."

Anthony fell back on the bed. He was feeble. He was undone. He was not himself. The little man advanced briskly and set down his bag. "Let me see your tongue." Weakly Anthony exhibited it. The doctor said, "Hum," thoughtfully.

He took Anthony's wrist in cool fingers. He consulted a large gold watch. He shook his head. He murmured, "Very rapid, *very* rapid. . . . Say 'Ah!' " he commanded suddenly.

"Ah," said Anthony docilely and opened his mouth. Then he shut it so suddenly that it was a good thing for Dr. Elman that, absent-mindedly, he had not put his finger in that yawning cavern. "What is all this?" demanded Anthony. "I'm not ill — where's my wife?"

The doctor shook his head. He opened the black bag. He brought forth certain pellets. He shook some into an envelope. He wrote upon the envelope with a fountain pen. He said, "Open your mouth," and when Anthony did so in order to roar like a wounded tiger, in popped a clinical thermometer. Dr. Elman then drew forth a blue pad of prescription blanks and filled one in with that not uncommon medical penmanship which resembles a wounded hen floundering out of an

189

inkwell and making tracks on unoffending paper.

Anthony made terrible noises.

"Please," said the doctor, "please, Mr. Smith, you *must* be quiet." He withdrew the thermometer. He reported, "No fever. But a very rapid pulse. Eyes staring, every symptom of agitation, skin dry and pale. Yes, Mr. Smith," concluded Dr. Elman with every symptom of satisfaction, "you are in a highly nervous state. Two of these every two hours. And have this prescription filled at once. That will be three dollars, please. I'd like to see you this evening."

Anthony leaped from the bed. He was absolutely ferocious. He shrieked. He ordered. "Get out — will you — before they have to take *you* to a hospital!"

The doctor was a mild man. Live and let live was his motto. He retreated. He went downstairs to the desk. He set his bag upon it. He said, "In my opinion that man in room thirty-four is in a dangerous state. Perhaps I'd better have a consultant. Charge my visit to him. *Five* dollars," said the little man firmly.

Anthony tore around the room. He threw the pellets on the floor, he ground them into the carpet. He muttered. He had every appearance of a man bereft of his senses.

Somewhat later, carrying his bags, he appeared at the desk. He demanded, "My bill, please."

"Have you breakfasted," asked the clerk, "Mr. — ?"

"Smith," said Anthony briefly. "No — I haven't time — I have to leave, at once."

The day clerk consulted a book. He said, "Mrs. Smith paid for the rooms when she checked out last night. There will be only the doctor's charge. Five dollars." He added timorously, "But — hadn't you better go back to bed, Mr. Smith? Dr. Elman said —"

Mr. Smith interrupted, and flung a five-dollar bill upon the desk, "No, I'm not going back to bed. I want to see the night clerk."

"But," said the day clerk, "Mr. Mannerly is asleep."

"He'll have to wake up," said Mr. Smith, "or else —" He loomed above the desk. He fixed the clerk with an eye which had cowed tigers, elephants, cobras, naked black gentlemen, and negligeed white women. He said, "I'll see him at once. Where is he?"

Gasping, the clerk mentioned the room number and tottered to the telephone as soon as Mr. Smith's formidable back was turned to call Mr. Mannerly and warn him. "Hal . . . sorry . . . this is Dick . . . there's a nut coming to see you, at once . . . name of Smith . . . shall I send someone after him?"

191

Mr. Mannerly responded, drugged with sleep, and beatifically, "Smith — lovely woman . . . say, Dick, she makes me think of . . . !"

Dick, shrugging, hung up. It was not his funeral.

Anthony pounded on Mr. Mannerly's door. Mr. Mannerly was still in a semistupor. He admitted him and then got back into bed and pulled the covers around his ears. What was that Dick had asked? He wished heartily that he had agreed to the head porter, the house detective, and the manager.

Anthony sat down on the bed. He put a twenty dollar bill on the coverlet. He said, mildly enough, "I'm sorry to wake you, but I understand you can tell me about — er — Mrs. Smith. When did she leave, where did she go, what did she say? Everything you can recall. And at once."

So it *had* been a quarrel. Mr. Mannerly was on Mrs. Smith's side. "I'm sure I don't know. She came to the desk, with her bags, shortly after midnight. She asked about train connections. There were no trains. She paid the bill and hired a car to drive her to Boston."

"I see," said Anthony. "She — she left no message?"

Mr. Mannerly, sitting up, the cover clutched to his skinny chest, eyed his unpleasant visitor with dignity and disapproval. He said, "She did not. She said you weren't well — that if you hadn't called down by seven to please send the house doctor up."

"Hell!" exclaimed Anthony violently. "Damnation!" He then muttered to himself in a strange tongue, which may have been Cantonese, Hindustani, Afridi, or merely Arabic.

"I *beg* your pardon?" said the clerk.

Anthony reached out his hands. He shook this little man. He asked, and he shouted it, "Where was she going — where was she going?"

The clerk cried, gasping, "Let go of me! I'll call the manager. Let me go! She was going," he managed to articulate, as Anthony's hands fell from his shoulders, "to — to her sick child."

"Her what!" asked Anthony, incredulous.

He threw back his head and he laughed. He roared. The clerk blinked and quivered. The man was out of his mind. Still laughing, Anthony rose and went to the door. "Her sick child!" he said. The door slammed. His laughter was loud in the echoing corridors. It died away.

The clerk was alone with twenty dollars.

He plucked at his lower lip. He thought, *That's right. I wonder if she got a phone call? No wires came to the desk.* He made up his mind to ask the night operator if a call had come through for Mrs. Smith before midnight. Somehow, with the remembrance of Mr. Smith's Gargantuan laughter in his ears, Mr. Mannerly was sure there had been no call.

He put the twenty dollars in the drawer of the night table and, even more exhausted than mystified, rolled over and fell asleep.

At the desk Anthony was making demands. The driver of the car Mrs. Smith had hired. Fetch him here, at once.

The day clerk shook his head. They wouldn't have reached Boston till early morning. It would take them better than four hours, five, he thought, would be more like it. And the man wouldn't turn right around and come back. Even if he had, he wouldn't be here yet.

Anthony asked for the name and address of the garage, and the clerk gave it to him and sighed with relief when he departed. He marched himself into the dining-room, ate an enormous breakfast, paid the check there, and leaving his bags to be called for, walked over to the garage.

Yes, they knew the car and the driver. Reliable man. Oh, no, they didn't believe he'd be back today. He had a married daughter in Boston. He'd go there and stay.

Anthony thought, *What's the use?* He thought further, *By the time I get to Boston after waiting for this fellow to show up and tell me where she went, she can be anywhere.*

He asked about trains. The garage man told him, and fluttered a timetable in his face. Anthony said, "I might drive to Portland and take the night train to New York from there." He thought that driving would be better than the slow travel by day coach, the interminable pressure of people about him. He added, "I think I'll go back to the hotel now. I've changed my mind. I'll wait till late afternoon, in case your man comes back from Boston."

But when he reached the hotel he overheard the day clerk talking on the public telephone as he passed the booth. "Simpson's . . . is that you, Mitty?"

So they knew, or would in a minute. Miss Hambridge would weep with pity and gape with excitement, Mr. Hill's teeth would misbehave.

Anthony whirled. He retrieved his bags. He snatched them from the boy's astonished hands. He sailed down the street back to the garage. "I've changed my mind again," he said. "Get me a car and driver now, will you? I'm going to Portland."

There were hours to kill in Portland. He got his publisher on the telephone. The other man's voice came across the wires to him amiable, faintly relieved. "Oh, it's you, Amberton . . . I was beginning to worry . . . haven't heard from you . . . how'd you like Simpsons?"

"Fine," said Anthony grimly. "Look here, I'm in Portland. Leaving tonight. I'll deliver the manuscript in the morning. Meantime have someone look up sailings for me."

"But," expostulated the publisher, "you know you have a lecture engagement next week —"

"I'd forgotten," said Anthony, and indeed he spoke only the truth. "Tell them I'm ill. Black water fever. Zengue. Malaria. Smallpox. Nervous breakdown. I'm leaving."

"But where are you going?"

"I don't know. Have someone find out what boats are going and where. No, not a direct boat. Not one of those damned cruises either. I'd rather take a tramp. Get me a passage on one that's not going any place in particular. Cargo boat. Just as long as it's clean and comfortable."

He thought of his secretary whom he had left in the Orient and who had by now returned to his home in Scotland there to await further orders. He would have produced a passage, out of a hat, and no questions asked. Anthony shouted, "I'm fed up, I tell you. I'll stop in town just long enough to wind up those infernal legal matters and then — I'm off." He hung up.

Now let her try and find him if she wanted to, he reflected with gloomy satisfaction. He wouldn't lift a finger to find her. Not as long as he lived. She could go somewhere and divorce Samuel Smith if she so desired — but he thought, enjoying himself, it would be rather hard to serve papers on the missing husband. No, she could not divorce him. It came to him suddenly and unpleasantly that there were annulments. Let her try that if she wanted. Where is this man? I don't know. Where did he live formerly? I haven't the least idea. What did you say his name was? Smith. Samuel Smith.

He doubted if she had looked at the marriage license save to set down her signature. Born, U.S.A. Residence, he had written, New York.

Fine. If she wanted him back she could look for him. Feeling like the needle in the haystack, pointed and sharp and incredibly hard to find, he composed himself to wait for his train.

For the rest of his life a man with Something in His Past. For the rest of his life a man who murmured to woman, "I'm incapable of love — the love you demand — I am not free. Women are the brief bright spots along a dark

197

way — the charming playmates of a moment's loneliness — but, darling, do not ask me to love you —"

Finis.

He thought, looking at his watch, *Where is she?*

She was at home in the Van Steeden house. She had been there quite a while, after flying fleetly from Boston. She had taken a taxi from the field and given an address some blocks distant from the Van Steeden house. She had permitted the driver to carry her bags up the steps of the brownstone dwelling. She had rung the bell. She had asked the maid who appeared, "Is this Mrs. Clark's?" And then, "oh, I'm so sorry. It must have been East. This is West." And then, staggered by her own duplicity, had set off down the steps again and walked to her grandmother's.

The butler opened the door cautiously. For once he showed some emotion. His old face broke up into lines of relief. It looked like a fine piece of porcelain which has been mended none too skillfully. He exclaimed, "Miss Sarah!"

"Yes." She patted his arm absently. "Where's Grandmother?"

"In the white room. She's — she's been worried." He took the bags and turned. "I'll tell her you're here."

"Never mind."

Lucy Van Steeden sat writing at her desk. She turned as Cherry spoke. Cherry's heart sank. It seemed to her that her grandmother had aged in something over a week. She had thought, all the way home in the plane, *I'll tell her. She'll know what to do. She can help me get out of this. Divorce. Annulment. Anything. I never want to see him again as long as I live.*

No. She couldn't tell her. It didn't make sense. She fancied Lucy's cool black eyes on her own. You didn't know anything about this man? Just the name he gave you — not what he did for a living, where he resided, who his people are? Nothing! He might have been anyone — a person one reads about in the papers — thief, murderer, bigamist, blackmailer. He didn't know who you were? Nonsense. My granddaughter! And a motion picture actress! Sarah, have you lost your wits?

No. She couldn't tell.

Lucy Van Steeden said sharply, "So, you've come home." She did not rise. She just sat there looking at her granddaughter. She felt a little faint but she wouldn't show it. "Will you kindly have the goodness to explain what you meant by leaving the boat and why you left it?"

Cherry sat down on the floor. She felt tired, lost, utterly forlorn, completely miserable. She put her head against her grandmother's knees. The hot tears soaked through the fine black silk, and her slender shoulders shook. Mrs. Van Steeden bent down. She put her thin hand under Cherry's chin and wrenched it sharply upward. She demanded, half whispering, "What has happened? *What has happened?*"

All sorts of insane visions raced through her tired old brain. The child had been kidnaped — escaped. The child had —

"Nothing," said Cherry. She got hold of herself somehow. "Nothing. I'm so sorry, Granny," she said, in the old term of her childhood. "I —"

"Where have you been?"

"In a farmhouse, in New England."

"Why, Sarah, why? Marian was frantic. She telephoned me as soon as she docked, before I could see the papers, before those vultures started pounding down my door. Who else knew about this? Was it something they call a publicity stunt?" Her voice wavered on the unfamiliar words, her mouth writhed as if she tasted something very bitter.

"No, truly. I — Granny, I didn't mean to upset you and Boycie and promote all this newspaper gossip."

"You are rather late," said her grand-mother. "After all, you have had some experience with the press. You must have known Marian could not conceal your absence — after landing."

"I didn't think —"

"Obviously. This place in New England? Where and why?"

"Just a farmhouse. They take boarders. There — there was no one else there," said Cherry faintly. "I'd heard about it. I — I didn't want to go abroad."

"Nonsense, you fretted yourself thin because your sailing was delayed. There's a lot more in this than meets the eye," said the old lady sensibly.

"No. No. I *swear* it. I was tired. Of everything. People. Interviews. You know what it would be like over there, with Sylvia and Gerhard. People — hotels — I got on that boat but I knew I couldn't stand it. I had Hilda pack a bag, give me some of her things. I knew about this farmhouse —"

"From whom, may I ask?"

"A friend — in — in California. I thought, if I could just get away for a little while — It was heavenly there," she said, and choked miserably to recall how heavenly, "so peaceful. No one knew who I was. I ate and slept and went out in the snow. I didn't see the papers. When

201

I did, I came straight home."

Her grandmother said, "Normally I wouldn't believe a word of this. But since you elected to make a public show of yourself you haven't had even an average mental equipment. Your explanation is fantastic but like the sort of life you live, it probably has a certain amount of reality — to you. Go upstairs and to bed, I'll send for Dr. Cummings."

"Why?" asked Cherry, and got to her feet. "I'm perfectly well, Granny."

"No," said her grandmother, "you are not. I will send a statement to the papers this evening. I will also send messages to the urgent gentlemen on Broadway and in Hollywood who have been making my life hideous. You have returned home. As Miss Boyce-Medford told the press, you went away for a rest. You are now at home under a doctor's care because of the hounding of the papers. As soon as you are well enough, you will sail for Europe, to join your mother. Is that quite clear?"

"Quite," said Cherry dully.

CHAPTER ELEVEN

THE GIRL IN THE MOON

Cherry's return did not entirely solace the hungry newsgatherers. Her arrival at the Van Steeden house was heralded far and wide but there were plentiful speculations in black and white. Where had she been? And with whom? Was it not true that the director of her last picture was known to be in love with her? One bright lad thought to interview Horace, not for the first time. Horace kicked him down the steps — that is, by proxy; he delegated his manservant to do so. Personally, he would not soil his polished boots.

The director in question gnashed his excellent teeth and spent three hours and four thousand dollars convincing a certain blonde that he disliked Cherry Chester: *No, of course she hasn't your talent, sweetheart, or your looks either — she just got the breaks. No, I can't endure the woman. No, naturally I won't direct her next picture. How in the world could I have been with her, haven't I been here all the time? Yes, I know, I flew to Palm Springs for a day. But Chester's east. My angel, do be reasonable!*

She was not reasonable; she was very expensive.

Cherry stayed in bed for almost a week. That is, so far as the public knew, she stayed in bed. Actually she kept to her rooms except when she dined with her grandmother in Lucy's sitting-room. Higgins came to see her, and Mrs. Higgins. The chauffeur came. Cherry said wildly, "I think I'll take the car over — arrange it, somebody."

It was arranged.

That she was in Coventry she well knew. Her grandmother said nothing further, merely looked volumes when the speculations were at their height. But a nice sack murder crowded Miss Chester off the front pages.

The Broadway manager came to call. He was admitted as if he were something which reeked unpleasantly. Cherry received him in the white room. He was a very nice person, as it happened, and a good friend of hers. He had given her her first chance. He had lost money on her and he had made it all back. Now he was a little worried. "This new opera, it doesn't look so hot," he said cautiously. "The public won't like seeing you jump off cliffs and things, Cherry, just because you're in love with your stepbrother!"

It was tragedy. It was gloom. It was dark purple. Cherry adored it. She desired to play it. She said so. "And that's flat, Gus — that or nothing."

"Okay by me, baby. Anyway you've got a swell buildup if the public doesn't forget too soon. By the way, sweetheart, tip me off. I won't tell a soul. Where *were* you?"

"In the moon," answered Cherry solemnly.

She wanted to laugh, she wanted to cry. In the moon indeed, wrapped about with moon magic, a honeymoon. What a honeymoon that had turned out to be! She never wanted to see honey again —

Some appeared on her breakfast tray next morning. Sage honey. Her grandmother's housekeeper had scoured the shops for this delicacy which she had once heard that Cherry liked. Cherry threw it on the floor. Sage honey is special, very special, but when it encounters a carpet it's just like any other product of the busy little bees.

The quiet dark gentleman from the New York staff of her motion picture company came to see her. He adopted a most curious attitude. For ten straight minutes he reproached her and for ten more he congratulated her. The publicity was, of course, enormous. However, as she wouldn't be doing a picture before the autumn, he wished she had selected a more opportune date to vanish.

After this meeting in the white study the room was aired out, on Mrs. Van Steeden's orders, for the second time. The first time was after Gus had departed.

Cherry saw few other people; not her many curious friends nor any reporters, no one else save one or two intimates. Lolly Harris was one of these, a bright-eyed young woman, with enormous means and a gift for enthusiastic friendship. She and Cherry had known each other since their childhood. And it was nice to see Lolly again, returned from a long cruise and looking so very chic that one forgot she wasn't particularly pretty, and being so amusing —

"Darling, must you go abroad — can't you come up to us?"

"No — later perhaps. After the show closes. I'll love it then," said Cherry.

"And you won't tell me a word, not even a little word about what you were doing while all this furor and fanfare was on? My dear, I'd be like the grave."

"Even the grave gives up ghosts," said Cherry, laughing.

"I wouldn't." Lolly made a sparkling brunette face at her. "But if you won't, you won't. But I'm not gulled by all this 'rest' business. Romance. I'll bet a cookie — a whole cookie jar. Wasn't that it — romance?"

"Of course it wasn't," said Cherry very crossly. "Don't be a zany."

Lolly kissed her and prepared to go, slender and elegant and smothered in silver fox. "I'll come see you off," she said. "Oh, did you know that Pete's brother has gone in for newspaper work?"

"Not really?" said Cherry. "I knew he wanted to write."

"If you'd give him an interview? He's dying to see you again. He's been talking about you."

"Oh, Lolly, spare me. Later perhaps, not now."

"All right," said Lolly, "I've known you longer than my young brother-in-law. Of course, he isn't doing anything much. Jerkwater town and paper. If ever he managed a real scoop he might get a job in town. But I don't expect that he ever will, poor darling. He isn't intelligent. None of Pete's relatives are. Nor is Pete. Look whom he married!"

She waved, she blew a kiss, she laughed and was gone. Left alone, Cherry curled up on an ancient chaise longue and moped. She wished she had dared confide in Lolly. She wished she dared confide in someone. Boycie for choice. But she didn't dare.

She opened a smart weekly magazine. She turned its pages. An advertisement leaped to her — the photograph of a scent bottle — squat and imposing, with a clever and adjustable atomizer top. *Cherry Blossom* she read — the latest creation — *dedicated to that incomparable star of stage and screen, Miss Cherry Chester.*

The magazine sailed across the room and brought up sharply against a whatnot, dislodging and completely ruining a pink-faced young man in porcelain, with a baby-blue lute. He shattered to the floor. Cherry wept stormily.

She talked to Sylvia, still in London, by telephone. Sylvia's voice came to her with its usual overtones of musical complaining over the thousands of miles of tossing water between them. "Baby? I was so relieved to have the cable . . . but why did you do it . . . when are you sailing?"

"Next week —"

"We'll wait. I'll meet you at Southampton."

"Liverpool," shouted Cherry.

"Liverpool, what's the difference?" asked Sylvia, geographically undaunted, "and we'll go right to Cannes. London is horrible. Fogs. Dull, terribly dull. I can't bear it anyway, until the season."

"How's Boycie?" shrieked Cherry.

"Who? Boycie? Oh, she's fine. At least,"

said Sylvia vaguely, "she's down with the flu or something silly. Not surprising, worried as she was, you bad infant."

Cherry hung up, remorseful and troubled. She'd aged her grandmother, if not in the wood, at least in a week. She'd worried Boycie into flu. She'd made herself the talk, if not the laughing-stock, of a couple of continents. And for what? For a young man with broad shoulders and curly black hair and hazel eyes, for a young man with very experienced arms and lips. For a young man who detested her, who had to manufacture the most absurd excuses in order to be rid of her, for a young man who —

Where was he?

She said, "Sammy —" into her pillow, and then threw the pillow on the floor and rose and jumped up and down on it savagely. Sammy! Hadn't there been a song once, long before she was born: *Sammy — oh, oh, oh, Sammy,* or something? Who could get sentimental over a name like that? Not she. She cast herself on the bed once more and murmured to the unresponsive coverings that she wished she were dead. She hoped the boat would sink. But if the boat didn't sink she'd have the time of her life in Europe. She'd flirt her head off. She'd lead men on and be cool and unfeeling and disdainful. She'd laugh at

them. "Of course you amuse me, Count —
but — No, I'm afraid not. You see, I've no capacity for love. It — disgusts me — rather . . ."

A woman without a heart.

Evenings she played cribbage with Lucy.
And she played very badly indeed. "Fifteen-
two, fifteen-four," murmured Lucy. "What's
wrong with you, Sarah, you are not keeping
your mind on the game," she asked, putting
the little pegs sharply and firmly into place.

"I'm all right, Grandmother."

"You look badly," remarked her grandmother. "As you know, I don't approve of
rouge. I dislike you to wear it. But please do,
I'll manage to overlook my disapproval. Just a
hint. You're gaunt and hollow-eyed — and
plainer than I've ever seen you. Horace is
coming to dine tomorrow night to say good-
by."

"What, again!" asked Cherry irrepressibly.

"Yes, again. The poor boy had been nearly
out of his mind. Think how unpleasant it has
been for him dragged into all this disgraceful
talk. I'll thank you to at least remember
your manners when he is here, provided you
haven't forgotten them altogether." She
added tartly, "I've accepted your explanation,
Sarah, and I have forced our friends and even
the press, to accept it — at least outwardly.
But I warn you that if I ever discover that you

have lied to me, that you have managed to involve yourself in something discreditable, I shall cut you off without a penny. Without a penny, do you hear me?"

Yes, Cherry heard. She had heard this threat a good many times since she had gone on the stage. But somehow it was sharper tonight and it was closer and there was a real disturbance at her heart.

She didn't care about the money.

That was a lie. She did care. The income which her grandmother had allowed her was very pleasant. To be sure, she earned large sums when she made a picture. Not otherwise. Her contract called for a certain amount of money per picture. She was paid an excellent salary when she was working in a stage production. But she didn't work very often and stage productions have been known to fold their distracted angel's wings within a few weeks. And into this new spring venture money of her own was going. Yes, the income from her grandmother was very acceptable. She could write her own ticket. She could dictate her own contracts, she could back her own shows. Without it —

Without it she would be one of many, and not terribly sure of herself. She wondered, shuffling the cards listlessly, what her new picture would gross. She had thought it very good indeed, her best. But one never knew. It would open next week, in New York. It had already been shown in the sticks and they had given her encouraging reports. After all a picture stood or fell on its reception outside of the big cities. She thought, *It doesn't matter —*

But it did.

She said, raising her green eyes to the black ones, "I'm sorry you can't trust me, Granny."

"Fiddlesticks. Of course I can't trust you. Never trusted a woman in my life — not even myself. Women are fools. You never know what they'll do next." She smiled brilliantly at the girl. She said gently, "I do believe you, Sarah."

Cherry smiled back at her with a mouth suddenly tremulous. What had she done? She had done something very dreadful. She regretted it with all her heart.

She did not regret it. She frowned at her cards. She thought, *If it hadn't been for that damned perfume — providing that it was the perfume.*

She'd never know. She'd never see him again. Wedded but no wife. Wife in name only. Suppose she advertised — *Personal — Samuel Smith, please write to Sarah Brown.* She supposed she'd get about eight thousand letters — from all the Samuel Smiths in the world except the one to whom she was married.

She sobbed, aloud.

"For heaven's sake!" exclaimed her grandmother.

"It's nothing, Granny, I'm tired, that's all." She rose and almost upset the table. "I'll go to bed, if you don't mind." She went to her grandmother's chair, bent down, kissed the old cheek, and fled. Mrs. Van Steeden sat there a moment, and then she put her hand to her face. The cheek was damp. Mrs. Van Steeden hadn't really cried in a good many years. Not really. She rose after a long time and went upstairs and knocked on Cherry's door.

"Come in," said Cherry indifferently.

Mrs. Van Steeden sat down on the edge of the bed. She took the two warm young hands in her cool dry clasp. She said, "If there is anything troubling you — My child, I am such an old martinet, are you so afraid of me that you do not dare to come to me when you really need me?"

Cherry kissed the hands. "Granny, I'm all right. No, I'm not afraid. You're — a lamb and a darling. I'm fine, really. Just —" she smiled a little in the darkness — "just a little temperamental."

"Not around me," said Lucy Van Steeden. "I've spanked you before. I'm not too feeble to spank you again." She rose. "Go to sleep," she said.

No, it wasn't really the money. It wasn't half the money. It was mostly hurting this upright old woman, with her sharp tongue and her back like a ramrod and her sudden, unexpected weakness, her vulnerability, which was Cherry herself.

On the following night Horace arrived, pink and prim. "Nice pickle you got us all into," he complained. "I must say, Sarah, you have very little consideration."

Mrs. Van Steeden ordered sharply, "Leave the child alone, Horace. I know where she was and why she was there. That should be enough for you."

Cherry looked gratefully at her grandmother and had never in all her life felt so guilty.

Her relations with Horace were very cool.

The last few days until her sailing were days of nerve strain. Every time the front doorbell rang, every time the telephone shrilled. It might be — he might have traced her. How easily he could have done so. He could have gone to Boston after interviewing the hundred dollar driver. He could have made inquiries at the Copley-Plaza, at the telegraph station, at the airport. Oh, if she had been a man she would have known a way, turned Philo Vance, Sherlock Holmes! She would have traced the taxi driver and the brownstone house which had not been the residence of Mrs. Clark. She would have found someone who had seen that girl in the tweed coat and carrying the suitcases, who walked up the steps of the Van Steeden house. She would have put two and two together from the headlines — *Where is Cherry Chester?* — and she would have made — just two again. Two, alone.

But he hadn't bothered.

She wished she knew where he was. Not in order to see him again but so that she might send him six forty-dollar bottles of *Cherry Blossom* perfume with her compliments.

When she drove out with her grandmother she kept looking from the window. There. There was a tall man. There was a man who walked hatless in the bitter wind, but his hair was fair, not dark, and he was shorter than the man she so disliked. There was one who walked as lightly as he but he was, strange to say, a fat man.

Then, the day before she sailed, she did see him.

He was standing on a street corner talking to a shorter man. A nondescript man who looked, Cherry thought bitterly, like a plainclothesman. That he happened to be a publisher did not matter. And as she looked, as she leaned from the window, to such an extent that Lucy Van Steeden demanded, "What is wrong with you, Sarah? You are making a show of yourself," he was gone. Gone, turning on his heel, lost in the crowds.

She wanted to shout, "Drive after that man!" She wanted to shriek, "Stop the horses and let me get out. Let me run after him!" She wanted to command, "Drive over him, stamp him to earth with the iron hoofs." She wanted to laugh and to cry, and her heart was giddy in her bosom and her brain was loose in her head, banging this way and that in tune with her heart. He was here, he was in New York!

That night after she had gone to her room she telephoned every hotel of any standing whatever and asked for a Mr. Samuel Smith. She got no less than eighteen Mr. Smiths, none of whom knew her. Six of them would have been glad to know her and said so. None of them spoke in Anthony's voice, a deep voice, a startling voice, an unforgettable voice.

Cherry hung up. She hadn't really wanted to talk to him anyway.

Legal business had, after all, kept Anthony in New York a little longer than he had expected. He was as jumpy as a boxcar full of horses. He insisted on canceling the speaking-engagement. He implored his publisher not to send out publicity items. The publisher nearly fainted. This from a man as anxious for publicity as any man he had ever known! No, no items, nothing about his stay in New Hampshire.

"But I sent that out when you went up there."

"That's all right, she wouldn't have seen it, and if she had at that time — Never mind, I mean, don't put anything more in," he said like a man distracted. "And no photographs and nothing about my sailing — until well after I've sailed, and tell them I won't give any interviews."

His publisher was bewildered. He thought, after leaving Anthony at his hotel, *What's come over the man?* He thought of breach of promise — farmer's daughter — but he said he wasn't going to use the Amberton name up there. No, it can't be, far too much like a traveling-salesman-smoking-car story!

Anthony sailed on a slow boat one afternoon, bound for sleepy little ports, and was the only passenger. Cherry sailed on a faster boat at noon on the second day. It would be pleasing to say that theirs were ships which passed in the night. But they didn't. They did not come anywhere within hailing distance of one another, and that was that. And Cherry, perfectly aware of the excited speculations concerning her on the boat, kept to her suite. She sometimes went walking on the deck very early, before most of the passengers were up, and sometimes late at night.

She did not frequent the lounge, she did not dance, she did not swim in the pool or come to the seat reserved for her at the captain's table. The passage was stormy but she didn't mind that. She liked it. Wind and the waves rolling, the pitching and rolling of the ship under her feet. She felt like that herself, stormy, unsettled, wishing to wreak vengeance on anything, anyone.

The passengers who could drag themselves to steamer chairs watched a redheaded girl in a heavy coat of marvelous English tweed buttoned high about her neck and her wild hair blowing in the breezes. An unfriendly girl. A girl about whom there had recently been much gossip, and who had shut herself away from all reporters and cameras on this second sailing. A girl who would presently land in England several weeks behind her schedule.

"I wonder where she was," they said to one another. "I didn't believe that newspaper yarn, did you? Of course not. There's a man in it somewhere."

There was a man in it, a man who walked the deck of another ship. And their thoughts were like radio messages which did not find their destination.

If you loved me, you'd come and find me . . .
If you loved me, you'd come and find me . . .

CHAPTER TWELVE

GAY JOURNEY

It is not too much to say that Cherry Chester carried the torch all over Europe, or at least over that part of Europe which her mother considered decently civilized. Cherry's torch carrying was a matter of singeing other people and burning down their defenses. She was extraordinarily gay. She had made up her mind to be gay, and gay she would be if it killed her. She was very like the old gentleman in the older story who remarked that he was going downtown to get drunk and, God! how he dreaded it.

Boycie journeyed up from quiet Sussex which exhibited in season the usual landscape of ancient lawns, cows knee-deep in something-or-other, willful trains, bull's-eyes, and potted salmon, in order to have a quiet little talk with her charge. This was difficult. Sylvia was superbly all over the place in the suite at the Savoy. She popped in and she popped out, sometimes with Gerhard in tow and sometimes along with three Pekinese, a devouring curiosity, and a razor-edged temper.

It irked her to the beautifully modeled bone that her child had seen fit to give Hilda a holiday. Sylvia could not possibly share her own stolid and unastonished maid with anyone and that Cherry should tour the Continent maidless was something too horrible for discussion. For three days before Cherry's arrival her mother had been interviewing maids, and having migraine.

Sylvia Van Steeden Brown von Waldheim, now Princess Gerhard Torkey Erik Gyllencrona, was forty-odd. Very odd. She was much prettier than Cherry ever dreamed of being, and much less beautiful. She had very fair hair cut short and worn with the least un-ostentatious ripple above nice ears. She had small accurate features of no especial value in repose. But they were rarely in repose. One of these days she would have to stop permitting them to flit about and remember her contours. As yet she could afford vivacity. She had a magnificent skin to which she catered with all the loving anxiety of a young mother bowing before the altar of childhood. That skin did not permit her either strong drink or mild tobacco; it put her to bed early and it looked after her diet and it saw that she had naps. It was a beautiful nuisance and took half the joy out of life.

For the rest, she had small bones, an almost

flawless little figure, good feet and better hands, the motions of a hummingbird, the mind of a grasshopper, and the calculating shrewdness attributed to the lowly pismire. She talked a good deal and listened rarely which was one reason why Cherry met her upon landing with much less trepidation than she looked forward to her encounter with Boycie.

Sylvia loved her daughter. If that love was not profound it was not her fault. She loved to capacity and that's saying a good deal. Few people love beyond the first ten rows in the orchestra. And so far as capacity is concerned, if a bathtub holds more than a saucer, why blame the saucer? It is doing its level best.

She loved her; she envied her; and it was not wholly delightful to her to realize that Cherry was twenty-six. It made her forty-odd, nearer fifty than she liked. But she bore this cross with a really commendable fortitude.

Sylvia had the voice of a plaintive silver bell which has been rung once too often. It chimed in Cherry's ears all the way between Liverpool and London, above the purr of Sylvia's expensive motor and ignoring the pleasant self-effacement of Sylvia's expensive husband. It continued to chime, for several days. The tune rang something like this — with changes:

"I can't understand you — whatever was your grandmother thinking about? I believe Mother is losing her mind. You know there is the least little hint of insanity in the family. Was it Cousin Jennifer? No, she only ran away with the groom — very good-looking he was, too, what is there about the smell of the stables which fascinates some women? Like men and hearty peasant girls, which reminds me I must get some of that new-mown hay perfume before we leave here — really, darling, it is England's contribution to allurement, reminds every man you meet of the first time he kissed the farmer's daughter under the haystack. What was I saying? Oh, yes, Mother. Poor Mother, I sometimes believe she is not as capable as she was. Boycie! What on earth was wrong with Boycie? I've always felt so safe when she was with you. But she *wasn't* with you. I've never seen her so upset, my dear, she was positively babbling when we met. Of course, if I hadn't been frantic — until she explained you were quite all right, and with friends, it would have been comic. What friends? Where were you? Oh, don't tell me, I know you won't tell the truth. You were always a most secretive child." Then she suddenly shrieked at the chauffeur "For heaven's sake, not so fast, not so fast, my nerves won't stand it. Darling, you are looking very badly.

You need a haircut, and you are absolutely haggard. Was the crossing terrible? Don't tell me, it is always terrible."

This went on for days. Between pauses for breath Cherry was able to tell her carefully Bowdlerized story. She was certain that her mother would accept it. Her mother never stayed long enough with any one topic to question it. But more than once she found her stepfather's amiable and handsome regard thoughtfully upon her. There was a twinkle in those eyes, a tolerant spark. Hastily Cherry looked away again.

Boycie was difficult. Boycie minced no words. Among other things she said, "You are a very selfish young person, Cherry. And I don't believe a word. Oh, yes, I presume that you went to New Hampshire! Heaven knows you've dates and trains and circumstantial data and evidence. You thought that all out coming over. Rather carefully, too. You went to New Hampshire to a farmhouse to rest. But why?"

"Boycie, if you can't *see* why — !"

"No," admitted Boycie, "I can't see why. If you were really as fed up and as miserable as you say, it could have been perfectly simple. We would have canceled this racketing around Europe trip and I would have taken you somewhere quietly and you could have rested until you were blue in the face. Sometimes I think you are perfectly mad; at others I believe you have merely too sharp a nose for news. Are you *sure* this wasn't cooked up in the publicity offices behind my back? You know I would never have approved. When I think of your grandmother my mind reels."

"Grandmother believes me," announced Cherry with hauteur.

Boycie regarded her. She murmured, "Then Sylvia is right, Mrs. Van Steeden is slipping."

"Boycie, don't — please don't nag at me. I've had enough." She was on the verge of throwing things. Boycie thought, *Heavens! Not in the Savoy!* She agreed hastily, "All right." Then with a sacrificial sigh from the depths of her troubled being she urged, "Give up this trip with your mother. Come with me. I can put you up comfortably. You'll have nothing to do but sleep and eat. You won't be bothered. In my little bailiwick people seldom attend the cinema."

"I'd go mad," cried Cherry; "I — I want to go to Paris. I want to dance and laugh and flirt —"

"Within reason, I trust," said Boycie austerely. "Your grandmother may have slipped once, but if I know anything about her, she will have recovered her equilibrium by now."

"I want to be gay," caroled Cherry, and promptly burst into tears. She cast herself at Boycie and clung to her. "Boycie, I'm so miserable. I wish I were dead. Boycie —"

Miss Boyce-Medford patted her back and gave her a clean handkerchief. She thought, *There* is *a man then! I knew it all along! And she isn't going to tell me, or does this mean that she will tell me?* Boycie pondered, emitting soothing sounds. *Whatever's happened, I'll get her out of it. I always have, haven't!? She's always come to me.*

"Cherry, my dear —"

"I'm all right," said Cherry with a sniff. She drew away from the older woman, moved over to her dresser, and did the usual things with a powder puff. Sylvia came in, like a warm south wind. She wore an enchanting negligee and a pleased expression. "Look," said Sylvia, "look what someone sent me. In honor of your arrival, I suppose. Dear Agnes Dawson Dawson!"

She held up a squat bottle, a lovely bottle. It was a bottle of *Cherry Blossom* perfume. She cooed, very pleased with the world, "It has an atomizer. Here — See, you screw it on."

She atomized. And Cherry gave one wild shriek and sprang toward her mother — "actually like a tigress bereft of her young, yes, a tigress," similied Sylvia with agitation, reporting to her husband a little later — and knocked it from her mother's hand. Henceforth the Savoy carpets would be as an orange grove in bloom and a couple of conservatories of gardenias.

"What in the world," mourned Sylvia, for once almost speechless. But Cherry had fled. She was locked, weeping, in a bathroom. Boycie rang for the maid, a dustpan, soap, and water. Boycie shook her head. "Don't be hard on her, Sylvia," she warned. "The child's half distracted."

"She must be in love," Sylvia deduced from some deep and innate wisdom. She herself had always been distracting but never distracted, which was part and parcel of her figure, her complexion, and her completely iron nerves. For although Sylvia fluttered like a bird and talked like a woman in a delirium, she had the inner placidity of a graven image.

"I'm sorry," said Cherry, emerging penitent, "I hate that scent. No," she added, while Boycie and her mother stared at her in bewilderment, "I don't. I adore it. I want some — several bottles — I'll replace yours, darling," she told her mother and put her long young arms around Sylvia's delicate person and hugged her soundly. And Sylvia said, "I've remembered now, it wasn't Cousin Jennifer, it was Great-aunt Anna Rose. She went just that way too. All of a sudden."

Cherry laughed.

She went on laughing, more or less all over Europe. She bade Boycie good-by almost casually. Boycie was hurt but would have perished rather than show it, and went back to Sussex where the spring was evolving in a succession of crocuses and bided her time and worried a good deal for she had not succeeded in extracting a confession either by wiles or by straight talking. And Cherry had been relieved to see the last of her, she believed. She was right. Cherry thought, *if she stays another ten minutes, I'll throw Sylvia out of the window — nothing would happen to her, a prince of the blood would be passing and would break her fall and accomplish his own — and I'd tell her. I'd Tell All! I'm too damned used to telling all to Boycie. By the time I see her again I shall have got myself together.*

They went to Paris. Sylvia didn't like Paris. It was shivery. They went to Cannes. It rained. They went to Nice. It was cold there and there were too many tourists. They went to Saint-Jean-de-Luz and that was a little better. Then for no good reason at all they went to Egypt. Sylvia hadn't seen the Sphinx for a long time and she had to see the Sphinx every so often or die.

That was Sylvia. She might be planning to

fly to Holland but break a fingernail and with no better reason than that she would cancel her tickets and go to the Basque country instead. A remarkable woman. She probably saw a picture of the Sphinx in an illustrated magazine at her hairdresser's and remembered that she hadn't asked a question or answered a riddle in a long time.

So they went to Egypt. In Egypt they encountered Nubar Pasha, who had just arrived, on matters of state, or income, or something. He had been pelting Cherry with wires, radio messages, and cables ever since her return from the unknown wilds. And here he was, very handsome, with fine teeth. Sylvia thought him rather divine and may have been right at that since he traced his descent — not too far down — from a god. But Cherry, regarding him over a tea table, commented, "Fancy running into you here." It was a perfectly reasonable thing to say. After all, one never expected to see people in their original settings, any more than rose diamonds. And so Cherry hailed him with as much astonishment as if she had encountered a Frenchman in the Ritz bar — and as if she had not received that last fervent message assuring her that he would be in Egypt.

"Really," said Sylvia to her husband, "the manner in which that child of ours treats men —" Sylvia had an engaging way of assuming that her first husband's child was her third husband's child. She'd done that to the baron also. Made them feel more closely allied to the family. "Modern girls are too amazing. Look at the poor young tea planter home on a holiday. You know, at Cannes. Something hyphenated, I don't remember his name."

"The younger son of the Duke of Albans," supplied her husband, "nice chap."

"Yes, that one. It was disgraceful. Yet she never does anything you can lay your finger on," said Sylvia, with vague amazement.

"No," agreed Gerhard, "she doesn't; and she doesn't permit them to, either." He smiled. "She will take care of herself, our little Cherry."

"Yes. Prettier than Sarah, isn't it? My idea entirely. She consulted me about a stage name, you know. And there was a Manhattan staring us in the face right on the table. I thought — Cherry, that's it — charming to see, youthful, sweet, but with a tang — oh, a certain tang — especially after being acclimated to the cocktail."

"You," remarked her husband, kissing her with great enthusiasm, "are really priceless. I hope you never tire of me."

Sylvia laughed a little. But she was somewhat anxious. She was afraid of that; afraid that after all she wouldn't tire of Gerhard, much as she disliked the antediluvian estates, all banquet halls, round towers, moats, and pewter, which, now and then, she had to inhabit. Life wouldn't be half as exciting if she couldn't tire occasionally. But Gerhard was a little younger than herself and a terrifically good shot. While he might appear rather docile on the surface his wife knew better. He simply couldn't be bothered to cross her in unessential matters. He saved his energy.

It was in Egypt that Miss Cherry Chester first heard about that sterling explorer Mr. Anthony Amberton. He had, it appeared, turned up out of the blue and from a cargo steamer and got himself into some extraordinary excitement in Algiers, involving a gullible tourist with too much heart and an itch for foreign travel which he now scratched once too often, a beautiful houri, imported straight from Marseilles, an angry gentleman with a fez, a couple of coffee-colored cops, and some revolver shooting. After rescuing the tourist, buying the houri a drink, knocking off the fez, and languishing in a singularly unpleasant jail, Anthony had managed to escape, due some said to the keeper's susceptible fifteen-year-old daughter, and had then disappeared again, looking, it was assumed, for more trouble. There was some talk of

Tibet, although in the last few years Tibet was no longer simon-pure virgin soil.

With the Gobi carefully combed of old-laid eggs and the Turks exhibiting motion pictures from the last explorer's generous hands, it looked as if Anthony would be hard put to it to find an unexplored tract of land. But that lost white tribe story had cropped out again, so Anthony had jumped off from Algiers into deepest Africa. At least so ran the last report.

Cherry wasn't interested. Nothing interested her. Shout "Amberton!" and she was deaf; whisper "Smith!" and she would swoon. Her mother never knew why she went over hotel registers with the fine comb of her ardent and narrowed gaze. Her triumphal progress, attended with all the usual fanfare through various portions of the long-suffering globe, could and did not succeed in effacing from her bruised memory one name, one countenance, and one week.

Even a motion picture actress, a stage star, Sylvia's child, and Lucy's granddaughter could not be expected to forget even an academic husband in a few weeks.

In April, Cherry returned to Paris, where, having said farewell to her mother and Gerhard and sixty-three devoted admirers, she whistled up Boycie and a rejuvenated

Hilda, still, however, conscious of her accessory before-the-factness, and embarked for the United States via Havre and a fast liner.

She went directly to her apartment which the patient Higginses, separated in the flesh, so to speak, but united in the spirit of service, had had redecorated in her absence and according to her orders. The car was shining, the chauffeur was glad to see her. Lohengrin and Elsa were fatuous, belly-crawling, tail-wagging, hand-and-face kissing to a degree. And, settling down with this menage, Cherry went into rehearsals.

It was understood that when she appeared as a public person in Manhattan, Park Avenue claimed her and the Van Steeden mansion disowned her for the time being, and except for occasional telephonic communications or stately luncheons on days which did not interfere with matinees. Horace was around a good deal. Balked by the antics of a whimsical stock market from running across the Atlantic Ocean, he found the apartment greatly to his liking and spent more time in it than was compatible with his hostess's good nature.

The rehearsals proved to be the usual dog-fight. Three leading men were fired but the fourth stuck to the bitter end. The amiable Gus lost six pounds in weight and dared not consider what he might lose in coin of the realm. But cheered, slightly, remembering that much of this coin was supplied by his star. The pretty girl who walked on in the third act sprained her ankle. "God, wouldn't you know it — why the hell didn't you write her a sitting part, Bill?" Gus demanded of the harassed author. The author quarreled with his new wife, who could not understand his irritability, after which he had a nervous breakdown to the relief of all concerned. The stage manager, in his own simple language, went nerts, and the girl who played Cherry's sister refused to speak to her off stage.

It was very lovely indeed and dress rehearsal was something that no one in the cast has ever been persuaded to mention from that day to this.

They had planned to open cold. But it appeared that opening cold would not be so hot. So they opened in New Haven and all of Yale University came. Yale University loved Cherry in her cinematic personality; it liked her so much that it cheered her through three acts of gloom which you couldn't cut with a knife, so no one ever did find out what the audience thought of the play. The New Haven critics used up their columns in criticizing Yale University.

A play doctor was called in to take temperature, to bandage, amputate, splice, poultice, and gland graft, as the original author was *non compos* almost anything. And then they opened in New York.

This play was like an inferior dumpling. It was half-baked and it was indigestible, and it lay heavy on the critical stomach. But it had something. It had Cherry.

Boycie, who had attended a few rehearsals in order to catch any props which the star might decide to sling, sat in the balcony on that first night and shivered. Either she was as crazy as everyone else or Cherry was turning in a bad performance. Cherry, Miss Boyce-Medford was able to concede, was no Duse. Nor was she a Cornell. But given the proper part with plenty of fireworks, she was a most creditable performer and she had a sense of timing which would have reflected credit on an adagio dancer. Moreover, she possessed the invaluable gift of infecting her audiences with her emotional reactions to a sentence or a scene.

But this play was as sorrowful, as melancholy as the man who has sold — and not short — just before the rise. And in it Miss Cherry Chester, her red hair in something approximating pigtails, and her long lithe body upholstered in a species of guileless gingham, became a female Hamlet, a Gloomy Gus, a

Mickey Mouse caught in life's trap, and with a bit of cheese at that, and a cross between Elsie Dinsmore and Hardy's Tess.

She was terrible!

Chapter Thirteen

A SECRET SHARED

The play was not a quick flop. It subsided slowly, almost, one might say, in circles. Nightly, for a good many nights, Cherry fell in love with her stepbrother, confessed to her sister, strangled her stepbrother's inoffensive wife, and hopped off a cliff. Why she had insisted upon this succession of disasters, no one knew. Her first Broadway success had been, to be sure, in a species of cheerful melodrama in which the hard-boiled baby of the better pavements turns out to be far purer than Manhattan snow and a Federal female dick to boot. Her second had been in charming, feather-light, and not too whimsical comedy. Her motion pictures, all three of them, had seesawed between the two and were hugely successful.

She had, of course, a tremendous following, and a much greater one than before her motion picture performances; and faithfully that following turned out; the little girls who adored her and who tried to arrange their hair after her altering fashions — the pigtails were difficult — and the young men who sighed in secret or not in secret, to say nothing of the older men. Gus kept muttering about the show — his star, he announced in private, raised Cain and to Cain's they would go, bag *and* baggage. And the cut-rate agencies looked smug.

The fearful thing about it all was that Cherry knew how bad she was but she set her nice square jaw and kept on flinging herself off cliffs. She had a lot of money in that show and she couldn't let Gus and the cast down any sooner than she had to. Gus and the cast envied her that cliff. Her theatrical step-brother went so far as to take a ride up the Hudson on a warm day and an excursion boat and look with longing at the Palisades.

Lolly Harris was a friend in need; in need of having her head examined, thought most of her acquaintances. She had a box on the opening-night and rows and rows of orchestra seats for nights thereafter. She saw to it personally that all of her friends, enemies, and their friends and enemies applauded Cherry, and Pete grinned and paid the bills. Lolly was warm-hearted and hot-headed. She didn't give a couple of whoops how bad the play and how shudder-making the star. Cherry was her concern and greater love hath no normally intelligent woman than to lay out her evenings in lavender for a play-acting pal. It got so that Lolly knew all the parts backward and indeed told Pete privately that they made as much sense that way as any other. She could have doubled for the stepbrother in brass and for Cherry in gingham.

Pete's brother Jerry came down from his New England hills long enough to be dragged to the theater. "And you must talk about the show in your column, lamb," said Lolly, giving him a very good dinner and plenty to drink — as drink does dull the senses, "because every little bit helps."

Unfortunately Jerry, a blond young man, not much stronger on chin than in head, partook too freely of Lolly's hospitality, with the incredible result that from the rise of the first curtain to the fall of the last, he sat with his head clutched in his hands and wept, to the great distress of the surrounding peasantry, who feared that this was a first night critic who had become slightly addled on dates.

Pete took his brother out a couple of times but that did no good. He demanded to return and indeed he was silent in his grief, and ushers merely shook their curly heads and did nothing about him. "It's so damned sad," said Jerry eventually, "poor lil' gal, in love with her stepbrother. Nasty cliff!" But in the car going home he sobered somewhat.

"Where have I seen her before?" he wondered aloud.

Lolly, considerably out of patience, told him in no uncertain terms. She named the plays, she named the motion pictures, she mentioned her town house and her Westchester place. "Take your choice," she generously offered.

But he shook his head. "Somewhere else," he kept repeating.

Pete uncrossed his long and lazy limbs. "Never mind, you'll feel better tomorrow. It's all a dreadful mistake. We haven't been to see Cherry Chester. That was Leslie Carter in *Zaza*."

"I thought I'd seen her somewhere," murmured Jerry, relapsing into vacuity.

By heroic and expensive advertising methods the show kept open until around the first of June. When it closed, almost soundlessly, Cherry, extraordinarily subdued, demanded of Boycie, "What next?" This was in itself an innovation, for as a rule Cherry could think of things to do faster than Boycie could listen to them. They were not due back on the Coast until September and the summer stretched endlessly before them.

Boycie was alarmed. It had been borne in on her more than once that, for all her earlier vaunted gaiety, Cherry had been very restrained — for Cherry — since her arrival in Europe. She suggested tentatively and with one eye on the nearest exit, that it would please Lucy Van Steeden very much if Cherry would offer to go with her to Riverview, and when Cherry nodded listlessly and replied that she, for one, didn't care where she went, Boycie almost had a stroke.

To Riverview they went, and for a month. For a month Cherry sat in the gazebo, selected blooms in the conservatory, walked on the country roads, and played cribbage with her grandmother.

Her grandmother was disappointed in Cherry.

"What's come over you, Sarah?" she inquired. "You do nothing but mope. It is that — that play of yours?"

"No, Granny."

"I'll send you packing," cried the old lady with almost religious fervor. "You've done nothing but 'yes, Granny' and 'no, Granny' me for weeks." She halted. She added, almost shyly, "You needn't feel badly about it. I understand that everyone has a failure now and then. Even in my day when the theater was a place of intellectual entertainment and when performers knew something about acting, that much was true. How much money did you lose?" she asked abruptly.

241

"How did you know?" said Cherry, startled.

"Never mind," replied the old lady. She chuckled. "It's good for you to lose money now and then," she announced. Pure generalization. She took as good care of her own money as of her eyesight. "But if you need —"

"No," said Cherry, "I don't need anything. Thanks just the same."

"I give up," said Lucy Van Steeden, and called upon heaven to witness.

She was almost glad when they departed. Cherry worried her and she hated to be worried. She cross-examined poor Boycie until that miraculous woman was ready to dig herself a nice quiet grave in the garden. "What's wrong? A man? It must be a man. Don't tell me it's that Abyssinian."

"Egyptian."

"All the same. Don't quibble."

Boycie shrugged wearily. "I don't know," she admitted, "but I don't believe so —" She added quickly, "I think it's just temperament."

"Bah!" said her hostess. Privately she liked Cherry's more sensational displays of a quality her grandmother had never admitted ever existed — "Temperament, nonsense! Sluggish liver!" — than this quiet pining.

Cherry pined in the gazebo and she pined

in the drawing-room. Of course, most people would pine in that drawing-room, it was eminently suited to pining. She pined even when Horace arrived for a visit. Not once did she offer him a really sound insult. Mrs. Van Steeden was troubled. "You don't believe she has become really attached to him?" she asked Boycie with such evident anxiety that poor Boycie began to feel herself permanently addled.

"Of course," the old lady hastened to add, "it had always been my wish that Sarah and Horace come to an understanding; one which would result in her settling down and giving up this theatrical nonsense. And yet," she admitted slowly, "I sometimes wonder whether Horace is really the man for her after all. She needs a very strong hand. I think this was amply demonstrated to us all last winter."

After much thought Boycie came to the private conclusion that Mrs. Van Steeden was not unlike the common or garden variety of mortals. Having worked very hard for something and now seeing it within her grasp, the goal appeared less desirable than at a distance.

I wish something would happen, Boycie told herself in desperation. This holiday at Riverview had all the symptoms of a slow collapse into dry rot coupled with more than a tinge of melancholia. You had but to look at Miss Cherry Chester and visions of weeping willows, mausoleums, and obituaries danced before your inner regard. She took to wearing dismally dark frocks, and parting her hair in the middle and plaintively inquiring of her companion why, after all, she shouldn't "do" Shakespeare. Had it been Rosalind, had it been Katharina or even Portia who appeared to her better nature it wouldn't have been so bad. But no. She rummaged through the heavy calf-bound volumes in the musty library and set herself the task of learning some of Viola's more unhappy speeches, and several times poor Boycie came upon her pacing the rickety wooden floor of the gazebo, uttering Juliet's more plaintive cries or indulging in one of Ophelia's more morbid moments.

The next thing, thought Boycie despondently, *we'll have black velvet and to be or not to be!*

Horace saved the day. The last person on earth who could be counted on to rescue even ten minutes out of the twenty-four hours, he became emboldened by Cherry's strange and gentle mood and decided that she was probably dying of love for him. Arriving at Riverview for a brief week-end, he found her at lovely dusk in the rose garden dressed all in virgin white and declaiming to the indifferent blossoms that if music be the food of love she would just as soon the orchestra kept on playing. Horace said, "Darling —" and cleared his throat and Cherry looked at him sadly. She was sorry for Horace. After all, he loved her and a good man's love is not to be scorned. With so many faithless wretches in the world, and so much black treachery, a good man shone like a candle. Or was it a good deed? "Dear Horace," she murmured, hoping that he would propose again. It would give her a subdued satisfaction to break a true heart because hers had been broken by falsity.

Horace misinterpreted his cue. He cast a hasty look around in order to espy any lurking gardeners and perceiving none clasped her fervently, and very suddenly, to his manly bosom. Cherry was much too astonished to defend herself. Also, Horace was a large and determined man and Cherry a somewhat weaker vessel than usual, having given up all but the most essential eating recently. She struggled a little, to be sure, and uttered the astonished cheep of a startled bird; but to Horace all this denoted a maidenly modesty which well became her, considering the fact that she had for some years comported herself in public as no maiden should. Thus heartened, he pressed upon her drooping lips a large, ardent, and entirely uninteresting kiss.

"I *knew* you loved me!" he said, as soon as he could speak.

"Love *you!*" cried Cherry.

Color blazed in her pale cheeks and she scrubbed violently at her affronted mouth with the back of a rather grubby hand. Then she swung upon her devoted lover and smote him on the ear. She hit him very hard and Horace saw stars which hadn't appeared as yet, and were therefore much ahead of schedule. His head rang like a carillon and he heard the sound of harps. By the time he had somewhat recovered Cherry was sailing down the garden path, under full canvas.

She burst into the house and up the stairs. She galloped into the room where Boycie sat reading a detective story. Boycie looked up and dropped the book. Something had happened at last! What were a few ax murders on a printed page? The celebrated Miss Chester looked like a couple of the more appalling Furies. She screamed at the startled lady. She announced, "We've got to get out of here!"

"Why?" asked Boycie in measured tones.

Cherry looked around. There was a footstool handy. She hurled it. She said, after the dull sickening thud, "Horace! He kissed me! He thinks I love him!"

"And don't you?" asked Boycie.

Cherry glared at her. "Don't be a damned

fool. This place is getting on my nerves."

"You're telling me?"

Cherry dashed into her own room and yelled for Hilda. "Pack," she commanded. "We're leaving — at once!"

Boycie followed her. "May I ask where we are going?" she inquired courteously.

"To Lolly's," said Cherry, having thought of Lolly at that instant. "She's been begging us to come for weeks. Get her on the telephone. Call the apartment and have the car come out."

"Tonight?"

"Tonight," said Cherry firmly.

"What about your grandmother?" inquired Miss Boyce-Medford, for once not caring.

Cherry grinned. "You'll have to handle that."

Boycie did so. She suggested "— a lover's quarrel and I think we'd better give her her way," and other vague things. Mrs. Van Steeden was wickedly amused. She had seen Horace stalk through the drawing-room, his hand to his ear. She had listened to his curious excuses. Business, said Horace, called him back to town. "So sorry, Cousin Lucy."

"She slapped him," Mrs. Van Steeden reported to Boycie, with a sadistic satisfaction. "Business? Tomorrow's Sunday." She sighed. "Well, perhaps she'll be happier with

247

that Harris minx," she conceded. "I must say she's caused me considerable anxiety of late. She's so unlike herself."

"When," asked Boycie with asperity, "was she ever like herself?"

They packed, the car arrived in the evening; and at a very late hour Mrs. Peter Harris's large Georgian house received them.

Lolly knew her Cherry. She asked no questions. She escorted Boycie to a room — "I can't give you connecting suites," she said. "Hope you don't mind, but Pete's brother is here for a week-end, and a few other imbeciles. They'll all clear out Monday morning and then there'll be house parties and such. Think Cherry'll mind?"

"She'll love it. The wind has changed. Sure you want to bother with me, Lolly?"

"Perfectly," answered Lolly. "I wouldn't dare have Cherry under this roof long without you. You're the red flag beside the keg of dynamite."

But the dynamite wasn't Cherry after all. It was Pete's brother Jerry, who among other duties conducted a column on a local newspaper in New England.

He had met Cherry before this, but always regarded her at a distance, either surrounded by people or across the footlights. When she came downstairs the following late morning, he was lying in wait for her. He said, "Look here, Miss Chester, may I talk to you?"

Cherry bestowed upon him her second best smile. It worked. Jerry wriggled and looked completely idiotic. Cherry, in a green frock and with her face done up to perfection, was very special. Jerry shook his head. He said, "I can't believe it and yet —"

"And yet what?" asked Cherry.

"Look here," he said, "you've a right to know this. I — I wasn't sure until I saw you in *Forbidden Love* —"

"If you don't mind we won't talk about that," said Cherry hastily.

Jerry took her over to the tennis courts. He sat her down on a green bench under an orange umbrella and sat down beside her. He said, without warning, "I saw you in a hotel in Plymouth one night last winter — you and a man. I thought — I didn't recognize you then, but I heard you laugh. I went over and read the register. I wasn't sure in the least. I just knew that I'd heard you laugh before. Next morning when I came downstairs they told me you and — and your husband had left."

Cherry sat very still. After a moment she said, "I think you're crazy."

"No," denied Jerry, "I'm not. I was sure, when I saw your show. But I thought — if I were mistaken? But I wasn't. Lolly's told me

249

you were in New England that time you disappeared. I'm just back from there. I've been to the hotel. I've seen the clerks and the doctor and the chambermaids and I've seen the Simpsons. It was you, all right. There's no getting away from it, Miss Chester. I even saw a copy of Sarah Brown's license and talked to the minister."

Cherry asked after a moment, her face a mask, "What are you going to do about it?"

Jerry said, "I was going to drive over to your grandmother's place today if you hadn't phoned you were coming. I — I wanted you to give me permission to announce your marriage. You don't know what it would mean to me, Miss Chester. The biggest scoop since the crash. Boy, a little lousy New England paper is the first to get wind of Cherry Chester's secret marriage. I thought I could get exclusive interviews and pictures — with you — and with him. I — It would make me, Miss Chester. I'd get a job down here. If you knew what it means being buried alive in that little neck o' the woods." He looked at her hopefully, a blond young man staking a claim to a gold mine.

Cherry thought. She thought fast. She thought, *Well, why not Samuel Smith! He's dead — dead to me, isn't he? But if this ever gets out —* She thought of her grandmother and of

Boycie; she thought of Samuel Smith learning whom he had married, and how much, returning on the fastest train to establish his legal rights. She asked slowly, "Have you said anything to anybody about this — Jerry?"

"Why, no," said Jerry flushing, "I haven't. I —" He swallowed hard. "I wasn't entirely sure until I made the inquiries — and then — well, you're Lolly's friend. I thought it was only decent to tell you first and ask your cooperation."

To his infinite and painful astonishment, Cherry began to weep. She wept without any distortion of her features. Fascinated, he watched the bright tears well from the green eyes and run down her cheeks. He said, "Oh — I mean — look here, stop crying, won't you?" in desperation.

Cherry choked back the sobs. She said after a minute, "Jerry, you can't — you mustn't say anything. You're the only person who knows, you *can't* tell, Jerry!"

"Why not?" asked Jerry. He thought, *She can't trick me — turning on the waterworks — I won't be tricked.* He shoved his hands into his pockets and looked at this seductive Niobe belligerently. He said, "Well, if you won't give me permission and the interview — I guess it can be done without permission. I can produce the witnesses and the photostatic copy of the license; and I can go see your husband."

"No," said Cherry, "you can't do that." She put her hands on his arm and brought her little face close to his own. "Jerry, you've got to listen to me. We quarreled — that night — and separated. Jerry, I've never seen him since. He's — he's dead!"

"Dead!" cried Jerry, stupefied. *"Dead!"*

"Yes." She nodded. "Pneumonia. Oh, Jerry, you must understand. I was going to keep my marriage a secret, there's a clause in my contract forbidding me to marry for a term of years. And my grandmother considers me as good as engaged to my third cousin. She'd cut me off, she'd never see me again, if she knew. I thought I could keep it a secret — and later that she could meet — Sam — without knowing — and that she might get to like him. Oh, I know I was insane," admitted Cherry, "but we were terribly in love."

"Poor kid," said Jerry. His eyes smarted. He was a kind young man. He asked, "But how did you — find out — I mean, about his death?"

"He'd gone home," she said. "I — I saw it in the paper. He lived in the West. I couldn't even go to the funeral. I couldn't claim his body. Jerry, I've been so wretchedly unhappy. I couldn't even shut myself away with my sorrow. I thought, it's like a dream, and perhaps after a very long time I'll awake. I couldn't go out there and face strangers — his family — and tell them. What would be the use with Sam dead? There was a girl, too, who had expected to marry him. She would be wearing the mourning and — and —" She began to cry again. "It was madness, we — we hardly knew each other. But we were so in love and now he's dead and he'll never know how much I loved him and how bitterly I regret the dreadful things I said. If we hadn't quarreled — if he hadn't gone away — if — He caught cold," she cried tragically, "walking for hours in the snow, after our misunderstanding. He was ill on the train going home — and died almost as soon as he got there. Jerry — I don't care about the publicity, I don't even care about what will happen to me any more. I don't care about anything. It isn't that. But if you print that story, I'll be hounded by curious people. I'll kill myself. Think of his family and that other girl. What good would it do, Jerry? He's dead, and he died hating me, and it's all over."

By now she believed it. She was a heartbroken widow bereft of love. This was real, this desperate sorrow, this face, drenched and forlorn, which she turned to him, the face of a lost child.

Smoke got in his eyes, or something. He

253

rubbed them with his hand, and swallowed. And up in smoke went his dreams of the city desk and headlines and the scoop of the season. Cherry's hands were on his arm again. She was saying, "Jerry, for my sake — let me keep what I have — in secret — my own — it doesn't belong to anyone but Sam and me. And he's dead. I'll make it up to you, Jerry. I'll get you a job. Horace has a brother who owns a lot of newspaper stock. Please — Jerry — *promise?*"

Huskily, he promised. He felt like a million dollars. He felt like the gentleman in the *Tale of Two Cities* — a far, far better thing. He would lose his scoop and keep the secret. He would be the epitome of honor, the honor of the press. He said, and held out his hand for hers, "I swear it!"

He got more than her hand. He felt her lips fluttering against his cheek. She said, after a moment, "I'll never forget, Jerry. I do trust you. Please go now and leave me."

He went, a man in a dream. All knighthood in flower. And Cherry blew her nose and propped her chin in her hand and thought. *He might tell. Not because he meant to but — There must be another way.*

Lolly. Lolly was the only way. A secret shared is no secret but Lolly was all wool and a yard wide. It had to be Lolly. Lolly and Pete.

Chapter Fourteen

"CAN'T WE TALK IT OVER?"

Late that night Cherry sat with Lolly and Pete in their small sitting-room. They looked very comfortable, Cherry in negligee, Lolly and Pete in pajamas. She began her attack by asking, "Look here, is Jerry trustworthy?"

"Well," said Jerry's brother, while Lolly widened her dark eyes in amazement. "I don't know. When he's sober he is. When he's drunk he has no inhibitions. Why?"

"Because," said Cherry gravely, "he knows something about me which would ruin me if he told it."

"Holy smoke!" uttered Pete, and Lolly cried out with shock. They stared at her. Cherry hurried on. "I never meant to tell a soul. But you have to know. You must help me. You're my best friends except Boycie. And I can't tell her. She'd never forgive me and she'd think it her duty to tell Grandmother. You and Lolly know the terms of Grandmother's will and my income. You know all there is to know about me except that I'm" — she paused — "a widow."

After the earthquake had somewhat subsided, she told them. She told them more
than she had told Jerry. She told them almost
all. She told them that she had met Samuel
Smith before sailing — she didn't say where
— and had fallen in love with him. She told
them that Samuel Smith had had no idea who
she really was. She told of the snowy idyl in
the mountain rendezvous and of their marriage. She told them of the quarrel but not in
detail. She let them assume that he had discovered who she was and had refused to husband a woman of stage and screen. But from
then on her story deviated from even partial
truth and was word for word as she had re-
hearsed it to Jerry.

Lolly was speechless. Lolly was in tears.
Lolly cried, "Oh, my darling, my poor sweet!"
and seized her in her loyal arms and rocked
her and wept with her. Pete shook his head.
"This is a hell of a mess," he commented
gloomily; "might be legal complications.
Damn it, you're the man's wife — widow, I
mean — you're entitled to his estate!"

Cherry stamped her foot at him. "As if I
wanted it!" she cried. "I tell you he was poor
— that was another thing which parted us.
And he had a family," she explained, "a
mother and father to support."

"What was his business?"

Cherry shivered. She looked wildly around her. After a moment she said weakly, "He had — he had a drugstore — perfumes, drugs, you know."

Lolly said in horror, "You'd fall in love with a man in a drugstore!"

"Why not?" asked Cherry haughtily. "Wasn't Keats —"

Lolly asked, "You really loved him, Cherry?" softly.

And Cherry nodded. She said, "As long as I live. Oh, Lolly, if only I hadn't sent him away!"

She left them together an hour later. The council of war was over. She stopped at Boycie's room. Boycie was reading in bed. "Wherever have you been?" she asked, and Cherry said, "Oh, just gossiping with Lolly and Pete." She went on to her own room at the end of the corridor. It would be all right. Lolly and Pete were the best friends you could wish for. If only they could handle Jerry.

Pete handled him. He went into his brother's room and shook him wide awake. He sat down on the edge of the bed and he said, severely, "Look here. Cherry's told us. If you ever breathe a word of this, I'll break your neck. What's more, I'll stop your allowance. If you think you can buy bonded whisky and toothpaste smiles on fifteen a week, you're crazy. Get me?"

Jerry said, hurt, "She needn't have bothered. I wouldn't tell." He thought after Pete had left him, *Perhaps when years have gone by and I'm city editor of the "American" — no, managing editor — she'll realize all I've done for her and come to love me.*

He had the fiction mind.

He left the next day. He didn't see Cherry again. Pete looked him in the eye and asked, "Sure you know what you're *not* to do?" and Jerry nodded.

But he went back to his job the most enviable of men, a man to whom a beautiful and famous young woman had trusted her reputation. He deeply resented that some threads of it had been confided to Lolly and Pete.

Cherry stayed on at the Harris's. They were very good to her. They watched over her with such astonishing care that Boycie's brows were permanently wrinkled in perplexity. She noticed, moreover, that on occasions when Cherry seemed to be feeling especially gay she would look up and see Lolly or Pete watching her, and would give them the strangest, bravest, saddest little smile Boycie had ever seen. Boycie thought, *I believed I knew her in all her manifestations, but this defeats me. Is she out of her mind or has she something on it?*

Toward the end of July, Boycie left Cherry with her friends and went out to Ohio where she had an uncle who had migrated many years before from England. Once a year Boycie paid him a duty visit. This now seemed indicated as in September she and Cherry would once more head for the Coast. She said to Lolly, on her departure, "Do look after her, Lolly. I can't tell you how she worries me. She hasn't broken anything for weeks."

Lolly thought, *Except her poor heart!* She kissed Boycie. She said, "We'll do our best."

After Jerry's departure, Lolly had cleared the house of guests and canceled her house parties. But Cherry insisted that she mustn't. "You must lead your own lives," she said solemnly, "or else I'll have to go away somewhere. Please, Lolly — It's better for me too. To have a lot of strangers around, to try and forget."

So after a week or two of calm the guests began coming again. Tennis, golf, swimming, riding, motoring. Contract, guessing-games, charades. Dances and dinners. A very gay Westchester season and Lolly and her house guests tremendously in demand. "It's you, of course," she told Cherry. "This is what I get for harboring a lion under my roof. But the minute it bores you, the second you can't stand it, we'll call it all off."

"I can't think just of myself," said Cherry valiantly.

Boycie had been gone about two weeks when a wire came for Lolly. She opened it and gave a large and enraptured shriek. She cried, "Listen, everybody, you all remember that graceless cousin of mine, Pat Thayer. He's just back from abroad. Seems he's become a great friend of Anthony Amberton's. They sailed on the same boat and he wants to know if he can bring him up here. Isn't that marvelous?"

The two other married women at the table screamed with delight and their husbands looked bilious. Pete said, "For God's sake, the boudoir explorer?"

"Don't be nasty, Pete, he's marvelous-looking really. Cherry," said Lolly, "he's good-looking enough to be in the movies. I've seen his pictures."

"Who is he?" asked Cherry indifferently.

Everyone answered at once. The accounts of the men differed a little from those of the women. Cherry said after a while, "Oh, I remember — I heard about him in Egypt. Sounds dreadfully attached to himself."

"Sure, he married himself some time ago," said one of the men. "I've met him. He's never been a faithless husband. Talk about a life romance!"

"Oscar Wilde said that first and better," Lolly reproached him severely. She rose.

"They're staying in town. I'll wire them at once. Gosh! I haven't been so thrilled since I stepped on Clark Gable's foot in the lobby of the Los Angeles Ambassador one day."

That night she came in and perched herself on Cherry's bed. She said, "They say he's awfully difficult. Women are crazy about him — there was a duchess once — they say she tried to drown herself because of him. And I've heard," whispered Lolly, her eyes wide, "that he's had — dozens of black girls!"

"How very unpleasant," commented Cherry. "He sounds terrible!"

"He can't be. He's divine. I tried to meet him in London a couple of years ago but he didn't turn up. It seems he forgot to come to the party. The next day he sailed for some God-awful place." Lolly gave a little wriggle. "Of course," she said, "Pete is the world's lamb, but really, Cherry, he isn't awfully exciting." She looked at her friend. She said thoughtfully, "You'd make a marvelous couple."

Cherry smiled. Then she frowned. She turned her head away with an expression of utter distaste. "*Please*, Lolly," she said faintly.

"Darling," said Lolly contritely, "I'm so sorry. For a minute I'd forgotten."

Anthony Amberton arrived on the evening train. Cherry did not see him until dinner time. She effected a late entrance, late entrances came naturally to her. She came down the wide, curving stairs with casual grace, her red hair demurely smooth across her brow and breaking into a surf of curls behind her ears. She wore white starched chiffon, with a tiny jacket, and a belt of peacock blue. She looked down into the living-room from the stairs. They were all standing, talking, with cocktail glasses in their hands. The long windows were open to the sweet breath of a very warm night and the room was full of flowers. Someone was at the piano. A very tall man with a dark curly head was standing by the mantel talking to Lolly.

He turned. Cherry's hand tightened on the railing. It was suddenly wringing wet, that hand. Her heart was almost physically in her throat. She stared, incredulous, and the color drained away back of the delicate rouge. A tall man with dark curly hair, in white flannels and a blue coat. It *couldn't be.* But it was.

She thought, *I can't. I'll die first. I'll go upstairs again. I'll say I'm ill. I won't see anyone. I won't leave my room until he has gone. I won't.* And then she thought, *Darling* — DARLING —

But Lolly heard the crisp sound of her wide skirts as Cherry moved, and looked up. It was too late for escape. Lolly called and waved. "Cherry, you bad girl, you're almost late!"

Cherry came slowly down the stairs. Anthony Amberton stood quite still and the slender stem of the cocktail glass snapped in his hand. The glass fell and shattered. He apologized, stonily, "I'm terribly sorry, Mrs. Harris"; and Lolly said, "That's quite all right, we really shouldn't buy seconds." She smiled at him and asked quickly, "But you didn't cut yourself, did you?" The butler came forward to remove the remains. And Lolly said, "Come with me. You must meet my dearest friend."

He asked, "Who is she?"

But he had known her at once. Powder and paint and the curled charming hair and the lovely gown. These didn't matter. He saw a girl in a green ski suit with her hair brushed back and freckles on her nose. He saw a girl in a white woolen robe with her hair about her shoulders and her eyes shining.

"It's Cherry Chester," explained Lolly. By now they had reached her. Lolly said, "It's always exciting when two people as famous as you two are meet for the first time. Cherry, may I present Anthony Amberton?"

Cherry held out her hand. It was like ice. She smiled. That was like ice too. She said, "So nice to know you, Mr. Amberton. You paint, do you not?"

Lolly could have shaken her. She'd seen

Cherry turn perverse before this. But Amberton only replied apologetically, "No, I'm sorry. I have no creative gifts." And as Lolly turned away to speak to the servant who approached, he added, "But I perceive that you do."

"Do what?" asked Cherry coldly.

"Paint. It's rather becoming," he added. He laughed at her very effectively. He said, "I suppose you'll think me very old-fashioned, but I wouldn't permit *my* wife —"

"Oh," said Cherry, "so you're married?"

"Just technically," replied Anthony and accepted another cocktail from a tray. He added, "I'm afraid I didn't quite catch your name, Miss — Miss — ?"

"Chester," supplied Cherry with refrigerated brevity. She added, "I'm starved. I hope we'll have dinner soon."

"So do I," agreed Anthony politely. He added, "Cherry Chester, charming name. It seems to me that I've heard — You sing, do you not?"

Her high heels clicked on the polished floor as she turned and walked away. Anthony stood looking after her, smiling a little. He drank the cocktail. He didn't need it for exhilaration. Here she was, he had found her again. And by no effort of his own. He'd made her pay, he thought grimly. Cherry. Cherry Chester.

Cherry Chester was talking to Pat Thayer. "How do you like my prize celebrity?" Pat asked her, smiling. Nice person, Pat. Cherry shook her head. "Not much, I'm afraid," she said. "He — he thinks very well of himself, doesn't he?"

"Oh," said Pat, "that's just a pose. Underneath he's swell. You'd like him, Cherry." He looked at her a moment, a fat, pleasant man. "You're rather alike, you two."

"I — like — like him?" said Cherry indignantly.

"Yes. Good-looking, charming, celebrated, temperamental —"

"You didn't mean that."

"Perhaps not," said Pat, who had known her for many years, "perhaps I meant the posing. Remember how much in love with you I used to be, Cherry? You nearly drove me nuts," he added cheerfully.

"But you got over it," Cherry reminded him.

"Yes, thank God!"

At the table Cherry had Anthony on her right. She turned her bare and lovely back upon him and talked animatedly to Pat. Anthony devoted himself to his more friendly neighbor, a woman of uncertain years but certain experience. She must have been very entertaining, for Cherry heard him laugh more than once.

After dinner Lolly seized upon her. "You aren't being very nice to Anthony Amberton," she said reproachfully. "You behaved as if he had some peculiarly virulent disease."

Cherry said, "But I don't like him, Lolly."

"Why not?" asked Lolly. "I think he's divine."

"Perhaps. But I can't stand him. I don't know why. Just a case of Dr. Fell, I suppose."

Lolly looked at her. She said, "I don't think it's that at all." Cherry's pulse quickened. "What do you mean?" she asked. Lolly touched her cheek gently. "You know," she said, "darling — I used to feel that way about Pete. I still do if it comes to that. As if I had a — a sort of immunity."

A little later they all went to the game room. Here there was an excellent screen and an operator for their projection booth. As a very special treat they were showing Cherry's latest picture this evening. The guests settled down to armchairs and smoking-stands. Cherry found herself by Anthony in the intimate darkness. She moved in her chair as far from him as possible. He said, "Don't worry, I won't touch you. I've no desire to touch you."

She said furiously, "You lied to me!"

"How about you — Sarah Brown?"

"I *am* Sarah Brown," said Cherry, "but you —"

266

He asked, after a moment, "Ever hear of Smith bathroom equipment?"

So that was it. She had not married a shoplifter or even a writer. She had married a glorified plumber, who went exploring, as plumbers do.

She watched her own slim shadow dance across the screen, laugh and weep and rage and turn to melting tenderness in the arms of the leading man. She watched her shadow mouth lifted to the kiss and the close-up. Anthony said reflectively, "You are a better actress off stage, Miss Chester."

She said, under her breath, "How I despise you!"

It was a complete nightmare. She thought, much later, lying in bed and tearing a perfectly good pillowcase to pieces in a tempest of impotent fury, *I'll leave — tomorrow — they can think what they want.* But she knew she would not leave. She thought, *If Jerry should come back?* She hadn't asked Jerry if he saw the man with her clearly that night in the hotel. But he had snooped around, he had been given a description. A dozen things might happen. He could get fired as easily as not and return to his brother's house. And it wouldn't be very difficult to discover Anthony's ancestral name.

Just before she slept she told herself, *I'll*

stick it out. As long as he does. I wouldn't give him the satisfaction of outstaying me.

She went down to breakfast. Anthony at the laden sideboard turned to ask courteously if she had slept well. "Very well," she replied, so savagely that Lolly almost upset the coffee urn. Later, seated beside her in the breakfast room with the sunlight pouring over the glass and silver and honey in the comb, he said reflectively, "This reminds me of something very charming which happened to me long ago."

"What?" asked Lolly, hanging on his every word. "Please tell us, Mr. Amberton, I'm sure it's very thrilling."

"It was," he said. He laughed and shook his head. "But I'm afraid my lips are sealed."

Butter flew from Cherry's knife and narrowly missed the rotund façade of Pat's pullover.

"How about some tennis, Miss — ah — Chester?" Anthony asked her.

She shook her head. "So sorry," she murmured.

"I see," he said, "not athletic, are you?"

"Why," cried Lolly from the head of the table, "Cherry plays a marvelous game — she always has."

"All right," said Cherry, "I'll play."

Unfortunately, he beat her. Love sets.

Strolling off the court, he linked his arm in hers. "No, no," he admonished gently, "don't pull away. And don't look at me like that. What will people think? If anyone saw the hatred in your eyes they would know at once that we are married. If you don't stop I shall kiss you."

"You wouldn't dare!" she cried furiously.

"Oh, yes, I would. But I'd much prefer to kiss you in private," he said; and added carelessly, "By the way, where's your room?"

Cherry tore her arm free. "If you ever come near me!" she stammered, "if you as much as set your foot across my — my —"

"Threshold," he supplied helpfully.

She said, "If you dare! I'll scream, I'll pull the house down around your ears!"

"That would be unpleasant," said Anthony softly, "and very bad for your reputation, unless you wish to produce your marriage lines. That reminds me, where are they?"

"I burned them," she said defiantly, which was not true.

"That's good," said Anthony. He laughed at her. "An ideal arrangement," he told her lightly. "I am protected in the future from predatory females and you from moronic males. Really, it couldn't have worked out better."

She asked as they approached the house,

"How long do you intend to stay?"

"We have been asked for a week," he said, "and very pleasant I find it. Of course, if you are uncomfortable, there's no law against your leaving, is there?"

She said, "If you think you can drive me out you're very much mistaken."

By the fourth day she had lost four pounds. Thrice Lolly found her in tears, and the third time Anthony was a witness. Lolly said, brushing him aside, "Let me —" and ran to her friend.

Cherry was curled up on a bench in the garden with her head on her arm. She looked about sixteen in the short linen frock. Lolly whispered, "Darling, please —" and looked around to see Anthony still beside her. She spoke his name in earnest and Cherry looked up. Anthony asked, "Nerves, I assume? Is there anything we can do? I suggest a bromide."

Cherry jumped to her feet, slapped his face, and ran toward the house. "Well," said Anthony serenely, "that's that. I'm afraid Miss Chester doesn't like me, Mrs. Harris."

"Please," said Lolly, frantically embarrassed, "you mustn't think that. It's only — Cherry's so sensitive — she hasn't been herself lately. She — she's suffered a very great sorrow recently — a death in the family."

That much she could tell him safely. That she told him anything was due solely to her present nervous condition. She had never spent so hideous a four days. Cherry acted like a cat on hot bricks, she was insufferably rude to the most attractive man Lolly had ever seen. Lolly wanted to shake her and spank her. But she couldn't. She loved her and she was sorry for her.

"It's not the first time I've been slapped by a pretty woman," remarked Anthony, "but it's the first time I haven't had a reward first to take the sting out of it."

He amused himself further that evening by kissing Mrs. Henderson, the lady with experience, and doing it stagily and deftly in the corner of the veranda when he was entirely sure that Cherry would be looking. And looking she was. She went into the house at once, and presently Anthony and his companion followed. The others were playing contract and after a time Lolly, who was dummy, turned on the radio and danced with Anthony.

A little later Cherry approached them. "Pete's calling you, Lolly," she said.

Lolly excused herself. "Shall we dance?" asked Anthony politely, and Cherry was in his arms before she knew it. She loved it and she hated it. He remarked, "You'd dance a lot better if you'd learn to relax."

"I saw you," said Cherry, "with Sophie Henderson."

"I intended that you see me. Nice, wasn't it?"

She said viciously, "I hope she uses perfume."

Anthony said, "No, as it happens she doesn't. I made sure of that, first. By the way, I've noticed that you don't either."

"I didn't bring any with me. Look here, I wish you'd go away."

"And leave you?" he demanded. "I couldn't think of it. I never had such a good time in all my life. It beats head-hunting."

"But — if Jerry should turn up —" said Cherry.

"Who's Jerry? My good woman, you haven't committed bigamy, have you?"

"Don't be silly," said Cherry crossly, "once is enough."

Anthony danced her through the open French windows and to the veranda. "What's all this about? Who is Jerry?" he asked sharply.

She told him. Anthony began to laugh. "A widow!" he said. He looked at her and laughed again. "A widow!" Then he sobered. "Not while I live," he stated quite accurately.

Cherry turned without a word and went into the house and up to her room. She spoke to no one as she passed but Lolly saw her face. A moment later when the hand was over Lolly went out on the veranda and found Anthony smoking there, standing looking out over the wide green lawns which were very lovely in the starlight. "What's happened to you and Cherry?" asked Lolly. This business was getting on her nerves.

"Nothing. She was unhappy," he said soberly, "poor child. She told me something about herself. Confidentially, of course. She knew her secret was safe with me. You see, I happened to mention a man I'd known once — a man named Smith."

"Smith?" gasped Lolly.

"Yes," said Anthony Amberton. "Fine chap. I hadn't known of his death."

Later Lolly burst into Cherry's room. She cried, "What in the world made you tell Anthony Amberton about — about your marriage? He said he'd known your husband. Of course, he's never long in one place and I'm sure he won't say anything; I tried to explain to him how important it was that no one should know, and he said he understood."

Cherry was perfectly white. She said, "I — what *are* you saying, Lolly?"

Lolly explained, in detail. She tucked her up solicitously. "You look done up, you poor chicken," said she. "Try and get some sleep. I suppose the shock of hearing his name mentioned and all. And I don't blame you for confiding in him, personally I'd even tell him my age, without the asking."

Anthony's progress very late that night was one beset not with temptation but with difficulties. It was a night when others seemed inclined to flit. He had to go three different times to the library to fetch a book. And when at last the coast was clear, her door was locked.

He pressed the knob and spoke softly, "Let me in."

There was silence. Was she asleep? He turned the knob again.

"Let me in —" he said, once more.

He heard her now, by the door, he could hear her breathing, he could imagine her pressed close against the ungrateful wood. She whispered, "No — go away — I'll call someone."

He did not answer.

"Go away," she said again, waiting there, her hand on the key and her heart misbehaving. But there was no sound. He had taken her at her word. He had gone.

She cast herself upon her bed and wept.

"Don't cry," said Anthony, coming as easily as a cat through the open window. She sat up in bed. She had forgotten the balcony, she had forgotten a lot of things. She said furiously, "How dare you!"

"Very simple — a lead pipe, a balcony, a stout old rambler." He sat down on the bed, there in the darkness. He put his arms around her. She whispered, "Your robe's wet —"

"Bushes and such and a heavy dew. Here, let me look at you." He switched on the small shaded bed light. He looked. He said, after a minute, "You'll do. Stop struggling. Keep quiet." He put her down among the pillows. He sat on the edge of the bed, his hair ruffled and his eyes unruffled. He said, "Let's talk this over, shall we — not too sensibly?"

CHAPTER FIFTEEN

FRAGRANT NIGHT

"I don't want to talk," said Cherry sulkily.

Anthony looked at her with appreciation. Her red hair was in charming disorder, her small and lively face likewise. Washed clean of the artful touches which had enhanced, but not disguised her, her fine skin had the luminosity of pearl and the freckles were not apparent in the shaded and flattering light of the bedside lamp. From a delightful confusion of silk her shoulders rose, bare and smooth. Anthony bent and touched his lips to the one nearer him and straightened again, smiling at her gasp of — well, possibly — indignation.

"I don't blame you," he agreed smoothly. "It's a pitiful waste of time — nevertheless a brief conference is necessary. No," he raised a hand, "don't speak. If you speak you'll scream, and if you scream, people will come running, and if people come running, the cat will be out of the bag, the fat will be in the fire, and the beans will be spilled."

"You're terribly clever," said Cherry bitterly and low. "Please don't talk so loudly.

Someone will hear you — what will they say?"

"What will they think? Look here, Sherry —"

"Sherry?" she repeated, staring at him, her eyes enormous, the dark green of a stormy river.

"Why not — pleasant combination of Cherry and Sarah. Cherry!" He laughed, deep in his throat. "To think that the day would come when I would find myself legally married to a woman whose imagination was so lacking that she would name herself after a fruit. Yes, Sherry, sometimes warm and golden, sweet and heady. But at the moment rather on the dry side."

"Please say what you came to say and get it over," demanded Cherry. She yawned, ostentatiously.

"So sorry," said Anthony instantly. "We'll skip the mechanics of the plot which followed almost immediately upon our last — ah — encounter. I fell asleep, for which I doubt if you can forgive me, and you went to Boston which is somewhat analogous to slumber. I will pass over the incursion of a fat hotel medical man into my room at seven in the morning." Cherry giggled, and he looked at her sharply but went on, "Yes. Boston. I was able quite easily to trace you that far — with any intelligent effort I could have traced you back to New York, I presume."

She said, "You didn't try —"

"No, I did not. Look here, why form stately sentences? I — I could have strangled you. Some day I shall," he added parenthetically. "No, I went to New York and I took a boat. I didn't much care where it landed me. It landed me in jail, for one thing, but that's a minor matter."

She said, "I'm not interested in your excursions or if I am I imagine I can buy copies of your more popular books."

Anthony took her by the shoulders and shook her. "Shut up, we're behaving like a couple of crazy kids. Forget you're Cherry Chester, and try to remember the girl at the Simpson farm. I haven't forgotten her. Do you think that I haven't thought of her every day since then? Don't you know I've cursed myself for letting her escape me? *Has* she escaped me — for good?"

Cherry said, in a small voice, "I don't know."

"Yes, you do. When I looked up and saw you come down the steps I thought I'd gone completely mad — and when an instant later I learned who you were — well, even that didn't bother me," he said profoundly.

"Why should it?" asked Cherry indignantly. She added, "I would have told you —

in Plymouth — if — if —"

"Yes," he interrupted hastily. "I know. But you didn't tell me. As to why it would bother me, you ought to know what I think of modern women and more especially what I think of actresses. Not," he added, amused, "that you are much of an actress, darling —"

Cherry said, "Please, did you come here as a critic — ?"

"Not tonight. We have the rest of our lives for that," he assured her. "You understand, of course, that you'll give up the stage and the screen?"

"Are you going to give up exploring?" she inquired.

"Certainly not," he said at once. "I'm going on with it and you're going with me."

"Oh, no," said Cherry, "I'm not."

They stared at each other a moment. Anthony said finally, "We'll leave that discussion until later, too. Tomorrow you and I will leave here. When we return the hue and cry will be over — and we can settle down to something approximating a quiet life."

Cherry said, "You forget I have a contract. I shall be in Hollywood in September." She looked at him smilingly. "I'm not in the eloping mood," she said carelessly. "I never elope on Wednesdays. If you'd care to come to California we might arrange to meet again."

279

"What are you talking about?" he demanded furiously.

She answered, sitting up straighter. "I'm telling you that I do not consider myself your wife. I've had plenty of time to think. We don't know each other. Had we gone on together last winter we would have soon learned that. I'm trying now to give us a chance to know each other and to decide what we'll do —"

He asked, "Probation period, eh? And at the end of it either you say, I'm so sorry, but I find that after all you won't do or else — No, you don't," he told her, "you're married to me, and you'll stay married to me."

She said, "I've heard of divorce, haven't you? And of annulments?" and added, before he could speak, "You didn't act much like a bridegroom last night — on the veranda with that Henderson woman."

"You're jealous!" he exclaimed with delight.

"I'm not!"

He put his arms about her and drew her against his breast. He bent his dark head and kissed her. One regrets to report that she did little to defend herself. The moment after, she wept, with her arms around his neck. "Oh, darling, I've missed you so — !"

"Do you love me?" asked Anthony a little later.

"I love you," she admitted. She drew away and shook her head at him. "But I don't like you much. I think you're pretty insufferable — yet I love you —"

"Funny," said Anthony, "I feel much the same way about you. I don't suppose we'll get along at all — but — it's better to be unhappy with you than miserable without you."

She whispered, "Sammy!"

"What?" he asked, looking down at her bent head. He had never thought that he'd ever enjoy hearing anyone call him Sammy. He believed he had buried Sammy a long time ago. He hadn't.

"That perfume — was it really because you can't stand it or because there was another woman, once?"

He hesitated. He hesitated because she had given him such an easy way out. It is ignominious to confess to the woman you love that your internal mechanism is simply not attuned to the infinite in synthetic fragrance. A man would far rather confess a lax moral than a weak stomach. He said, therefore, "Please don't ask me about that," rather tragically.

"Then I was right!" said Cherry. With astonishing strength she pushed him from her. She said, "I thought that was it. You can't forget her, can you? You don't *want* to forget her. Who was she? One of your damned duchesses or your native women?"

"Listen to me," he implored her, unable to deny the duchesses or the ladies of color, having mentioned them, if delicately, in his books, having built a reputation on them so to speak. "Listen to me. I didn't mean —"

"I don't care what you meant!" Cherry slid from the other side of the bed. She rushed to her dresser, careless of her excessively informal attire. She picked up the first thing she found there. It had not been quite true when she had told Mr. Amberton that she had brought no perfume with her. The bottle in her hand was not *Cherry Blossom*, it was sandalwood, and it would serve. She flung it with remarkable accuracy. "Now get out," she said.

Perfume bottles when broken make a small splash but a loud noise. This one sounded like a gun going off. Almost instantly, as Anthony, drenched and unhappy, shivered and made frantic gestures and uttered improbable curses, doors opened on the corridors and there were sounds of running feet. Anthony glared at his wife. Then, feeling extraordinarily giddy, he made the necessary exit. By the window.

Hands thudded on Cherry's door. Pete said, "My God, Cherry, what happened, are you all right?" and Lolly's voice was urgent, over his — "Let us in, Cherry."

They were white with anguish. They had thought, *She has shot herself.*

Cherry called, shakily, "It's nothing. I got up, and when I passed the dresser I knocked a bottle off it — that's all. I'm so sorry, please go back to bed."

The other guests were assembling in sketchy costumes. Through the door Cherry explained, all over again. Lolly demanded, "Let me in. I've got to see for myself."

Reluctantly Cherry unlocked the door. Lolly and the others grouped on the threshold peered in and then fell back. The evidence was perfectly clear. "I must be getting nerves," sighed Lolly. She waved the rest back to their respective rooms, came in, and tucked Cherry up in bed. She said, "That's awfully strong, isn't it?"

"Someone gave it to me," said Cherry, clinging tightly to the last tattered remnant of her self-control.

Lolly giggled. She said, "It's a good thing Anthony Amberton didn't hear all the fuss and come galloping to the rescue. He must sleep pretty soundly — we woke everyone else up. Pat told me the maddest thing about him when he called up about my wire. It seems that he can't bear perfume — of any kind — it makes him deathly sick. On the boat coming

283

over he had to stop dancing with some woman. Haven't you noticed that Sophie left off that heavy scent she affects? She heard Pat telling me. . . . Oh, but I told you, didn't I? I warned everyone, as soon as I knew."

"No," said Cherry faintly, "you didn't tell me."

When Lolly had gone she thought, *Then, after all* — Poor lamb, she would make it up to him. Tomorrow morning. Tomorrow morning she would go to him and tell him, Yes, I was jealous. I thought — all sorts of things. I'm sorry. Let's tell everyone, let's go away from here, just we two — do you suppose the Simpsons would take us in? *I can handle Granny*, she thought. *I'll wire Boycie and cable Sylvia. I don't care what they do about my contract. Granny will forgive me, after a while.*

She fell asleep presently, worn out with the conflicting emotions of the last few hours, and never knew that Mr. Amberton was spending the rest of the night skulking about the grounds, contemplating suicide and nudity with equal fervor. For his dressing-robe reeked of sandalwood and he felt extremely low, both mentally and physically.

He couldn't get back into the house. His own room had no balcony. He wouldn't attempt Cherry's again. Moreover, he doubted whether in his weakened condition he could

284

make it. He felt like nothing on earth. He doubted whether he would ever recover. He thought, *Let her divorce me, and the sooner the better. As far as that goes, I'll divorce her, God knows I have grounds.* He dodged the Harris night watchman neatly enough and then wished he had not. Would it not have been simplicity itself to walk up to that astonished gentleman and say, "Look here, my good man, I came out for a little stroll and now find myself locked out. Could you let me in, with dispatch, and as little clamor as possible?"

He shuddered, picturing himself surrounded by all the perfumes of Hindustan, not to mention Araby, accosting a suspicious man very late at night, and pleading insomnia.

After a while he went down to the water. It was a happy thought. The Harrises possessed a strip of beach and the Sound lay dark under the night sky, beyond. Anthony stripped off his dressing-robe and his pajamas and kicked aside his slippers. It was a warm night and he was an excellent swimmer, as the Hellespont and Panama Canal bore witness. He waded in and the water was a cool benison about his fevered limbs. He swam, turned over on his back and floated. He thought savagely, *I wish to God I had some good salt-water soap.*

He had to put on the pajamas and dressing-gown again. He could not greet the dawn costumed as Adam before the fall.

Much later he regarded an exceptionally beautiful sunrise without any artistic pleasure. The warmth of the nearing planet was pleasant but he received it with no enthusiasm. A little after six o'clock a lone housemaid was sweeping the terrace and was amazed to see striding toward her the tall figure of her employers' distinguished guest, clad informally, and emanating as he strode a delightful fragrance which caused the excellent Norah to wrinkle her nose with responsive pleasure but to narrow her eyes with various surmises, all of them dark, and some of them uncomplimentary.

"I'm so sorry," said Anthony, smiling at her. "I came out just at sunrise for a little dip, thought I'd get back to my room without being seen. I hope I haven't aroused anyone."

He went past her through the open door into the house. Norah looked after him. She shook her graying head. Years of servitude in other people's houses had subdued her original wit but she could still put two and two together and make six. She had unlocked the doors this morning. Or did this distinguished guest add locking doors on the inside, after passing through them, to his accomplishments?

Anthony bathed, thankful that his room

was somewhat removed from those of the other guests. He then flung a perfectly good Charvet robe into a wastebasket and piled the silk pajamas on top of them. He shaved. His hand was unsteady, he cut himself twice. He looked pretty terrible, the mirror told him candidly.

This household rose late. He was very glad of it. Breakfast any time you wanted it. You rang and it was brought to your bedside or you strolled down from nine to eleven or thereabouts and helped yourself at a sideboard. Very English. A nice custom.

Only Norah and a second maid were about when he appeared again, correctly clad for town. He asked, still with his ingratiating smile, if he could use the telephone. Norah, still suspicious, conducted him to the small and unobtrusive booth. He shut himself in and phoned that long-suffering individual, his lawyer.

"Hello . . . can you hear me, Newton? This is Amberton. I want you to telephone me in exactly fifteen minutes and tell me that it is urgent that I return to town at once." He gave Newton the Harris number. "In fifteen minutes," he repeated, and hung up.

He was in his room, of course, when Norah knocked to say he was wanted on the telephone. Lolly, waking to sunlight, heard the knock, and heard Norah's message. She raised herself upon a pretty elbow and peered at her sleeping husband. She flung a pillow at him. He woke and cursed. Lolly said, "There's a phone call for Mr. Amberton."

"Well, what am I expected to do about it?" growled Pete, never at his best before breakfast.

Lolly sighed, "Go see what's the matter."

"It's probably a girl friend, he has quite a reputation."

"Pete! Get up and go downstairs. No one would call him at this unearthly hour unless it were vital."

Pete went down. He met Anthony emerging from the booth, and Anthony promptly arranged his features into an expression of proper concern.

"Did I wake you? I'm devastated. It's that confounded lawyer of mine; something's happened. You know I thought I'd wound up all this legal business last winter but, no, it needs must bring me back to the States this summer and now I've got to leave your delightful roof — and at once. Is there a train?"

Pete said, "I'll send you in by car. Meantime, while it's coming round I'll have Gustaf pack for you —"

"No, thanks, I'll manage that," said Anthony.

"Well, coffee, then," said Pete, "I could do with a cup myself. I'm sorry, Amberton. I hope you'll come back — surely it won't take more than a couple of hours, this business. The car can wait. Why bother with the bags?"

"That's very good of you," said Anthony, "but I'd better take them, just in case"; and Pete thought, *You can't help liking the man; personally I think he's phony, but there's something about him —*

They had their coffee. Gustaf, coming up to strap the bags, found them ready and was presented with a sweet-smelling dressing-gown and a pair of magnificent pajamas, as well as a substantial amount of cash. "Take these, will you?" urged Anthony. "I've spilled some shaving-lotion."

Gustaf said nothing, but he thought a lot.

In his own doorway Pete reported, "He's been called to town."

"Oh dear!" Lolly, distracted, jumped out of bed, ran a comb through her hair, and searched for a negligee and slippers. "Is he coming back?"

"He doesn't know. He's taking his bags. Say, here's a funny thing, when that call came he was all dressed," said Pete, scowling.

"Maybe he's an early riser. Jungle habits or something. Oh," mourned Lolly, "I'm *so* sorry. But at that," she added thoughtfully, "I think Cherry will be relieved."

"Why?"

"She doesn't like him — and his knowing Smith and all. Pete, doesn't it seem strange — Cherry, whom I've known all my life, married, actually married, to a man I've never seen?"

"Well, you're not likely to see him," said Pete practically, "unless there's something in this immortality business."

Lolly and Pete saw their guest depart. He leaned from the car to say, "Tell Pat I'll see him in town."

"Oh, but — surely you'll return?" begged Lolly.

"I hope so. I'll wire or call you," he told her. "You've been very kind. Present my apologies to everyone. Remember me to them — especially to Miss Chester," he said, smiling rather wickedly, "and tell her that I've been called to Boston."

The car drove off. "Now what did he mean by that?" asked Lolly as she returned to the house.

"How do I know?" asked Pete crossly. "Look here, there's no use trying to go back to sleep again. What about a round of golf before the others get up? I'll caddy for you."

CHAPTER SIXTEEN

A CHANGED WOMAN

Cherry had her breakfast served in bed. She ate a good deal and chatted so gaily with the little maidservant that that young woman was more than ever enchanted with this close-up of one whom she had long adored. So enchanted perhaps that she forgot to mention the departure of the other celebrated guest. Cherry said penitently, "I broke a perfume bottle last night, Martha, I'm sorry to give you any trouble, but could you sweep up the glass now? I'm afraid I'll cut myself."

Martha, going downstairs in search of broom and dustpan, encountered Norah and talked for two solid minutes of Miss Chester. "The prettiest thing I ever saw, and so natural, laughing and talking, sitting up in bed. Oh, I forgot, she broke a perfume bottle last night — it's all over the place. The room smells like heaven. I've got to sweep it up for her."

Perfume bottle? said Norah to herself.

Cherry thought, *I'll stay in my room till ten. He — he deserves to be frightened. But at ten I'll go downstairs and —*

She hugged her slim round knees, and bent her face on them. The red hair veiled her smile.

At ten o'clock Cherry came downstairs, just as Lolly and Pete returned from their golf. As usual they were quarreling over shots. "Six on the third," said Lolly. "Seven," said Pete, "or don't you count misses? How about some breakfast? I could eat a horse."

"Sorry, didn't order horse today. There's Cherry."

"Where on earth have you been," asked Cherry, smiling at them, coming across the room, "at this hour?"

"Playing golf. Amberton got us up before dawn, practically —"

"Amberton!"

"He's gone — a phone call from his lawyer," began Pete, and Lolly broke in, "I wonder what it was about."

"Oh, breach of promise, most likely," said Pete and turned to stride into the dining-room, there to lift covers off dishes and peer into smoking interiors. "Come on, girls," he shouted, "this looks pretty elegant. Where's everybody else?"

"Not down, sir," Gustaf said, behind his chair. Lolly, in the other room, linked her arm through Cherry's. "Come on, honey."

"Thanks, I've had breakfast," said Cherry with stiff lips. She said, with an effort at carelessness, "Is — is Mr. Amberton returning?"

"He doesn't know. He'll wire," said Lolly. She looked at her guest. She thought, *Why, she's ghastly — she looks as if she were going to cry.*

Cherry said hastily, "I did want to talk to him."

"Oh, of course," said Lolly, remembering.

"Hey!" yelled Pete. "What's the matter with you women?"

"Run along," said Cherry. She sat down and lighted a cigarette. A moment later she stubbed it out. She didn't, of course, believe the lawyer business. He'd done that on purpose, to show her, to pay her back. Well, if he wanted to be petty — Oh, if he'd only waited a few hours, a very few hours.

His wire came at noon. He was desperately sorry, he could not return. He would have to be on the spot for several days and then he was booked to visit in Canada. A thousand thanks for Lolly's kindness. And in the afternoon an enormous box of quite superfluous flowers, and a day or so later a five pound box of hideously expensive candy for Lolly, and a case of that liquor he had heard Pete say he liked.

Just before the arrival of the baked funeral

meats Cherry had made her inquiries. She talked to Norah and she talked to Gustaf and she heard about the bathrobe and the two telephone calls and she thought, *Just as I thought. Well, never again!* They were even now. She'd run away once and he'd run away once. But while it might be permitted the bride, no escape is permitted the groom.

She told herself, *He knows where I am, he knows who I am, if he wants me he can come and fetch me. But it won't be as easy as that.*

Three days later Boycie returned to find Lolly hysterical and Cherry sullen. The other guests had left, including Pat. Lolly took Boycie aside. She said, "I don't know what to make of her. Everything's been all right up till a few days ago. Now, nothing pleases her. She sulks. She won't eat. She won't meet people. She locks herself in her room for hours on end."

Boycie said, "It's high time I came back."

She marched herself into Cherry's room, after forcing her to open the door. She said, "I haven't been here two hours and I hear all sorts of rumors about you. What's the matter? Coming down with something?"

"No," said Cherry, "I'm not." She tried to smile. She wept instead. She howled. She sobbed. "Oh, Boycie, I'm so miserable. Let's go away somewhere. I adore Lolly and Pete but I can't stand this place any longer."

Boycie spoke soothingly to Lolly somewhat later. "It's nothing," she said, "I've seen it happen before. Just a spell. She'll get over it. I'll take her off somewhere and get to work on her. She'll be all right as soon as she reaches Hollywood again."

"No," said Lolly, "she won't. I — I do understand her."

"Now what," asked Boycie, "do you mean by that?"

"Nothing," said Lolly. She thought, *Poor lamb, I've been impatient. I suppose it's — it's that man. Oh, why in the world did that have to happen to Cherry of all people?*

Boycie said, watching Hilda pack, "Well, we're off again, Hilda. But where I don't know. How has — how has Miss Cherry seemed since I went away?"

Hilda said, "I don't know, Miss. Like a seesaw, maybe — up, down, up down —"

Packed, Boycie confronted her charge. "Now where?" she demanded.

"I want to go to the apartment," Cherry told her.

"But, my child, it's terrifically warm, you'll perish."

"I want to go to the apartment."

They went to the apartment and roasted. Dripping, poor Boycie employed her time with making long distance arrangements for their arrival in Hollywood. She said triumphantly, "Well, we've got the Benedict Canyon house you wanted and a hundred less a month than they asked originally."

Cherry didn't answer. She was sitting curled up on a broad window seat staring down at the traffic on the melting pavements. Boycie said, "I think you've lost your mind. Don't you *care* what house you live in?"

"No," said Cherry, "I don't." She turned and looked at the older woman. "Oh, Boycie," she begged, "don't look like that. I know I'm a wretch. I can't help it. I'll be all right when I get to work again. It's this hanging around and doing nothing that I can't stand."

That, for once, seemed almost sensible.

They were in town several weeks. Mrs. Van Steeden made daily demands on the wire from Riverview. What had got into the child, what was the idea of Manhattan in August? Boycie said she didn't know. Boycie said, "No, I don't think she'll come to Riverview, Mrs. Van Steeden, not until just before she leaves . . . No, I don't know what's the matter with her."

Horace came and was all but thrown out on his ear.

He came again and Cherry wouldn't see him.

296

He went up to Riverview and complained bitterly and his dear Cousin Lucy stamped her foot at him, looking rather like an ancient and withered Cherry at that moment, and cried, "Well, what do you expect me to do about it? If you aren't man enough to conduct your own love affairs, don't come sniveling to me. What that girl needs is someone who will beat her soundly and then run away with her, and I'm beginning to think, Horace, that you lack all the necessary qualifications!"

Affronted, Horace betook himself to the modest country house of a plump blond widow who had somehow annexed the best cook in six counties. He knew he shouldn't. He knew that if he stayed there a week he would probably marry the woman. He couldn't get the cook any other way.

Cherry asked Pat to dine. Pat came, pleased at the attention. They ate by candlelight and with the windows wide to the sultry air, the three of them, and the conversation was general in the extreme. But Cherry, Boycie was glad to see, showed at least some animation. And once she asked carelessly, "Have you heard from that comic friend of yours — what's his name?"

"You know his name," said Pat, amused, "Why didn't you like him, Cherry?"

"I can't bear a man as much in love with

himself," said Cherry. Boycie thought, *So that's it, who is this creature, I must get in touch with Lolly — is it possible that the child has at last met someone who hasn't fallen flat on his silly face at the sight of her?*

"He's all right," said Pat, "one of the best. Been up in Canada quite a while, I suppose he'll be back soon. Too bad he had to leave Lolly's so suddenly. You would have liked him, Cherry, had you really known him."

"Well," said Cherry, picking at a peach, "that's what *you* think. However, I shan't dispute it as I'm unlikely ever to see him again." She liked saying and thinking things like that. She liked the sharp, almost physical pain it brought her. She enjoyed the rack.

Later she asked casually, "Where does Anthony Amberton live when he's in town?"

Pat told her, raising an eyebrow but keeping his voice without inflection.

She had what she'd asked him to dinner for, and for the rest of the evening lapsed into an almost total silence. Boycie and Pat made faces and polite conversation at each other and finally Mr. Thayer took his departure with considerable relief. He wondered, walking down Park Avenue, how it happened that he had once been in love with this incredible and incalculable girl, and congratulated himself sincerely upon his complete recovery. A man liked to know where he was at with a woman. Moods were well enough, in their place, now and then, and lent a subtle charm, but when a woman turned out to be composed entirely of moods — and all conflicting — no man could hope to find any peace or security with her.

Cherry called Mr. Amberton's hotel, several times. The first three times he had not returned from Canada. The fourth time he was out. The fifth time he had left town. She replaced the instrument with such force that she put the telephone out of order for some time. She'd done all she could do. She wouldn't lift a finger.

Yet she wrote him that night. A funny, stilted little letter. *You needn't have run away . . . we can't go on like this . . . it is apparent that we'll never in all this world get along. We must see each other somewhere privately and talk things over. Couldn't you divorce me in — say, Holland . . . or Mexico or one of those places? No one would ever know. . . .*

She tore it up. He might take her at her word and go tearing off across the ocean or the continent, without so much as seeing her.

About this time she came upon Boycie perusing Anthony's latest volume. The fact that Cherry had every book he'd ever written, in or out of print, hidden in a bureau drawer, and had read each one from cover to cover since her return to town, did not temper her reaction. She snatched the volume from Boyce, exclaimed, "Trash!" and threw it on the floor.

"Well!" said Boycie, "it may not be strictly veracious. So many things couldn't possibly happen to one young man. But it's charming, nevertheless. I enjoyed it, Cherry. Do you remember the last time we came east? I spoke of a very handsome young man on the train with us? I feel sure now that that was Anthony Amberton." She pointed to the floor where the book lay open at one of the twenty-two pictures of Mr. Amberton in appropriate costume for the text. "It looks very like him."

Cherry said, "He doesn't look like that in the least. Touched up, I dare say. He's really rather repulsive looking."

She left the room hastily and Boycie looked after her. Then she bent down and picked up the book and went on with her reading. *Mercy,* she thought, *Anthony Amberton must be a very formidable young man.*

That evening, late, she met Hilda who, with her arms full of books, was walking down the corridor. Boycie stopped her. "What have you there, Hilda?" she asked, and peered through her pince-nez at the titles — *Brightest Africa* by Anthony Amberton, *Turkish Delight* by

Anthony Amberton, *East of Suez* by Anthony Amberton.

"Miss Cherry told me to burn them," said Hilda, "but I thought my sister's little boy —"

"By all means," agreed Boycie graciously, "your sister's little boy should enjoy them immensely."

On the following morning Cherry, breakfasting in bed with her newspaper propped up before her, tossed the paper aside. She said, "Look here, Boycie, what's to prevent us from going on to the Coast now? Think we could get in the house? It's not far to the first and they're in Europe, it must be in order."

Boycie said, "Of course, if you say so. I'll wire today."

"All right," said Cherry, "we'll run up and say good-by to Granny. Higgins can get the tickets. He can stay and close up and follow us, and the car — no — let's not go by train, let's drive."

Boycie, a little dizzy, said, "By all means. But you hate long motor trips."

"I adore them," said Cherry indignantly.

Boycie waited until Cherry had gone to take her bath. Then she picked up the paper. Nothing in the headlines. She searched diligently until she found an item under *Books and Authors*.

Mr. Anthony Amberton, celebrated explorer

and writer, left yesterday for a trip to Panama. It is rumored that he has been offered an interesting contract with Nationwide Pictures for a series of jungle shorts.

"Well, well!" said Boycie reflectively.

When Cherry returned from her tub Boycie said cheerfully, "Certainly, let us start for the Coast as soon as possible. I've been thinking it over. You won't begin production much before the end of next month, of course, but it will mean only a matter of a week or two before we had planned to start anyway."

Lolly came in to say good-by. She and Pete would be in Santa Barbara during the winter and so they would all see one another soon. Boycie and Cherry went up to Riverview and informed Mrs. Van Steeden of their change in plans and said farewell. The exodus began, bag and baggage.

At Chicago, Cherry decided she didn't care for travel by automobile. It was too slow. It gave her a headache. People stared at her in the hotels, and reporters besieged her. They deserted the car, repacked their luggage, and went on via the *Chief.*

The house was lovely. It was a house Cherry had coveted on each of her previous trips. Now it was hers for a term of months. She hardly glanced at it. The turquoise tiled swimming-pool, the palm gardens, the rose gardens, the motion picture theater equipment aroused no enthusiasm. She said briefly, "I suppose it will have to do," and Boycie clutched her head in despair, thinking, *We might as well have saved the money, a bungalow would have served nicely.*

Their arrival had been attended by the usual festivities and the usual business of cameramen and reporters and publicity department didos. Cherry's employers welcomed her back with orchids and admonitions. She faced the producer of her latest opus across his desk a few days later. The producer looked upon her and smiled. "This new story has everything," he said, "it has sex, romance, drama, pathos — it's swell! You'll lay 'em in the aisles, Cherry. I've got Meader and Harcourt on the script."

Cherry listened while he outlined the story. The delicate daughter of riches, she was to go forth into the jungles in search of the man she was to marry, only to discover that he had made the expedition a form of escape from her because he loved a woman whom he could not marry. With Cherry, by some astonishing twist of the plot, would be a poor young newspaperman who would accompany her upon her mission. Horrors would overtake them, storms, wild animals, natives gone berserk — there was to be a sort of voodoo ballet in the middle of the picture — and Cherry and her reporter would become separated. Eventually rescued, they would find the man to whom Cherry had been engaged since childhood, upon his deathbed — it was indicated that this deathbed business was purely sacrificial on his part — and the final close-up, with Cherry in tatters and not much else, in the arms of her reporter, would certainly send an audience home satisfied.

Cherry said, "It sounds terrible."

"No, Cherry," begged the producer, looking hunted, "you mustn't judge by the bare bones of the story. Wait till it builds up. We engaged Lothar Sanchez for the lead and David Mortimer for the older man."

Cherry shuddered. The producer said quickly, "You and Lothar are a box office team."

Cherry rose and looked down at him. She said, "It's all right, Jack. Who's directing?"

"Burns," almost whispered the producer, waiting for the explosion. It didn't come. He wondered if he was dead and transported to some new heaven in which the stars were harnessed and docile and did not toss ink bottles on being told that their next director was to be Mr. Burns. Not that Mr. Burns was not popular on the lot. He was. Only he had directed Cherry in her first picture and the echoes of that encounter had not yet died from affrighted ears. And Burns had said very recently, "Sure, I'll do it. If you think that little nut can intimidate me! Only she's got to toe the mark, Jack. Sure, she can have music with her big scenes, but it will be music that I'll direct too."

They'd spent a lot of money getting this story. They were prepared to spend a lot more. Most of the jungle scenes would be done on location. This would be a feature picture. It would give Cherry every chance in the world, she would be called upon to weep, to rage, to suffer, to surrender, to escape, to flee, to face death gallantly and love with recklessness. It couldn't miss.

Cherry left the office. The producer stared after her and mopped his brow. "Wonders," he remarked to a secretary, "will never cease."

CHAPTER SEVENTEEN

"WE BELONG TOGETHER."

Cherry talked over the picture with Boycie. Boycie commented, "It sounds utterly unreal to me. After all, Cherry, you can exercise the clause in your contract which states that you are entitled to have the final word on the selection of your pictures."

"I don't care," said Cherry, "it doesn't make much difference. If I did that it may be weeks before they'll find another story." She turned on Boycie with sudden fury. "I've got to work," she said, "or go crazy!"

Boycie said, "Here, lie down. You're worn out. We can't have you facing production in such a state."

But she wouldn't lie down. She drove herself, from day to day. Fittings. Hairdressers. Parties. People. Stills. Interviews. Conferences. The studio began to believe in Santa Claus. Their most difficult star as amenable as a plow horse! It wasn't possible. The great designer of cinema fashions reported that not once had she made an objection — not even to the careful physical exposure afforded by the tatters. He designed the tatters too.

"You must rest," begged Boycie desperately, while Hilda followed her around with cushions and eggnogs. "You're smoking too much. You'll look — a wreck. You've lost more weight than you should. You can't keep things up like this. When you start production you know what will happen. You'll break down."

"No," said Cherry, "I won't break down."

Where was he? Where had he gone? Did he think seriously that he could get away with this? He had to come find her. Not that she'd — No, of course she wouldn't. She'd keep him cooling his heels on the doorstep, she'd laugh at him, she'd humiliate him.

She couldn't do that. It had been her fault too. She had to be fair. There was a sturdy strain in her that spoke warningly of justice. Much of Boycie's early training had fallen on good soil and the creeping growth and undergrowth of something called temperament had not choked it all out. And only Boycie, Mrs. Van Steeden, Cherry, Lolly, and perhaps Pat Thayer really knew that much of this temperament was superimposed. As a youngster playing her first bit on the English stage, harassed by her grandmother's rage and real distress and by the amusement of her friends — "Oh, it won't last, she'll give it up" — she had set her little jaw and told herself that she wouldn't give it up, that people would hear of her some day. You couldn't make them hear by the small voice of talent alone, you had to shout to attract their attention. And so Cherry had shouted. And when she made her first picture shouting was encouraged. Now, of course, it had become second nature to shout — to storm and scream, to laugh and cry, to throw things and to assume the attitudes required of her.

Sometimes I pose and sometimes I pose as posing. Cherry had never read Stella Benson but she would have understood a sentence which stands on the title page of a little green book. *Sometimes I pose . . .*

She gave a little dinner for a visiting novelist. She went to Lothar's big housewarming. And Lothar said, smiling at her, "Well, how about it, Cherry?" and she had smiled back at him. Several people reached hastily for stimulants. The last time Lothar Sanchez had been Cherry's leading man he had carried the marks of her fingernails upon his handsome face for several days and had contemplated suing. That was the picture before the last. They hadn't spoken until now.

"What's come over her?" asked her friends. "What's the new disguise?" inquired her enemies who were, for the most part, women.

Location was established. A wild strip of coast with white sands and plenty of palm trees. It was not too far away, it would do nicely, and a comfortable camp could be set up. Everything would be jolly. Everything but Cherry.

The picture went into production. The interiors were shot, the routine things took place, the story unfolded itself in jigsaw puzzle pieces as stories do. One day it would be assembled and the pieces would fall into their proper place. But what was the matter with Cherry Chester?

Not that she didn't act. She did. With fire, with tears, with agony. She had never acted better. Her scene in which her fiancé leaves her for this sudden yachting trip almost on the eve of their wedding was most affecting — Cherry's deep hurt, her astonishment, her lack of comprehension. Not that she loved this man passionately, that much was made clear to her audience, but because she was so alone without him, her guardian since her parents' death, the one guiding hand in a difficult world — or words to that effect.

And the scenes with Sanchez taken on the lot were charming. Her interest in him after he had come to her rescue in a street fight when her own yacht was in port, her growing interest in him, the dawn of young love, the struggle against it —

Boycie came and watched. Boycie said to herself, *She's cutting something genuine from this shoddy cloth. It's real. Her tears are real — the gestures of her hands —*

Burns could be well satisfied with her. He was. This would be a picture without retakes, he promised himself, and they'd finish well ahead of schedule. But — what was the matter with Cherry?

It wasn't that she kept to herself, between her scenes. She generally did that. It was that something had gone from her, some inner drive, some flashing thing which they had all come to look for, to dread and to admire. Only when the cameras ground and the lights beat down upon her red hair did she seem to come alive again.

Then they went out on location. Boycie went with her and they camped together comfortably enough. On location things began to go wrong. Whatever was keeping her up, whatever had animated her, now perished. Her scenes were the acme of listlessness. She infected her fellow players. The picture fell to pieces. It was lousy.

Burns tore his hair. He shook his fist at Boycie. "What in hell is wrong with her?" he demanded. "We can't go on like this. She

310

starts out like a million bucks and ends up like a slug!"

Boycie said, worried, "I don't know, Mr. Burns. She isn't well. I'll talk to her tonight."

But talking did no good. She lay there on the camp bed and wept soundlessly. And after a while she said, "I know, Boycie. I can't help it. I thought I could go through with it, I thought I could put everything in it and get rid of it that way — but I can't!"

She's delirious! thought Boycie.

The upshot was that production ceased; and Cherry went home to the house in Benedict Canyon. Doctors came and went. They shook their heads. "Complete nervous collapse," they said. Organically Miss Chester was perfectly sound.

Rest was indicated.

That was just dandy for the studio. Officials stormed the doors and shouted in whispers at the unfortunate Boycie. How long? Did she know how much money this whim was costing them?

It wasn't a whim. The physicians, the two nurses could testify to that. The child was ill.

They'd scrap the picture, they threatened, they'd give it to Alma Davis.

Alma Davis was the new discovery. The runner-up. The latest redhead who, the critics said, reminded them of Cherry Chester.

"Then," said Boycie, "you'll have to do as you think fit."

The officials departed in a dark cloud. If they scrapped it — if they gave it to Alma Davis? But that would cost as much as waiting for Chester to recover from whatever ailed her.

Later Boycie tiptoed into Cherry's room and the pretty nurse sitting beside the bed smiled at her, raised a warning eyebrow, and went out. Cherry turned her head wearily on the pillow. She looked badly, yet not worse than when she had come out to the Coast. Boycie said briskly, "They're talking of giving the picture to Alma Davis."

Cherry simply registered a shrug under the covers. Boycie drew a deep breath. She said, "By the way, here's something that might interest you. Anthony Amberton — you recall meeting him at Lolly's? — is on his way to the Coast."

Cherry sat up in bed. She repeated, "On his way — ?" Then she sank back against the pillows. She said, "I hardly know the man." Boycie perceived her voice was stronger. After a minute she said, "Tell them to wait — a few days; they can't give that part to Alma. I — I liked that part, Boycie."

There was really nothing wrong with her. She was merely tired. Tired of thinking, tired of being unhappy. Tired, after a while, of the only antidote she knew, which was work, and flattery, and acclaim. So she had gone to bed. Because she didn't care. Because nothing mattered. But if Anthony was on his way west — if he heard, if he read — *Cherry Chester is suffering a nervous collapse* — As if she would give him that satisfaction! She'd show him!

She looked at Boycie. She said, "I'd like something to eat. Steak. Rare. And a pitcher of milk. And a custard. And a glass of sherry."

Miss Chester was on the road to rapid recovery. The news went forth to the studios and the studios rejoiced. The officials said, rubbing their pleased palms, "I thought that Davis business would make her snap out of it."

When next Cherry made her entry into the studio she was greeted with what amounted to three rousing cheers. She looked swell, they told her. No one would ever dream that she had been ill; indeed, no one did. When would she be ready to go to work again? Things had to be speeded up. It had been decided that the location would be ideal for the first of the Amberton pictures.

"Amberton?" said Cherry indifferently.

Anthony Amberton. He would reach Hollywood the following afternoon. The publicity department was taking a cageful of tigers down to the train, just to make him feel at home. Someone had sent a marmoset to his temporary suite at the Ambassador. A couple of cobras and honey bears were on the way. Boy, would the women go for an Amberton jungle short! It would be terrific! Cherry said, "I'm ready to go to work in the morning!"

Before morning the studio had a marvelous idea. "This business where Cherry is rescued by the explorer," said the publicity man raptly, "what's the matter with Amberton? Just that one scene, where he finds her, and in her delirium she believes him unfriendly and struggles with him — after wandering around for days separated from the heart interest, lacking food and water, and scared to death. There's not much footage in the sequence where the explorer discovers her and carries her to his camp — Sanchez bursts in right after that, you know. There's a million dollars' worth of publicity in it."

There was.

Cherry and Boycie were on location when Anthony arrived. He greeted the tigers — they were very small tigers — with an amused lift of an eyebrow, which was promptly snapped by the cameras. He welcomed the monkey with a slight smile but asked that it be removed to less formal quarters. After all, he hadn't come to Hollywood for any monkey business. He had come for two reasons, both of them good: a wife and a large sum of money.

He made his inquiries carelessly. Miss Chester? Oh, he knew Cherry Chester? She was on location just now, finishing a picture. She'd been ill and production had been held up.

"I see," said Anthony. So she'd been ill, had she? He frowned and walked to the long windows and looked unseeingly at two pretty girls putting on the Ambassador green directly below him. Vines in blossom caressed the windowpanes and the outlook was entirely charming. He didn't see it. She'd been ill, had she? Somehow he'd never thought of anything like that ever happening to Cherry. When people were ill they sometimes died.

The men with him spoke twice before he answered. Departing, they shook their heads. "Looks like we have another Chester on our hands," sighed one. "Wish I'd gone in for chicken farming."

Mr. Amberton was in great demand. Parties were thrown for him, high, wide, and handsome. Now and then he attended one. He thought, this location business, don't they ever come back? But she wasn't at any of the parties.

He talked with the gentlemen who would write his scripts and he looked at the docile animals to be largely identified with them. He blue-penciled certain absurdities and found himself taking an interest in what was going to happen to him. He took a screen test and afterward regarded the result with some amazement. His employers went into a couple of pleased huddles. Anthony screened like a box office dream and he had a voice that reproduced magnificently. Such equipment was wasted on a mere explorer. He could name his own price and get it if he wished to become an actor. He didn't seem to wish it.

And then he was summoned to meet the Higher Ups in order that he might be offered an amazing sum for a few minutes' extra work. They explained the situation to him. The Chester script was given into his astonished hands.

He found himself saying in a voice unlike his own, "I've met Miss Chester."

Everyone assured him immediately that she was a grand person and a great actress. Would he consider this bit? It would mean priceless publicity, not only for the Chester picture but for his own.

Anthony expostulated, "But, really, I am not a motion picture actor."

"You could be," cried one enthusiast,

"you've got what it takes. I saw your tests."

Anthony said, "Gentlemen, I'd like to think it over."

But he couldn't do that. There wasn't time. Burns had signaled from location that if they were going to bring on their importation, they'd better do so, and at once. The bit actor engaged for the part was even now sulking, and literally, in his tent. He'd draw his salary all right. But they hadn't dared to let him go until they knew with certainty what Anthony would do.

Anthony rose and ran his cool eyes over the flushed faces. He said, "I think it might be very amusing."

When he had gone everyone looked at everyone else. Two large and efficient gentlemen made brief remarks, they were thumbnail sketches merely but they served to scent the air with sulphur and brimstone. "I thought," said one, at last, "that actors were the final word in this and that. But I take it all back. An explorer," he added, "is pure essence of actor."

Anthony drove out of the lot. He had rented a car immediately upon his arrival, a small open two-seater, fast and powerful. He smiled at the guard who popped out of his sentry box and challenged him. The guard touched his hat and Anthony drove on.

Anthony arrived at location on the following morning. He was not alone; an assistant director had been sent with him. He regarded with some astonishment the really wild loveliness of this little spot, within motoring-distance of Hollywood. To be sure, he had had to rise at five o'clock to get there in time but it had been worth it. He had driven so fast that the assistant director feared his own naturally ruddy complexion would be permanently blanched.

"There's Chester," he said, gasping for breath.

Anthony saw her. She was standing in a group of people and she was stamping her foot and raising her voice. "I won't!" she was saying. "I won't!"

It was quite evident to Anthony as to the assistant director that Miss Chester had just been informed of a change of actors.

Anthony walked toward the scene of battle rather swiftly. The assistant director had to trot to keep up with him, on his short fat legs. Anthony saw Cherry stop shouting to stare at him — as if she couldn't, after all, quite believe her eyes. He said, "Hello, Miss Chester, nice to meet you again, like this."

Cherry turned her back.

Mr. Burns, sweating profusely, shook Anthony's hand. "So glad you've come," he said. "You've read the script? How about the lines — there aren't many. We'll take them slow in rehearsal. Miss Chester," he said, turning.

But Cherry had disappeared.

A short pleasant-looking woman standing beside Burns looked at Anthony with small, shrewd eyes. "So you're Anthony Amberton," she said slowly. She waited for Burns to make belated introductions. "Cherry's spoken of you," she said, smiling. "I'm her companion, you know. By the way, I think we traveled on the eastbound *Chief* together once; Cherry didn't see you. Or did she?" she asked, perplexed and as if to herself, though aloud.

Mr. Burns seized upon Anthony and took him around the beach and environs with as much pride as if he had planted the bending palms, the twisted inland thickets. "Couldn't have been better if we'd gone to the spot," he said briskly. "Suppose we sit down and go over this part, Mr. Amberton. It won't take much of your time. We'll run it through rehearsal a couple of times till you get used to the tempo and everything and then we'll shoot."

Anthony said, "I'm afraid Miss Chester will do the shooting. She didn't seem overjoyed to see me."

"I was just telling her about you when you

drove up," said Burns. He looked at Anthony and spoke as man to man, forgetting the chivalries. "Don't mind that baby," he said confidentially, "she's nuts. I directed her once and I'll never forget that madhouse till my dying day. She's always been haywire but since she came back this trip she's been haywire *plus*. At first it was all peaches and cream. I hadn't a bit of trouble with her. Then she goes blooey, pulls a nervous collapse and now — look at her!"

Anthony would have liked to, but he couldn't. She wasn't there. She was in her tent, tapping her foot on the wooden floor, a Fury in rags, glaring at Boycie.

"If you think I'll go through a scene with that insufferable idiot —" she was saying.

Boycie said, "He seems a very personable young man, to me. Look here, Cherry, you march right out there and behave yourself. It means a few hours at the most. You'll never have to lay eyes on him again."

"Why he thinks he can use my picture as publicity for his own stupid, idiotic —" began Cherry.

"Be reasonable," interrupted Boycie, knowing this was the last thing Cherry would ever be, by nature, "it isn't his fault. It wasn't even his suggestion. Burns has explained all that to you. Be a sport, Cherry, do you want the man to go away saying that you were afraid of the competition?"

Five minutes later, her make-up adjusted, her hair in its state of artificially wild dishevelment, Cherry took herself out of the tent again and up to Mr. Burns. "I'm ready," she said abruptly.

Mr. Amberton, it appeared, was not. He was busy watching his own excellent features in the process of becoming jaundiced. A little later and he was donning the discarded explorer's equipment complete to shorts and pith helmet, to say nothing of several guns and a short black whip. "What's that for?" asked Anthony in mild amusement, wondering if he was to play Simon Legree.

A little conversation with Mr. Burns resulted in the laying aside of the whip. Anthony did not, he averred firmly, go about beating his boys in odd moments nor did he flick a passing lion on the sensitive part of his nose when the fancy took him.

He went over his lines with Burns. There were very few. The part called for action. Explorer stumbles over body of girl who has crawled on hands and knees for, it is assumed, several miles. Explorer falls on own knees, exclaims, seeks for signs of life. Girl stirs. Explorer murmuring, "Easy does it," or something equally casual, lifts girl in arms, and starts toward his camp which is nonexistent, being beyond camera range. Girl comes to life, high fever, wild delirium, fights savagely — explorer struggles with her off scene. Cut.

This was all there was to it. The next scene, once assembled, would show Sanchez breaking through the underbrush in search of Cherry; and would show their happy reunion in the camp of the explorer, its owner having stepped out to shoot a gazelle for breakfast, or something. "Well," suggested Burns cheerfully, "suppose we get going."

Cherry, Anthony saw, was shapely in her rags. He thought, furiously, *Every yap with a few dimes in his pocket will be able to look at her! Her bare slender legs, the not-too-infrequent glimpses of rounded bosom, the beautifully modeled back.* He thought further, *I'd like to give her a damned good hiding!* and bitterly regretted his whip.

Even under the make-up she was enormously attractive. She was *café au lait*, with great green eyes and disheveled red hair. She was a witch. She was also his wife and it was about time he did something about that.

Burns was sweating. This was the last sequence. Barring accidents and retakes they would be through once this was over. He liked Amberton. He'd like to direct him in a real picture. The man had intelligence. He mopped his brow. He thought, *If this goes okay we can get through, and back to the lot and see the rushes tonight.*

"Ready, darling?" he asked Cherry.

Cherry was ready. She cast herself upon the ground, obediently. She cast herself so hard upon the ground that she bruised her tender anatomy and grunted with astonishment. "Now, Mr. Amberton," said Burns.

Anthony came through the wood trail. He didn't see the girl. He actually stumbled over her. "Ouch!" said Cherry, forgetting her coma. Anthony looked down, exclaimed, and knelt. He put his finger on the slender wrist. He thrust, with a certain satisfaction, his hand beneath the tatters and held it over the heart which leaped furiously at his touch. This was certainly more realism than Burns had hoped for. Then, and with due care, Anthony, telling all and sundry that easy did it, lifted the body of the girl into his arms and rose.

He walked with her for the stipulated number of paces. Then Cherry went into action. She stirred, her lids rose, she struggled. She screamed, her eyes wide with a delirious horror, she beat at him with small weak fists, and she clawed his face with her small sharp nails.

Anthony dropped her unceremoniously and put his hands to his face.

From the ground she smiled up at him maliciously. Burns hurried up. He said, "That was swell, Amberton. You too, Cherry. Lord!" He looked with astonishment at Anthony's bleeding countenance. "For God's sake, Cherry," he expostulated feebly. And then when Cherry rose without a word and fled past them into her tent, where she proceeded to have hysterics, the director became apologetic. "Lord," he said, "I'm sorry. She — she does let herself go in a part, you know."

"So it would seem," agreed Anthony grimly.

"Come on, we'll get those scratches fixed up," said Burns, "they'll never show."

"That's all right," said Anthony, "providing she hasn't poisoned me."

A little later and they were all set for the take. Burns had decided to risk it without another rehearsal. Boycie had taken him aside. "If it's to be done at all," she said, "you'll have to do it now. She seems," explained Boycie, swallowing, "to have taken an active dislike to Mr. Amberton."

"You're telling me?" inquired the director.

There were the cameras, on the path and up the trees — from the trees the camera would get a very good shot of Cherry, forlorn and unconscious, lying beaten and ill in the jungle. The wind sighed in the palms, not too loudly, and the sound of the surf came muffled to their ears. The underbrush crackled under Anthony's feet and one twig snapped sharply and then it was all to do over again. It would reproduce like a pistol shot.

Back he came, along the path. Now he was beside her, now he went through the medical motions, now he had her in his arms, now he walked with her, the cameras swinging to follow. Now she had awakened, and was beating at him and her cries resounded through the woods and now she was scratching him again and calling her lost lover.

He began walking a little faster. That was all right too, a good piece of business. Naturally he would hurry, to get the girl back to the safety of his camp. But even when Burns yelled, "*Cut!* Swell, you two," Anthony kept on hurrying.

"What the hell!" exclaimed Burns.

Cherry cried, "Put me down. Put me down, I tell you!"

"No," said Anthony, "I won't."

He ran. He knew how to get back to the car which was parked on the little side road. He had an infallible sense of direction. He was Anthony Amberton.

"Put me down," screamed Cherry and flailed him with her fists. "Put me down."

"Shut up," said Anthony, "or I shall gag you."

He was a little out of condition, but not very much. He could make the car.

Burns was running. The assistant director was running. The cameramen were running. Boycie stood still and yelled at them. "Stop!" she commanded. "Come back here, all of you!"

Yet they heard Anthony's crashing progress clearly; heard Cherry's screams.

"He's lost his mind," panted Burns, completely white. "He's abducted her. It isn't Amberton at all — it's some phony — a plot. My God, what are you all standing around for, have you gone nuts too?" he demanded of Boycie.

"No," said Boycie. "I haven't. That's Anthony Amberton, all right. I'm sure of that. Don't worry, it's quite all right. Your picture's finished — and you'll have more and better publicity than you bargained for, I think. Cherry and Anthony Amberton are — old friends," said Boycie. She smiled at Burns and incredibly the lid drooped over her left eye. "What you've just seen, and what the camera had just recorded, is not an abduction but, unless I'm very much mistaken, an elopement."

"Holy Moses!" said Mr. Burns weakly.

"Don't follow them," said Boycie. "Not yet. Let them get a good start. Listen." They all listened, straining their ears, even the sulky and discarded explorer. They drew together, the handful of technicians necessary for that scene, and heard the sound of a motor starting. Boycie began to laugh.

Presently they were all laughing, their arms around one another, rocking with mirth. Why, they couldn't say. They would never know. But the sound of their laughter triumphed over the sound of the surf on the sand.

Ungently Anthony put Cherry in the car. He reached in the pocket of the door before she could move, whipped out two pieces of common rope, and tied her legs and then her hands together. He took out a piece of clean cotton waste and stuffed it in her mouth. Then he got in the car, stepped on the starter, and they roared off, rocketing down the long side road, emerging finally into the main road and headed for Hollywood.

Cherry choked. She kicked with her bound legs. She sputtered. Anthony reached around behind her for a topcoat. He put it about her shoulders.

He said, driving, his hand steady on the wheel and his eyes on the road, "You may as well face it. You're moving into my suite. Or

I'll move into your shack. It doesn't make any difference. We'll send out the announcements and we'll go off somewhere in the car for a week's honeymoon. Can't be any longer than that. I've got to come back and make those blasted pictures. There's a limit to everything," he said, "dammit, my forehead's bleeding again."

He wiped at it with a handkerchief. Cherry choked furiously. He said, "I'll remove the gag but you can't talk yourself out of this."

He took out the cotton waste.

Said Cherry, spitting, "I wouldn't live with you if — if —"

"Oh, yes you would," said Anthony. "You will, and like it." He slipped an arm around her, and slowed, a very little, the pace of the car. He said, "They'll be after us presently. It won't do you any good, Cherry."

After a while she said, "If you'd stop a minute — and untie my hands —"

He looked at her. "You won't get far walking in that costume," he told her.

"I don't want to walk," she said.

"All right." He slowed over to the side of the road and cut the knots which confined her hands and feet. He said, after a moment, "Dammit, I thought I could go through with this. I can't. You're free, I'll drive you back to location if you want. You can explain that I had a touch of the sun. Maybe you really hate me, after all."

She said, "We'll go on to Hollywood. I can't honeymoon in rags by Adrian, can I — Sam?"

Now she was in his arms. She was crying a little and laughing a great deal. She was being kissed. Then she drew away. "Hurry," she said, "hurry!"

They drove on. Anthony said, "We'll get along about as well as a barrel of wildcats. You're the last sort of woman I ever dreamed of marrying. I loathe your movie manifestation."

She said, "Well, I wouldn't like exploring. What are you going to do about that?"

"I don't know," replied Anthony thoughtfully, "maybe I'll give it up and take a turn at your racket myself. I've an idea I'd be pretty good." He looked at her sidewise. "Competition might keep you in order, Mrs. Amberton."

"It might," she admitted. She thought, *Boycie! Granny!* But Boycie would understand, Boycie would break it to Lucy Van Steeden, and Lucy Van Steeden —

She said, "My grandmother will probably cut me off —"

Anthony said carelessly, "I've more money than is good for you. When she finds that out, cutting you off won't have much point, will it?"

Cherry said, "Look here. I'll probably leave you a dozen times a year and you'll leave me a dozen times a year and —"

"And we'll always find each other again," prophesied Anthony soberly. He held her close and drove precariously with one hand. He said, "We're both of us crazy and we belong together. We know that. We knew it when we sat on a hill in New Hampshire and talked about simplicity. We'd hate simplicity, you and I. But we love each other."

"That's pretty simple," said Cherry giggling.

Anthony stepped on the gas. He asked, "Warm enough? We've got a long drive before us. I'll take you home and wait while you pack. I'll give you half an hour. Then we'll pack up my things at the hotel and —"

"Where do we go from there?" asked Cherry. "Heaven or hell?"

"I haven't the remotest idea," replied the great explorer, "do you care?"

"No," said Cherry, "not if we're together."